NOT ENOUGH ROPE

J.T. FOX

Copyright © 2023 J.T. Fox.

All rights reserved. No part of this book may be reproduced, stored, or transmitted by any means—whether auditory, graphic, mechanical, or electronic—without written permission of both publisher and author, except in the case of brief excerpts used in critical articles and reviews. Unauthorized reproduction of any part of this work is illegal and is punishable by law.

This is a work of fiction. All of the characters, names, incidents, organizations, and dialogue in this novel are either the products of the author's imagination or are used fictitiously.

ISBN: 979-8-89031-613-4 (sc)
ISBN: 979-8-89031-614-1 (hc)
ISBN: 979-8-89031-615-8 (e)

Library of Congress Control Number: 2017912862

Because of the dynamic nature of the Internet, any web addresses or links contained in this book may have changed since publication and may no longer be valid. The views expressed in this work are solely those of the author and do not necessarily reflect the views of the publisher, and the publisher hereby disclaims any responsibility for them.

One Galleria Blvd., Suite 1900, Metairie, LA 70001
(504) 702-6708
1-888-421-2397

Hello friends, there are a few points I would like to hit on. First, I need to say my thanks to my family. They are always supportive of my writing projects. Thank you, to my friends who also encourage me. A special thanks to Mark Domyan who took many hours out of his life to edit my manuscript. His encouragement and advice kept me going when I wanted to give up. Which brings me to my second point. It was very difficult to write this novel. It deals with suicide, which is a very serious subject. Many times during the writing process I wanted to stop. I continued, hoping to show people that taking your life is not the answer. Never give in, we all touch people in ways we never expect we could. The last thing I want to mention is to my friend. He is even bigger in life than I could ever write in book. He has talked me off the ledge once or twice. The other day I was thinking about your friend Axle. I don't know why, but that's another story.

J.T. Fox

CONTENTS

Chapter 1	Death By Hanging	1
Chapter 2	How's Your Father?	21
Chapter 3	Death By Jumping	45
Chapter 4	Officer Murphy	61
Chapter 5	The Birth Of The Monster	83
Chapter 6	Olivia	96
Chapter 7	Enter The Governor	110
Chapter 8	Will It Be Murder Or Suicide?	125
Chapter 9	Murder	144
Chapter 10	"You" Are Invited To An Anniversary Party	159
Chapter 11	Jump	177
Chapter 12	Tuesday September Eleventh	194
Chapter 13	The Sky Is Falling	207
Chapter 14	One Nine Seven Eight One	216
Chapter 15	September Twelvth Two Thousand And One	225
Chapter 16	The Funeral	233
Chapter 17	Starting Over	242
Chapter 18	Good News	251
Chapter 19	For Sale	257
Chapter 20	September Eleventh Two Thousand And Two	270

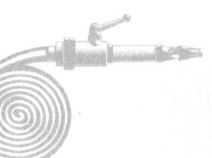

CHAPTER ONE

DEATH BY HANGING

June 8, 2001

My dearest Michelle if you're reading this note then you know what I have done. I'm sorry; it wasn't something I felt comfortable talking to you about. I wasn't happy with the way things were. I'm sure you thought it was time for a change too. I couldn't stare at the same four walls in the same empty house anymore. After enough time passes you'll get used to it. You may even think it was the right thing to do. In the end, I think we will both be happier.

Your loving husband;

Joe

Joe held the note in his hands. He felt them shaking slightly. The paper felt crisp in his trembling hands. He stared at the words with a blank expression on his face. His mouth was slightly open as he looked down. He felt something building at the corner of his mouth. He quickly tried to suck back a stream of drool before it fell on the paper. He read the note over, and over again, he wanted to make sure all his feelings were expressed and no blame was placed on anyone. He convinced himself it was perfect. A better conceived, heartfelt, and thoughtful suicide note has never been written. He folded it in half making a sharp crease in the middle of the paper. Then folded it again so it would fit neatly in the envelope. His hands started to shake more as he fumbled to open the legal size white envelope.

He was starting to breathe faster and could not stop it. Ironically his respirations were faster, but he was taking in less oxygen; try as he might, he could not fill his lungs with enough air to slow his breathing. As a long-time paramedic Joe realized what was happening. He was starting to hyperventilate. His hands were shaking violently as if he were having a seizure. He dropped the note onto the kitchen table and took a step back. Without panicking, he did his best to work out the problem. He attempted to slow his breathing and calm himself. He was too far gone, he needed to find another solution. His eyes scanned the room. He knew what he wanted, but could he find it? His fingers were tingling now and he was losing feeling in them. Like a fish out of water, he was struggling to catch his breath. Then he saw it. Quickly he shuffled his feet to the kitchen counter. Next to the toaster was a brown bag with a few stale bagels in it. He grabbed for it but could barely feel it with his numb fingers. He picked it up more with his eyes guiding him, rather than his sense of touch. As the bag left the counter two stale bagels fell to the floor with a thump. He hurriedly placed the bag over his mouth and nose and started to breathe into it. Within a few seconds Joe started to breathe in the carbon dioxide he needed to slow his respirations down.

As his breathing became more regular the tingling in his hands subsided. With his hands feeling normal again, he put the empty bag on the counter. Leaving his hand on the counter, he started to steady himself. His mind started to clear and in an audible voice he said. "Holy shit, that was scary, I thought I was gonna die!" He walked slowly back to the kitchen table and picked up the envelope with the suicide note in it. He reached down and picked up his pen. He wiped the sweat from his eyes. With his hands still slightly shaking he addressed it to his wife, ***Michelle.***

He held the envelope up with his right hand. He started to fan himself with it as he looked for a place to put it. As he gazed down at the kitchen table, he took note of how everything was in a specific place. Michelle liked that. Everything had a place and should be returned to its proper spot. The placemats were neatly placed at either end of the table. The empty chairs were pushed as close to the table as they could be without touching it. The wooden napkin holder was just about as close to dead center of the table as the human eye could get. The salt and pepper shakers were pushed back against the far edge of the table against the wall. Again, as close to center as could be.

A sly smile crossed his face. He knew how to place the note so Michelle would see it. He started to rearrange the layout of the kitchen table. He worked like a chess master. Moving pieces around the board to trap his opponent. In this instance, he moved the napkin holder against the wall.

He brought the salt and pepper shakers into the middle of the table. A blatant disregard of her A.D.D. But even that wasn't enough. He went even further and flipped the place mats over to expose the underside of them. With the table in total disarray, he placed the envelope between the salt and pepper shakers. She couldn't miss that. He slowly took a few steps back, staring at the table, admiring his handiwork. In his mind, he knew, Michelle would have a meltdown when her brain processed this mess. That devilish smile crossed his face again. He wanted more; he went for her King. He leaned over to the right side of the table and pulled out the chair that was neatly tucked in. Then he went to the left side and pulled that chair out as well. He took one more second to admire his end game. Then he turned, still smiling, and started to walk away. In a loud sinister voice, he said, "CHECKMATE!"

He strode out of the kitchen proud as a peacock. As he crossed into the dining room he stepped on something and almost twisted his ankle. He looked down and saw a stale bagel lying on the floor. "Oh shit!" he exclaimed. "I forgot about these if Michelle see this she'll kill me," he said. He bent down and picked up the stray bagel. Then he returned to the kitchen to look for the other one. He saw it next to the stove and picked that one up as well. He took the bagels and walked them to the trash and dumped them. He noticed the trash was kind of full. He stared down at it. Should he just leave it? He tried to walk away. He looked like a Cha Cha dancer as he tried to walk away shuffling his feet and turning his head back and forth. Then in frustration he reached down, pulled out the bag, and walked out the back door to throw the trash away.

It was a beautiful June day. The sun was out and it was not too hot. Summer was on the way. Joe started to reflect on his life with Michelle. In only a few months, August fourteenth to be exact, it would be their tenth wedding anniversary. It was surely the best of times then. Joe fell so hard for her. He loves her more now than he did then. Suddenly he heard a voice in his head.

"You know this is the only way. She doesn't deserve to live with me. I'm a monster and must die. Don't make her have to live with me. Be a hero and kill me."

Joe shook his head and snapped back to reality. With a low sad response, he answered the voice in his head, "You're right, you are a monster, you need to go."

That's exactly why he had to be brave and do what he had planned. She'd have plenty of time to move on and find a better life. Joe saw the symbolism as he dropped the trash into the can. Soon Michelle would be free of her trash.

He entered the house through the back door into the kitchen. He admired his set- up one more time. Michelle was all about routine, and Joe knew her habits well. She would park her car in the front of the house. Then the car door would open slightly. She would use her foot to kick it the rest of the way open. She would stand up, smooth out her clothes, and walk around the front of it toward the mailbox. She would rest her bag and purse on the hood of the car. She would bend forward slightly, and her beautiful brown hair would fall in front of her. She would pull the box open, reach in and grab the mail. As she thumbed through it on the street in front of the house she would tilt her head slightly to the right. After picking up the mail she would collect her things off the hood of the car and walk down the driveway. She always used the back door to enter the house. That would bring her into the kitchen. She would pull the chair out from under the table and rest her things on it. With her hands free, she would pick out the mail she felt was important. Joe had observed this behavior countless times through the years. He loved the way she would move her full red lips as she read the envelopes and bat her beautiful eyes as she shuffled the mail through her hands. Then with a small frustrated sigh, she would flip it onto the table.

That's when she would find the note he left for her. He was so proud of himself. If he could reach it he would give himself a pat on the back for knowing his wife so well. He was so proud of his plan, and the weeks of preparation. It would all pay off now. He took a quick glance at the kitchen clock. Michelle would be home soon, and there was still much to do.

In his mind, it was the most honorable thing Joe had ever done in his life. He was putting someone's else's feeling ahead of his own. He felt it was the selfless act of a selfish man. Two weeks ago, he gathered all his personal papers, his life insurance, mortgage, annuity, and his bank statements. He made a ton of phone calls. He made appointments with his lawyer, accountant, and his human resources department at work. He asked all kinds of hypothetical questions. He wanted to make sure Michelle would get her full benefit. The last step was to sign over all his financial holdings to her. He did all he could to make sure that Michelle would be well taken care of when he was gone. He signed all the papers and carefully placed them in a plain folder. Now Michelle would get everything. He took the folder and placed it in their bedroom on the king-sized bed in which he mostly slept alone in.

With his life insurance policy and his fire department death benefit Michelle would receive more than five hundred thousand dollars. With the monetary aspect in order, the last step in Joe's plan was to run to the hardware store and buy the rope. He knew he saw his wife this morning for the last time. Suddenly it hit him hard; he was going to be taking his own life. The suicide note was written the papers were in the folder where Michelle could find them, the house was in order. Joe could now prepare for phase two of his plan. He needed to buy a good strong rope.

Joe got into his car and started it up. He sat for a minute or two and thought. It might not be a good idea to go to the local neighborhood store; he might run into someone he knew. When he was dead they may feel some guilt if they were the last person to see him alive. More importantly, Joe did not want to speak to anyone. No quick hellos, or how's the family, no mindless banter with the man behind the counter who had seen Joe come to the store for years. Today he was focused, with one thought on his mind. He pulled his car out of the driveway. It was forty minutes out of his way, but he decided to go to the hardware store in the next town. It would take more time, but it was worth it to keep from seeing the people he might know.

It took longer than he thought with the traffic but he found a store that should have what he needed. It was a red brick building with a large lot attached for parking and storage. He had passed it many times before but had never stopped in. The lot was filled with grass seed, flower pots, soil, and several other large bulk items stacked on pallets. Very few cars were parked there. He parked his car way in the back of the parking lot. It sat all alone in the hot sun. He half- jogged up to the front door thinking he needed to make up time.

It was Paul's Hardware; a mom and pop store. It was perfect for him. He could zip in unnoticed, get what he needed, pay, and leave. He peered into the store from the glass door to see how crowded it was. Other than a few workers walking around in red smocks and a handful of customers, the coast looked clear to him. He took a deep breath in and pulled on the heavy glass door. The door made a loud rattle but did not open. Slightly frustrated, he tried to pull on it again with the same result. Then from behind him a small child accompanied by his mother moved past Joe. The boy pushed on the door and it slowly started to open. Joe cowered in embarrassment and tried to make up for his impatient gaff by pushing the door all the way open. He was startled at the loud buzzing sound the door made when he opened it. Then he was even more startled when the little boy fell to the ground from Joe pushing the door open so fast. Everyone in the store turned to look at the boy lying on the ground crying. Joe stood over him dumbfounded.

The pretty young mother swooped past Joe and scooped up her little boy. She turned to look at Joe still holding the door open as the buzzer continued to sound. "Thanks mister, you really made my day today," she said to him with anger in her voice. Still not exactly sure what had just happened Joe sheepishly replied. "You're welcome."

Joe's hope for a stealthy entrance was thwarted. The lady, with her son still crying hurried toward the back of the store. Joe stepped in and the door slowly closed behind him. All the eyes that had been watching the scene unfold in the front of the store had gone back about their business. An older lady working the register in the front of the store greeted him with a loud and friendly. "Good afternoon sir. Welcome to Paul's Hardware store. Please let us know how we can make your shopping experience a pleasant one."

Joe put his head down and started to rapidly walk. Without making eye contact he answered the lady as he passed her. "Good afternoon miss." He turned his back to her and stopped to get the layout of the store. A sign in the far back corner caught his eye, ROPE, CHAINS, AND BINDINGS. His mind flashed with a bit of nervous humor. He thought, was this a family hardware store or an adult book store. Joe started heading in that direction. When he arrived in the rope and binding section he stood motionless; his lips were moving but no sound came out. He was lost in his own thoughts, unaware of anyone else in the store. He was impressed with the nice selection of ropes. He knew about ropes from a happier time in his life, when he was a firefighter. They had nylon, hemp, thin, and thick. Joe knew he could find what he needed. He was looking for a very thick, heavy type of rope. He picked up a strong sample and was stretching it across his body to test its strength. He started to make a noose with it wondering if it would be strong enough to hold his dead weight. Suddenly he was startled with a tap on his shoulder. He jumped and turned at the same time and came face to face with a young pimpled face boy who was trying to get his attention.

"I'm sorry, sir, I just wanted to know if you needed any help with anything." Joe saw the kid was wearing a red smock with a name tag that read Kyle.

"No, Kyle, thank you I'm fine," Joe answered, but Kyle was one of the more persistent kids who worked for Paul's Hardware and followed up Joe's reply. "Are you sure, sir I've been watching you hanging around by the ropes for a while, so I thought I would swing by to see if you needed help?" Kyle paused for a second and then said. "See what I did there. Hang around and swing." Then Kyle burst into a deep and nasal seal- like laugh that had every person, customer and employee alike looking at them.

Joe's face turned beet red with embarrassment. He reached for the heavy rope he had been eyeing and took it off the hook. He left Kyle still seal barking at his own joke as he power -walked to the front checkout counter. He kept his head down while he waited in the short line for his turn to check out. When his turn came up the lady at the counter greeted him again. "Hello, sir. Did you find everything you needed?"

Joe answered politely, and without looking up said. "Yes, thank you."

The woman took the rope from him and started to look for the barcode then spoke again. "Did someone help you today?" Joe answered again without making eye contact. "No, not today."

"Oh, I thought I saw Kyle back there. Let me get him up here," she replied, "it's not like him to let a customer wander the store without any assistance." Joe again started to get red and quickly said. "No that's not necessary… yes, Kyle, was very helpful I just couldn't remember his name. Thank you."

She smiled back. "Oh sir, you're so welcome! Your total comes to $22.25; will that be debit, credit, or cash?' It is our policy not to accept checks." Joe looked up for the first time at the woman. It was the older woman who had greeted him when he entered the store. She had short gray hair and lots of white powder on her face. She wore bright red lipstick which made her yellow cigarette-stained teeth stick out. The name on her red smock read PIPEMMA. Joe thought she looked like a villain from a comic book. "Cash!" Joe answered sternly.

"Thank you, sir. Do you have our customer loyalty card? It can save you up to twenty percent on all purchases including sale items in the entire store." Joe looked at her and with a forced smile said, "no."

She quickly turned and took down a folded pamphlet and started to speak again "Okay, sir, would you like to sign up for our customer loyalty card? It just takes a minute." As the line behind him started to grow. Joe started losing his patience. He looked at his watch and thought he had less than two hours before Michelle got home and he wasn't even close to being dead. He looked at Pipemma and in a restrained, calm voice said. "Listen," he glanced again at the lady's name tag and continued, "Pipe Mamma, I can't hang around here all day." He stopped short in mid-sentence shook his head, and continued. "I'm in a big hurry. I just want to buy this rope please."

Now Pipemma looked annoyed and in an indignant voice replied. "Sir my name is pronounced Pip Emma not Pipe Mamma! It was my Great-Grandmother's name who happened to be one of the first settlers in this community. I happen to be very proud to be named after her."

Joe looked back, just as annoyed and said. "I don't care if you and the old bag came over on the Mayflower, I just want to buy my friggin rope. What ever happened to the days you could go to a store and buy whatever you dam-well wanted. Pay for it and walk out?"

Then she raised her voice and in a tone that was all business she asked. "May I have your phone number and zip code please?" Joe placed both of his hands on the counter and looked directly into the face of Pipemma. He had now totally lost his cool. He was frustrated and running out of time. Not caring anymore who heard him or how much of a scene he made he lashed into the old lady. "Look ma'am I have one, twenty-foot piece of rope which I was planning to use on myself, but the longer you keep me here the more I start to think of what size neck you might be. Now I am not giving you my phone number or my zip code! I will give you thirty dollars and you can keep the damn change! Maybe you can do something about those yellow teeth, or buy another pound of flour for your face. I really don't care. I do not want or need a bag, and please don't tell me to have a nice day because I am not planning on being around long enough to enjoy it."

Pipemma took the cash and threw the rope at Joe. Joe picked up his rope. By now he realized that every eye in the store was on him. He held his rope tightly in his hands and straightened himself up. He gave one last, nasty look at Pipemma and with all the dignity he could muster walked to the door and pushed on it. The door frame rattled and the glass shook as he went face first into the glass and let out an audible "ump." He looked over his shoulder at Pipemma. She looked directly at him and said. "You have to pull it you dumb FU…" Just as she was finishing her sentence Joe pulled the door open. The door started to BUZZ and he walked out.

When Joe finally pulled back into his driveway his frustration had faded. His mind was consumed with the remainder of his plan. He had less than an hour before Michelle would be home from work. He took his rope and tucked it under his shirt. Then he quickly ran into the house. He sat down on the grand wooden staircase in his living room. It was the focal point of the house. It was a beautiful oak structure with bannisters running up both sides. It curved slightly as it rose to the second floor. The upstairs had a wooden railing with decorative slats. It stood about four feet high. The vaulted ceiling had a huge wooden beam running across it.

Joe sat on the steps of the staircase under the huge beam. He started to make the noose and knot. After the noose was made, he worked on the knot. He wanted to wrap the rope above the noose thirteen times. That would be more than enough to hold his weight. But he was running out of time and rope. He settled at seven wraps and hoped that would be enough to hold him. As he finished preparing the rope his mind started to wander to what had brought him to this act of desperation. A smile crossed his face.

Joe and Michelle met in 1989. Michelle was a nurse and Joe was a fireman; it seemed like a match made in heaven. Joe was very popular with his fellow firefighters; he was one of the youngest captains in fire department history. He was a good-looking man but he was never comfortable with his appearance. He was built very much like his fictional hero, Captain James T. Kirk of Star Trek fame. Average height and muscular build, with long dark hair which he rarely kept combed. Joe was known as a friendly, kind man, but he was far from perfect. He was known to be very opinionated and could be obnoxious. He saw the world as black and white. There was right or wrong; there were no shades of gray. It made him a good captain since everyone was treated the same. It was also a major struggle outside of work. He had problems dealing with people's interpretations of the rules. His best feature was his ability to keep calm in even the tensest situations. He was a natural leader whom the men and women of the fire department looked up to.

Michelle was a buxom girl with a beautiful face. She had long dark hair and wore tight clothes that hugged every curve of her magnificent body. That girl could have easily been a famous and successful model but the good Lord also blessed her with intelligence. Michelle was the type of girl who never had a problem getting a date. Her downfall was her drive to succeed. The men she dated could not deal with her ambition. She felt the pressure of being a woman in a man's world. Deep down, she wanted more than love from a man. She wanted respect.

Joe and Michelle married in 1991. It was a storybook wedding with the fire trucks outside the church sounding their lights and sirens when the priest pronounced them man and wife. When the newly married couple walked out into the bright sunshine they were showered with rice. As they walked down the church steps wiping rice from their faces they saw two huge red fire trucks. They were the department tower ladder trucks. They were parked several feet apart from each other back to back. Both trucks had their ladders fully extended and crossed at the top. The couples wedding car, a white Rolls Royce, was parked below waiting for the newlyweds.

The wedding reception was just a huge party. Everyone had a great time. Joe even invited the people working at the catering hall to join in. The highlight was the toast. Ten years later whenever the wedding is discussed people still talk about it. It was given by Joe's best friend, Gary Murphy. They had known each other since they were kids. He took a quote from one of Joe's and Michelle's favorite movies, "The Wizard of Oz." When the time came, he stood up from the dais. He looked so sharp in his classic black tuxedo. The room went quiet and he started to speak.

"We've all seen the classic movie "The Wizard of Oz". It's one of Joe's and Michelle's favorites. At the end of the movie the Wizard gives the Tin Man a heart. He looks the Tin Man in the eye and says, a heart is not judged by how much you love, but by how much you are loved by others. Today, Joe and Michelle, you are surrounded by love," Gary raised his glass to the couple.

As time moved on Joe and Michelle seemed to drift apart. Michelle seemed wrapped up in her career. Joe was having his own problems; he was depressed when he was forced to leave the fire service. He started working crazy hours as a paramedic. As time wore on he started to have conversations in his head with The Monster. They were angry talks at first. Joe hated The Monster for having him relieved of duty from the fire service. But he tried to live with him.

When she wasn't working, Michelle started to get involved in computers and social media on the internet. Joe had no patience for the new technology and preferred to watch television. After a few years their lives became stagnant with no one willing to give in to the other. Michelle would stay up late at night on her computer and in frustration Joe would turn off the television and just go to bed. In the morning Joe would walk down the steps to find Michelle fast asleep on the couch with the lap top computer still humming. Michelle seemed to lose interest in anything that had to do with her husband. They had virtually no love life. Joe missed that, but Michelle didn't seem to mind. Joe felt constantly alone and he blamed The Monster. He loved Michelle too much to not see her happy and he hated being the cause of it. Once Joe was gone Michelle could go on with her life and he would not be alone anymore.

The kitchen clock chimed at the half hour and Joe was startled back into reality. By now he had less than thirty minutes before Michelle came home. All that was left to do was throw the rope over the huge crossbeam that ran over the master staircase. He ran up the steps and leaned over the wooden rail that kept people from falling to the first floor. He threw the rope over the crossbeam and reached out to grab the noose. Employing a special slip knot, he learned during his years in the fire service, he was able to secure the noose over the beam.

Then he heard the voice in his head, "Good, good, hurry she'll be home soon."

"Shut up! I'm working as fast as I can asshole."

"Hey, language dude. I'm just trying to help," The Monster replied.

He took one last look at his watch. Time was running out. He looked back up at the rope. His noose was hanging a little higher than he had wanted. The plan was simple; reach out, grab the noose, stick your head in it, and swing out. With any luck his neck would snap right away. Joe leaned over the rail but the noose was still too high to reach. He tried again, really leaning far over and straining with his fingers. It was still just inches away.

"Jump for it!" The Monster yelled in Joe's head.

"Are you nuts. That's a long jump." Joe answered.

"Climb on the rail, asshole. Yeah, that's right I said it. How do you like it?"

Unsure of himself and shaking his head. He climbed up on the rail and like an expert tightrope walker, he found his balance. Now he was even further away because he could not lean as far forward as before.

"Now what Einstein", Joe said to The Monster.

"Do your knees bend? Now is the part when you jump," The Monster replied.

He carefully bent his knees and started to swing his arms back and forth. In his head The Monster counted, one, two, three. Joe lunged across the gap over the master staircase. He kept his eyes glued to the rope and grabbed it as he went across. Holding on to the rope he discovered the fatal flaw in The Monster's plan. His momentum brought him across the gap over the master staircase twenty feet above the living room. His legs were bent behind him as he swung across. He quick tried to bring them forward to brace him from slamming into the wall. He just didn't have enough time. Still holding on to the rope, he slammed into the wall on the other side. He hit the wall with the left side of his face. He yelled out a quick, "OH SHIT!" as his grip was jarred loose and he fell. The rope swinging above mocking him and getting smaller as he accelerated towards the hard-wooden steps.

He fell, landing spread eagle, flat on his back. The impact took his breath away. He struggled desperately to gulp oxygen back into his lungs. Finally, his internal systems caught up with his struggle to take in air. He started to breathe. The next step was to try to move. He rocked his feet back and forth then he bent his knees slightly. The check list in his head was relieved; no lower body injury. Then he moved his hands and arms. Ironically, he was thankful he was not seriously injured. Slowly he tried to pick his head up. His vision was blurry at first. Slowly he focused his eyes on the rope swinging back and forth above him. As his breathing became more regular, the pure pain kicked in. Joe lay on the steps, arms and legs throbbing, then he heard the back-door open. His face grew hot and red with embarrassment. Michelle was home! He tried to move but the pain was too much; all he could do was lie there. How was he going to explain this without her thinking he's lost his mind? Michelle was too smart for a flimsy explanation. When she sees the suicide note, Joe sprawled on the staircase, and the rope swinging above him she'll figure it out. Joe closed his eyes, too ashamed to look her in the face and waited for her to enter the room.

He could hear as Michelle put her purse down and tossed the mail on the kitchen table. Then he heard the panic in her voice.

"Oh my God, what have you done?" He knew she was reading the note. Then he heard her again. "My table, it's in shambles. Oh my God, we were robbed!" She brought her hand up to her face in horror. Then she saw the clean white envelope. Her hand trembling she reached down for it and opened it. As she read it she started to shriek. "No, no he didn't! Please God, tell me he didn't."

She threw the note down and ran into the living room. She walked about five feet into the room and stopped. Joe lay about ten feet in front of her, sprawled across the bottom of the steps. She had a blank expression on her face as her eyes scanned the room. Her heart was beating like a jackhammer in her chest and her breathing was erratic. She made no move to go to her husband. Her face slowly started to relax, and a smile started to form. She brought her hands up across her heart and let out a sigh of relief. By now she had wandered into the middle of the living room. She looked down and saw Joe lying on his back.

"What did you do?" She asked him.

Joe summoned his courage to explain to his wife what had happened. "Well, it's like this."

Michelle cut him off before he could finish. "I like it," she said. Joe looked puzzled. Then, he saw her eyes looking up at the hangman's noose. There was a moment of awkward silence and then she continued. "It's a little creepy and you need to center it better, but it's a conversation piece. I have to say, you scared the shit out of me with that note. My God, I thought you bought new furniture or something."

She walked closer to the steps where Joe was lying, looked down at him patted him on the shoulder and said. "Good job, honey, but it must have been a bitch getting that rope up there."

Joe looked up and said, "You have no idea," then Michelle stepped over him and walked up the steps to the bedroom to change out of her work clothes. Joe started to move slowly and pick himself up off the steps.

As he got to a sitting position, he heard Michelle yelling from the bedroom. "JOE! YOU LEFT YOUR IMPORTANT PAPERS ALL OVER THE BEDROOM, DON'T COME CRYING TO ME WHEN YOU CAN'T FIND THE DAMN THINGS!"

He sat silently, hunched over, his face buried in his hands. Then Joe heard a familiar voice in his head. "Well you cocked that one up."

"SCREW YOU!" Joe said in a loud and angry.

From the top of the staircase Michelle yelled down, "What did you say?"

"Nothing dear. I was talking to someone else."

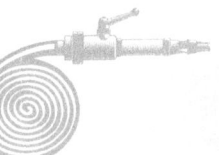

CHAPTER TWO

HOW'S YOUR FATHER?

It took Joe a few days to physically recover from his tragic miscalculation with the rope. He did have a few things to be thankful for. First, he was happy but a bit confused that Michelle had no idea he was trying to kill himself. He was also happy that he hadn't quit his job as a New York City paramedic. Today was his first day back to work and he was still hurting from his fall a few days before. He would also be thankful if his first day back would be a slow one. But this month Joe was working day tour which historically is the busiest shift of the day. With commuters rushing to work and not paying attention, they were bound to either cause, or be involved in accidents. The mornings usually had people waking up with chest pain, difficulty breathing, or other maladies that require emergency medicine. Yes, the seven to three-day shift could be very busy.

Joe was lucky, so far it had been slow. He had two calls; the first was an elderly male having an asthma attack. It was no wonder the elderly man had problems breathing. It was still early in the morning and already a hot, sticky, day. The patient tried to do the right thing. He got up early and tried to beat the heat by starting his errands before the real heat kicked in. He had to climb three sets of stairs to get to his apartment. He was dragging a shopping cart. A small metal cage about waist high. It had two wheels on the back end and a handle to pull it. It was a common sight in the city, with almost anything you could want or need within walking distance. When empty, the cart folded and was very light to carry. It was just a matter of grabbing your cart and go. It could easily hold more than a person could carry. It was also convenient if you needed to take a bus or train because it neatly folded so flat.

The cart was loaded with three bags of groceries and the poor man had to pull it up three flights of steps. With one hand on the bannister and the other on his shopping cart he would strain to pull it up. One step at a time, bump, stop, bump, stop, bump. When he finally reached a landing, he rested and caught his breath. The elderly man was also carrying a few extra pounds around his gut. By the time, he reached his apartment the strain and the heat were too much for him. He sat on his kitchen chair, sweat dripping down his face. He was trying to cool down and catch his breath. He tried to fan himself with a placemat on the table. The more he fanned himself, the more exhausted he became. Still, unable to catch his breath, he called the paramedics.

Joe got the call. He was only a few blocks away. A few blocks in Manhattan is not as close as you would think, with the traffic and people rushing back and forth. He made good time though, and arrived in front of the brownstone building. As usual the narrow street was jammed with parked cars. New York City has strange parking rules. It's called alternate side of the street parking. During certain times of the day cars could only park on one side of the street. When the time expired, the cars would have to be moved to the opposite side of the street. It was a sight to see. Flocks of people leaving their buildings. Running to their cars, driving around the block and trying to find a spot on the other side of the narrow street. Joe parked his ambulance across from the building. He was mostly on the sidewalk. At least the street was clear. He ran to the back of his rig and grabbed his med kit and the oxygen cylinder. He ran up the front stoop and into the building. The buildings Super met him at the entrance and led him up the steps to the apartment.

When he reached the apartment, he was out of breath. He found the elderly man still sitting on the chair struggling to breathe. As Joe tried to catch his breath he set up the portable oxygen. He took a quick hit of the O2 himself before placing the mask over the patient's face. The man tried to breath in the air but he felt very claustrophobic with the device over his mouth and nose. He kept pushing it off his face. Joe held the mask in front of the man.

"It's okay, pal, I'll hold it. You just think about taking some deep breaths. In through your nose and out your mouth," he told the old man. Then he looked over to the Super who was standing behind the patient. "Hey, do me a favor, look in the freezer behind you and see if there's anything we can put on this guy to cool him down." The Super pulled out a bag of frozen vegetables and placed it on the back of the man's neck. It didn't take long before the patient started to feel better. His breathing slowed down and become more regular. Joe took a set of vital signs and they were in the normal range. The old man felt so much better he refused to go to the hospital. After a few minutes, Joe convinced him that he may need further evaluation. Fortunately, the patient felt well enough to walk down the steps to the ambulance. It would not have helped Joe's back to carry that man down all those steps.

The second call was a very obese woman well known to the medics. She is one of a handful of people who call the medics several times a month for one malady or another. In the paramedic community, this person earns the nickname of a frequent flyer. She is so well known that when her address is called over the radio two police cars are dispatched to assist the paramedic. Standard operating procedure has the medic working alone in the ambulance. When a call goes into the dispatcher the ambulance and a police car are sent to the location. The police officer assists the medic. The officers are trained in C.P.R. and basic first aid. The officer also helps in moving the patient to the back of the ambulance. Then the officer hops into the driver's seat of the rig. While the medic cares for the patient in the back of the ambulance the police officer drives it to the hospital. When the patient is delivered to the emergency room the medic restocks his supplies then drives the police officer back to the address of the original emergency. The cop can then return to his car and his other duties.

Joe was the first to arrive at the apartment of the woman. He knocked on the door and announced himself. The door was open and he could hear the woman moaning in the back bedroom. The apartment had a foul smell to it. It was like an ammonia and urine mixture. There was another odor that was not identifiable but very unpleasing. As Joe walked past the kitchen he saw three overflowing litter boxes but he continued. Cats were everywhere. You couldn't swing a dead mouse without hitting a cat.

He got to the bedroom and yelled out. "Mabel it's Joe from EMS. I'm coming in." The paramedics have been coming here so long most of them knew her by name, and she knew most of them as well.

A high-pitched squeaking voice answered back, "I'm here Joe. Thank God, it's you! Help me please, I'm in such pain!"

"Okay Mabel, I'm here. Let's see what's going on." Joe opened his medic box and started to assess his patient. Most of the time Mabel's symptoms came from watching medical shows on television. He took her pulse and blood pressure which were in the normal range for her. She was breathing regularly wasn't diaphoretic, and her skin color was good as well. Joe started to ask her some questions. "Where are, you having pain, honey?"

"Oh, my belly. It's terrible! I think I have, um, have…" Mabel stopped and looked for a piece of paper on her night stand. Her fat fingers pushed some pill bottles and cotton swabs out of the way and she found what she was looking for. She unfolded the paper and read what she had written on it. "Upper abdominal distention secondary to aortic aneurysm." Joe put his head down to try and hide his smile. He scanned the room quickly and saw a large empty

Chinese food container, an empty ice cream box, an almost empty liter of diet soda, and a fat gray cat pawing at a half-eaten plate of crumb cake.

When he composed, himself he asked Mabel, "What was on television last night?"

"Not much." Mabel said. "Just some rerun of one of them medical shows," she answered back.

"I see," Joe answered back. "Well, Mabel, I think you have a belly ache and you should take some antacid and stay in bed for a while."

Mabel looked up with a look of relief on her face. "Are you sure, Joe?"

"All of your vital signs are good, your skin is not cold or clammy. You're okay." Joe said.

Mabel looked at Joe and snapped her fingers and with some embarrassment, she said. "That's right, the man last night on the show was very sweaty. Thank you, Joe, you're so kind and patient." Joe started to pack up his medical kit when he heard loud coughing behind him. It was the police officer dispatched to assist him. Joe had seen him before; he was a rookie officer. He tried to remember his name. He thought it was Kevin, or Kenny, or something like that. Whatever his name was, this was his first visit to Mabel's house and the odor was overtaking him. The officer was gaging so much that his eyes were watering and he was almost vomiting. Joe told the kid to wait outside and the cop ran for the front door. He left so fast he stepped on one of Mabel's cat's tails. The cat let out a horrifying screech.

Joe stood up and started to leave. Mabel called out to him once more. "Joe, thank you so much again. Just you coming here, makes me feel better."

"Anytime Mabel, but could you do me a favor please?" Mabel looked at Joe with a puzzled look, what could she do for him? "Sure, Joe, what can I do?"

Joe looked her dead on and said. "Can you switch to watching westerns instead of medical shows?"

Mabel started to cackle loudly as Joe turned to leave. She lifted her huge flabby arms and waved to the exiting paramedic, yelling to him. "Oh Lordy, that's a good one, Joe, but you know I can't take all that violence." Joe started to laugh as he walked outside.

When he was outside he could read the name tag on the rookie cop's uniform, and he told him. "It's okay Connor we don't need to transport her."

Connor had a look of relief on his face and said. "Thank God, I'll call off the other unit."

Joe patted Connor on the back and told him. "Get used to that, we're here a lot. She's a lonely lady who wants attention."

"Thanks for the warning, but how can you take that smell?" the officer replied.

Joe looked at him and smiled. "I have a trick. You should never go to work without your bag of tricks."

"Please, please, tell me what the trick is. I can't take that smell." Joe reached into his left front pocket. He pulled out a small tin container and held it up in front of the rookie policeman. The cop looked at it and read the label. "Vicks vapor rub!" he said, surprised.

"Yup, just a little bit under your nose, that's all it takes." Joe smiled and put the tin back in his pocket. They walked off the porch together and got into their vehicles and drove off.

Joe was sitting in his ambulance. His lower back was still sore and aching, but it was getting close to lunch time. He drove the rig over to a park he liked to sit in during his break. He parked it, grabbed his portable radio and his lunch bag, and walked over to a shady bench that had a magnificent view of the city. He pulled out his bologna and ketchup sandwich. He sat watching the young lovers walking past holding hands. He watched as young parents sat on park benches watching their children playing in the playground. He stared off at the city taking in all the joy and beauty around him and tried to come up with another idea to end his life.

While he was lost in thought his eyes caught a glimpse of the Palmer building; thirty-three stories of solid granite and steel that housed most of the major insurance companies in the world. "Wow," he thought, "How ironic would that be to kill myself at an insurance building? If I was lucky, beside the insurance payoff, maybe Michelle could sue them for another couple of million."

He smiled as he looked closer at the old majestic building and chewed his sandwich. All of a sudden something looked different to him. He looked at some of the other building's around it. Then he looked back at the Palmer building. Joe wiped the sweat off his brow, then it clicked. All the other buildings windows were closed. Sealed shut; they had air-conditioning. But the Palmer building had open windows. Joe counted and he saw open windows up to the tenth floor. Above the tenth floor the windows must have been sealed shut. Or maybe the extra floors were added on later. A light bulb went off in his head. That was it! He could walk into the building, get up to the tenth floor, sneak out a window and take the deadly plunge. It would be over in seconds. Joe sat back on the park bench, his head nodding up and down very pleased, a smile crossing his proud face. He had a plan. Now he just needed to pick a day.

He sat back on the bench very content, almost relieved. This idea was fool proof, and nothing could go wrong. Knowing he was going to end his life soon, he started to think back to his younger days. They say when people are about to die they see their life flash before them. Maybe when you plan your demise you slowly watch your life unfold. He was thinking of his best friend, Gary Murphy. Gary is a New York City Police Officer and that was all he ever wanted to do. Joe remembered back to when they were kids and their other friends wanted to be football players or astronauts and other big dreams. Gary always told people he wanted to be a policeman.

No one really remembers how they met, or how old they were, all anyone remembers is that they were always together. It was always Gary and Joe, or Joe and Gary, you never said one name without speaking the other. It was no secret what drew the two of them together. Joe idolized Gary, and Gary knew that Joe needed to be looked out for. They lived on the same block and spent every summer together. They would lift weights in the morning and after lunch run laps around the high school track. In the evening, they would meet up with some of the other kids in the neighborhood and play a game they created and named Off the Wall.

Off the Wall was a hybrid game. It was an ingenious game that took advantage of the odd shape of the schoolyard and the proximity of the tennis courts. The field was half concrete, and half dirt, and rocks. The tennis courts at the end of the field were too close to play stick ball. Added to that the pitcher had to pitch from a large divot below where the batter stood. Their solution was to use an old beat up softball. They would play two guys on a team, a pitcher, and an outfielder. The pitcher could lob it up to the batter without hurting his arm. The ball was so dead and misshapen that it took a mighty swing to hit it over the fence into the tennis courts. It was a good shot for a fourteen-year-old. That's not to say it never happened.

Gary was a strong kid. His hitting style was very awkward, but when he hit it, it went. There were times when all three tennis courts were occupied, and softballs would fall in there like meteors. The kids' hearts would pound as they watched a softball take off. Sailing high above the fifteen-foot fence separating the tennis court from the dirt and rock field. In one loud voice, all the kids would scream out, "HEADS UP!" All they could do now was hope it didn't hit anyone. Sometimes it did.

Gary was the first to bonk a tennis player. He hit a ball right into the center court. Two big college kids were playing on the court at the time. The ball sailed, and the cry went out. "HEADS UP!" The men kept playing. It appeared every eye in the schoolyard turned to see what was going to happen next. Even the birds sitting on the telephone wires high above quickly turned their heads to look into the tennis courts. The silence was deafening as the ball zeroed in on the player in the forecourt who just about to hit a crosscourt winner. Then, THUD! The ball struck him square, between the shoulder blades. He stood stunned for a second then started to search the tennis court to see what had hit him.

The silence of the schoolyard was broken by Joe's voice who quickly yelled out. "I'm not gettn that ball."

The big tennis player turned around and faced the dirt field, looking through the fence across to the stone wall where Gary stood holding a silver aluminum bat. Gary could instantly see that the tennis player was not happy.

"WHO HIT THAT FUCKING BALL?" He yelled out across the field.

Standing by the batter's box Gary held the silver bat up in his right hand and started to walk toward the tennis courts. At the top of his voice Gary yelled back, "HOW'S YOUR FATHER?"

"What? You, asshole, I should go up there and kick your ass."

That was not the response Gary was looking for. He started to wave the bat back and forth and yell back at the older, bigger, and angry, man. As he started to walk down to the tennis courts, bat in hand, he responded, "I'm on my way down. Don't go anywhere."

As Gary passed the pitcher's mound the tennis player yelled back. "Never mind, moron. I'm not risking gettn arrested for beating up a minor." Gary continued to march towards the tennis courts. Joe's heart was pounding in his chest. All he could think was someone was going to get killed.

As Gary got to the fence he said to the man whom he had hit with the softball, "Can I have my ball back now?" The other fellow who was playing with him retrieved the ball and tossed it to Gary. Then Gary turned and started to walk back to the batter's box. As he passed Joe, he stopped and said, "That's how you get the ball back."

Joe shot back in a confused voice, "how's your father?"

"It was all that I could think of," Gary said.

The boys were also known for their long walks around the neighborhood. Maybe it was Gary's way of practicing walking a beat like a cop. Whatever the reason they both enjoyed their walks. One winter day in the late 1970's the boys were out on one of their after-dinner strolls through town. Gary was wearing his football jacket and Joe had a blue Snorkel Parka, which was very popular back then. They had been walking about two hours - just talking and joking as usual - when one of them decided to stop at the Seven Eleven. That was a mistake.

The two fifteen-year olds wandered through the store and picked up something to drink, then they walked to the checkout counter. Gary went first and paid for his drink and then Joe stepped up. When he placed his item on the counter a large arm came out from behind him and grabbed him.

"Hold it right their scumbag," the man attached to the arm said. Joe turned his head around and saw a huge six foot five, three-hundred-pound man grabbing him.

Without missing a beat Gary turned and approached the much bigger man, "Hey buddy let go of my friend!" Gary fired back.

The guy behind the counter, who also had a very substantial build blurted out. "This doesn't concern you tiny, you can go." Gary was average height for a fifteen-year-old. He was built on a very solid frame and was deceivingly strong. Most of all he did not like being called tiny. He jumped at the big man like a pit bull. He was only a few inches away from getting his hands on the big store clerk when the second employee jumped in. Like a well-choreographed SWAT team the two Seven Eleven clerks went into action. The big guy, who still had hold of Joe threw him with all his might to the ground. Joe hit the cold, dirty, tile floor, and let out an audible, "Ump."

As Joe tried to stand up the guy behind the counter jumped over and went to tackle him. The big guy went over to engage Gary. He towered over him and outweighed him by more than a hundred pounds. He took him and pushed him out of the store like he was a rag doll and started yelling, "I'm calling the cops, and if you try to come back in here I'm going to break your friends arm and you're going to get arrested with him. Now stay the hell out!"

Gary shot back, "Come out here so I can kick your ass!" The door closed and the two employees placed their focus upon Joe. They pulled him off the floor. Now he stood facing the two brutes still not knowing what they wanted with him. He knew he was scared because he could feel his testicles pulling up into his abdomen.

The guy who was holding Joe passed him back to the bigger guy and said to him. "Take care of this piece of shit, Wally, I'm calling the cops."

Joe started to speak as Wally took hold of him. "What did I do?"

"You know, kid. You tried to shoplift. That old lady that just left told us. Now empty your pockets on the counter."

Joe who was never known as a tough guy did have a huge streak of righteousness in him. He was proud of his willingness to stand up for what he thought was right. He loved the quote he learned in American History class that Andrew Jackson said. "One man with courage can make a difference." Although he was scared and was sure he was going to get beat up he knew he did nothing wrong. People can't be treated like this, it was time to show some courage. With the most indignant voice he could summon he said, "I absolutely will not. I didn't do anything. You have no right to do this."

Wally reached over the counter and opened the cash register. He pushed his fat hand way toward the back and pulled out a heavy rubber blackjack. As his hand came back over the counter he slammed it down onto the conveyor belt where customers put their groceries. It hit with a huge Bang and Snap. Joe jumped back startled and started to rethink his righteousness.

Outside Gary paced back and forth like a caged tiger. Steam literally shooting out of his mouth and nose as he breathe the cold night air. As potential customers approached the store Gary scared them off. He couldn't do much to help his friend, but he could still hurt the owners of the store. As he walked passed he would look through the large window making sure Joe was still safe. His anger was growing and he was ready to run in if they tried to rough him up.

The other fellow came back and told Wally, that the cops were on the way. "Thanks, Mike," Wally said. Then Wally, still tapping the black jack on the conveyor belt, turned back to Joe. "Now, one more time, empty your pockets."

Joe spoke again, "You're not scaring me with that."

Wally raised the solid black rubber blackjack and with all the force he could muster slammed it down on the counter. WHAP! The sound came as it hit, only inches from Joe's hand. Joe looked down at his hand, then up at Wally, then down again.

Joe reached into his pocket and said, "I'm gonna show what I have just to teach you a lesson." He reached into the right-side pocket of his blue parka with his right hand and spoke, "In this pocket I have some old gum and a baby Charleston Chew."

He grabbed the contents of his pocket and dropped them onto the counter. He was as surprised as Mike and Wally when he saw two individually wrapped packages of condoms and a stack of rolling papers appear on the counter. Joe reached into his left side pocket and in a slightly more nervous tone said, "In this pocket I have some baseball cards and my report card, which by the way if you look closely at it you will see I am an exceptional student." He pulled his hand out and placed a half a pack of cigarettes and a book of matches on the counter. Wally and Mike looked at each other. What kind of freak was this kid? Joe was confused and embarrassed at the same time. He looked out the glass doors and windows and saw his friend Gary outside pacing back and forth, his arms flying around erratically and the mist of the cold night air coming out of his mouth.

Joe looked back at Wally and Mike and said, "You shouldn't be selling this stuff anyway." Then Joe had an epiphany, he must have taken his older brother's jacket by mistake. They had the same color parkas.

Wally and Mike continued to look in disbelief at the crap on the counter. They didn't notice that the cash register drawer had been left open. With their attention, still on their suspect, a shady looking guy in a navy-blue hoodie walked past the counter on the opposite side. In what could only be described as a ridiculously stupid move, he reached in and grabbed all the cash he could and bolted out of the store. Mike and Wally were taken totally by surprise, but lucky for them someone else wasn't. As the thief fled the store Gary Murphy saw all that was going on and went into action. The guy in the blue hoodie thought he was free and clear once he got into the parking lot. Then from out of nowhere he was hit and taken down, hard. After tackling him Gary jumped on top of him and put his forearm across the back of his neck to immobilize him. Just as Gary had control of him two police cars came cruising into the parking lot with their lights flashing. It looked like a scene from a movie.

The police pulled Gary off the suspect and held both of them until Wally and Mike came outside. "That's him, officer, the one in the blue pullover. That other guy caught him for us." Wally looked at Gary and said, "thanks kid."

By that time, Joe had walked out of the store and stood next to his friend. "How's your father?" He asked.

"I'm fine. What about you, what did they do to you in there?"

"Nothing yet. Some lady told them I was shoplifting so they wanted me to empty my pockets but I took Billy's coat by mistake, so I was pulling all kinds of shit out of the pockets. They think I'm some kind of degenerate."

"That's bullshit! Your mother and me would kill you," Gary answered.

One of the police officers handcuffed the robber and took him to the squad car. The other cop pointed at Joe and asked Mike. "Is this the kid you called us about?"

Mike answered. "Yeah, but it was a mistake. The lady said the guy in the back of the store with the blue coat. She must have meant that asshole in the blue hoodie." He pointed to the guy sitting in the back of the police car.

The cop looked at Mike and Wally and asked them. "Are we done here then?" Mike answered. "Yes sir, thank you."

"You're welcome," the police officer said. Then he turned to Gary, and with a pat on his shoulder said. "Nice work kid."

The police drove away with their suspect and the four boys walked back into the store. Wally and Mike both apologized to Joe. He walked over to the counter and collected the contraband from his brother's pockets.

Gary looked up at Wally and said, "We're not done yet!" Joe hung his head. Just when he thought he was clear.

Wally looked down at Gary and said, "We're done, I'm not messing with you." Gary figured that was about as close to an apology that he was going to get so the boys left the store and headed home. As they walked home Joe was still shaking from the events that had just transpired. Gary appeared as calm as usual. Joe was amazed.

He asked his friend, "How do you do it? How can you be so brave? Nothing scares you. How is that possible?"

Gary thought for a second and answered his friend, "It's do or die."

Back in the real-world lunch time is just about done and the sounds of the park slowly fill Joe's ears again. He still smiles when he thinks of those childhood adventures he had with his friend. It's a shame they don't see each other that much anymore. It makes him think if killing himself is an act of cowardice or if, for once in his life he is being brave. "Let's face it, I've always been a coward," Joe spoke aloud as his thoughts wandered back to his years in ninth grade.

It was springtime in 1979, school was winding down and next year Gary and Joe would move up to the senior high school and be in tenth grade. Tonight they were hanging around the library not to study but to find girls. The library was a known hot spot for girls who weren't interested in studying either. It was close to nine o'clock and the library was getting ready to close so the boys decided to head home.

I don't want to say Gary looked for trouble, but sometimes he did. Tonight, he insisted on walking home through the short cut which took them down the alley known as Frat Turf. To walk down Frat Turf Alley, or FTA as the locals called it, you needed to belong to a fraternity and wear your specially designed jacket known as your colors. Many self-proclaimed tough guys tried to walk through FTA but most ran as fast as they could to avoid a beating. The slower ones took a beating and Joe was not a fast runner.

Joe did his best to convince Gary not to go down FTA but to no avail. Gary was in a mood. He had been trying for two weeks to get with this girl, Valerie. She was a statuesque brown-eyed beauty. On most of their neighborhood strolls lately all he would talk about was her. Tonight, she would be at the library and Gary was going to make his move. The plan was so simple it was genius. The boys would go into the library and search for her. When they found her, Joe would start a small disagreement with Gary. Then he would gently push him into her. Once contact was made, Gary could start his rap and Joe would disappear.

As they turned down the History aisle they spotted her. Gary's heart immediately sank. She was there looking pretty as ever, but hanging all over Danny Cullen. He was the biggest dirtball in the high school, and a frat boy. What the hell would a beautiful girl like that see in him? He was in his fifth year of high school. Not to be out done by his eleven years of grammar school and junior high school. His hair was so thick with grease you could drill for oil. Which would not be too bad except he never put grease in his hair. His personal hygiene was so bad they said he showers at the zoo. When the gorillas let him.

Joe tried to convince his friend to walk down and talk to her. Gary would have none of it. "Fuck her!" He turned and started to walk out of the building. Now he was in a mood. They walked a few blocks in silence. Joe knew Gary needed to work this out for himself. As they approached the corner of Prospect Street and Hastings Avenue Joe continued walking straight. He took a few steps and noticed he was alone. Gary had stopped and was taking a long look down Frat Turf Alley. Reluctantly, Joe turned and walked back to him. "What are you doing?" Joe asked.

"I'm going home," Gary replied.

"Are you going down FTA?" Joe asked.

"I sure as hell am." He shot back with anger in his voice. He turned right and started a nice, slow, even, walk. He kicked every can or bottle he could find, trying to make as much noise and draw as much attention as he could. Joe stood alone at the corner of Prospect and Hastings. He watched as Gary slowly walked, doing anything he could think of to draw attention to himself. He shook his head in disbelief and ran to catch up with his friend.

Most of the frat boys were high school dirtballs. They loved to bully the younger junior high kids or the poor defenseless nerds of the high school. The alley was not well lit. It had the stench of garbage and stale beer. The dirtballs would hang out in the sunken stairwells that made up both sides of the alley. Gary made a point of kicking empty cans and bottles down these stairwells. Joe caught up to him and walked along his left side. Joe walked down the alley with heightened senses, his adrenalin pumping and his body on high alert. Gary was looking for trouble tonight and he was going to find it.

Gary seemed calm and cool as usual. He was strutting down the alley at a very leisurely pace. He was also talking in a louder voice than Joe was used to. While Joe was doing all, he could to control his nerves, he started to pick up on Gary's conversation. "I wonder where the frat fags are tonight. Maybe they had to stay home with their mommies," Gary said.

Joe was starting to get the feeling it wasn't going to be his night. In his mind, he was already beat up. He was looking for excuses to tell his mom and dad how he got like this. He knew if he told the truth they would not want him to stay friends with Gary. Joe continued down FTA not listening to the one-sided conversation Gary was having with no one in particular. He was still a bundle of nerves. The way his shoulders kept bobbing up and down and turning his head side to side, it reminded Gary of a ventriloquist puppet. Joe was starting to feel at ease that they were almost out of the alley: maybe the frat boys weren't out tonight. Then he heard it.

"Hey boys, we have company."

It was a deep, raspy voice like someone who was a heavy smoker. Gary stopped dead in his tracks but did not turn around. Joe stopped as well. Every muscle in his body told him to run but he stood by his friend. Gary wanted to make sure the voice was speaking to them. Out of pure fear and some curiosity Joe spun around to see how much trouble they were in. From the shadows, he saw an orange glow; as it came closer he could see puffs of smoke, and then a silhouette appeared out of the darkness.

As the figure approached his features became more apparent; he was more on the short side but very wide. He wore thick black work boots that added some elevation. As he walked. He had a bounce to his step that made the chain holding his wallet jingle back and forth. His black and red leather jacket made his shoulders look extra wide and gave his body a V shape. He had long, brown, greasy hair that was very unkempt. Joe marveled at his face. It was unmarked; he thought a tough guy like that would be full of scars and cuts. Joe wasn't sure who this guy was. His eyes were drawn to his grin. He had a tough guy posture and a confident smirk on his face. Joe could not stop staring at this guy's mouth. He had brown teeth with green and black spots. He knew he was about to get beat up yet he felt he was being rude staring. The tough guy took another puff on his cigarette, took it out of his mouth, and flicked the ash off. Then he placed it back into his mouth and started talking.

"Well, well, looks like we got us some trouble makers walkin on our turf."

Now Gary was sure who they were talking to, and he started to smile as he slowly turned around. As he faced the thug in the alley he spoke. "Richie Sylvester, are you still with that Sorority, the Alphas? Where are the rest of the girls? Changing their tampons?"

Richie's face grew visibly red. He took the cigarette out of his mouth threw it to the ground, and started to walk towards Joe and Gary.

In a very shaky trembling voice Joe spoke, "Oh, don't worry. I'll get that for you." Joe walked slowly and deliberately towards the burning cigarette lying on the ground. He thought he was being clever because it gave him a chance to get behind Richie. Out of the corner of his eye Gary could see a group of the Alphas standing across the alley. Joe was scared. He wanted to run but he could never leave his friend alone.

He stood his ground and listened as Gary told him, "I'll take this dirtball. You cut in front of me and slow his girlfriends down."

Joe turned around and faced Gary in disbelief. "The plan is for you to beat up Richie and me to beat up the rest of the guys?" Joe asked.

"This won't take long," Gary replied.

Joe turned and muttered to himself, "Motherfucker, how does this happen? This fucking guy."

He didn't know how but Joe walked a few feet up the alley across from the small group of Alphas as Gary started to walk towards Richie Sylvester. Sylvester took a quick look to see if his back up was coming but saw no movement. Richie was used to people backing down to him, he was all bluff and bravado. Most of his fights were with younger kids too scared to fight back. Today he was going to have to fight, because Gary kept coming.

Now as Gary came closer Richie was feeling nervous. He started to reach into his pocket; he removed his right hand and pulled out a shiny object. When he pushed the button, it made a distinct sound; there was no mistaking it, it was a switchblade. Gary saw the weapon and kept coming at him.

"You better back down man or you're gonna get cut," Richie said. He took a swipe at Gary but he blocked it with his left hand, he placed his right leg behind Richie's leg and pushed him over it, and Richie went down. Gary now had the advantage as he was towering over him. Richie started to sit up but Gary reared back and with his right hand punched Richie right in the face. The greasy dirtball fell to the cement in a heap. Now he had a mark on his face. Gary stepped over him and picked up the switchblade.

He headed over to where Joe was standing. The Alphas started to appear more visible in the alley, moving towards Joe. They started to walk across, although they did not seem to be in a hurry to help their comrade. As Gary and Joe started to walk towards the rest of the frat boys crossing the alley, the night became silent.

Gary broke the silence when he said, "I hope you dirtballs are comin over here to help this dipshit find his teeth!" He pointed to Richie rolling and moaning on the ground.

A voice could be heard from the back of the group. "It's cool. We don't want no trouble with you. You know Richie he's got a big mouth. We'll take care of him."

"We don't like being hassled every time we come down the alley," Gary yelled back.

The voice yelled back. "You guys are all right. There's no hassle, come down anytime. It's cool man."

Gary and Joe walked away. Joe suddenly felt as tough as Gary; he started to walk with a swagger. As they walked side by side down the alley Joe spotted something out of the corner of his eye. He walked away from Gary and stood over a half-lit cigarette. He turned to see the Alphas picking Richie up off the ground. He never broke eye contact with the group picking up the beaten thug. Then he lifted his foot and stamped out the burning butt with authority. When he lifted his foot off the expired cigarette he kicked it back down the alley. The Alphas continued to drag a bloody Richie off the ground and went back into their dark corner of the alley.

Joe and Gary didn't speak much the rest of the way home. Joe was still in awe of the way his friend handled those thugs. They turned down Central Avenue, the block they lived on. The night was still quiet. As they approached Gary's house Joe looked over and said, "Ya know, Gary, I thought we were going to get killed earlier."

Gary answered with confidence, "No chance. As long as we stick together no one can beat us."

Joe looked at his friend and a smile crossed his face as he said, "How's your father?"

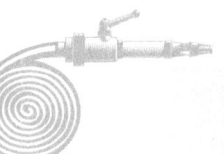

CHAPTER THREE

DEATH BY JUMPING

A few days later Joe was sitting in his house. He was alone at the dining room table. Michelle wasn't due home from work for quite some time yet. He was deep in thought and doodling on some scrap paper. He drew a crude upright rectangle. Inside the rectangle, he drew some small squares. The doodle was starting to take shape. He was drawing windows on a tall building. It was his interpretation of a skyscraper. On the top of the building he made a capital P. Outside the building was a stick figure standing on a ledge about ten floors above the ground. He made a dotted line from the stick figure down to the ground and wrote the word SPLAT! on the paper. At the bottom of the page he wrote, his next day off from work Tuesday. As he wrote he heard a voice in his head with a sinister laugh, "Heh, heh, heh."

His next thought was how to get there? He figured the best way was to take the Long Island Railroad. If he got off at Penn. Station, he could take a subway train downtown to Bowling Green Station. Then it would just be a short walk to the Palmer building. Tuesday is just another work day, he could walk into the building unnoticed. Then it was just a matter of taking the elevator to the tenth floor and finding an open window. Perhaps there would be an open bathroom window or cleaning closet. He could sneak into it open the window, crawl out onto the ledge, and, Bob's your uncle, splat!

He took his pencil and scribbled out the rough drawing then pushed the paper to the side. His hand hit a heavy object buried under some papers. When he lifted the papers, he saw a book he hadn't thought about or seen for many years. It was his and Michelle's wedding album. He reached for the album; it was faded with age not the pearly, white color that he remembered. A smile crossed Joe's face as he slowly opened the book and heard the spine creak. The color pictures looked back at him. They had a thin layer of plastic covering them. He looked at the first picture; it was his lovely bride staring at her reflection in a mirror. She was holding a huge colorful bouquet of flowers. Just looking at the picture made Joe remember the fragrance it carried. She was, of course, stunningly beautiful in her white satin wedding gown. It truly looked like the happiest day of her life.

As he continued to turn the pages, he thought how this simple but elegant album was like a time machine. It transported him back to much happier days when he was starting a new adventure in his life, with the love of his life by his side. He continued to look at the pictures and his mind drifted back to that hot, hazy day in August when he and Michelle took their vows. It all came rushing back to him; like it was yesterday. He was standing in the church sacristy when his younger brother came running in and told him told him, "Joe, we can't find your wedding rings!"

Joe kept his cool, a trademark he developed during his years in the fire department. He looked at his brother and with a calm demeanor said. "Who's we? I gave the rings to you to hold, Jack."

Jack stood scratching his head thinking; he looked at his older brother and sheepishly said, "That's true, I can't find the rings."

"When did you last have them?" Joe asked.

Jack thought for a moment and said, "I had them yesterday when you gave them to me."

Joe let out an audible sigh and started to think about what should be done. Just then another man wearing a black tuxedo entered the sacristy. It was Joe's friend Gary.

He asked. "Is everything all right back here? Do you need anything?" Joe felt instant relief at seeing his friend; he would know what to do, just like a super hero.

"Well," he started, "Jack can't find the rings for the ceremony so now I'm going out there with nothing but a smile."

Gary looked at Joe and his brother and said, "I'll be right back." He flew out of the door of the sacristy as Joe and Jack stood silently listening to the organ playing. In the church people were shuffling back and forth finding their seats. After a few minutes, Joe noticed, the organ music had stopped. That meant the Wedding March was imminent.

The organist fingers had just hit the ivory keys to make the first familiar chords when Gary entered holding two golden rings. Huffing and puffing he said. "Here, I found the rings," and handed Joe two beautiful diamond crusted gold wedding bands.

"Just in time. Thanks, you saved the day again!" Joe said.

Gary answered, "That's what I do."

Joe took one last look at the rings before placing them in his pocket, then he noticed something. "Hey, Gary, these aren't my rings."

"Yeah I never said they were your rings."

"Where did you get them?"

"That's not important."

Gary approached Joe and put his arm around his best friend. He guided him towards the corner of the room away from the few people milling around. "Joe, we've been through a lot of shit together so you know we can be honest with each other." Joe stood looking quizzically at his friend. Gary continued, "What I'm trying to say is if you don't want to go through with this I'll get you outta here and no one will see or hear from you for a month no questions."

Joe gave his friend a hug and said, "Thank you buddy, but she is the best thing that's happened to me since I met you."

"I know, but I had to ask."

The ceremony was going very well. The bride was radiant, the groom handsome, and the bridesmaids and ushers looked stunning. The happy couple exchanged their vows for better or worse, and before they were pronounced man and wife the priest asked the guests gathered for the ceremony, "If anyone here knows of any reason this couple should not be wed speak now or forever hold your peace."

As expected the church was quiet until a middle-aged obese woman shot up from her seat like she sat on a tack. "I object!" she blurted out. Every head in the church spun around at the voice in the back of the church. The woman pointed directly at the almost married couple and shouted, "Those are my rings!"

Joe shot a look at Gary who just said, "I'm on it." Off the Altar he went, down the aisle, which was covered from back to front in a beautiful white carpet. As Gary ran, his feet kicked up the white carpet. He looked like a cartoon character running as fast as he could, but not getting any place. His feet were moving so fast he was bunching up the white runner behind him. The church was quiet except for the sounds of his feet and the low whispers of the stunned guests.

When he finally reached the rotund woman, the church went silent. Everyone listened as Gary quietly whispered to the lady. All that could be heard were the loud responses of the woman who kept saying "hum." Every person gathered in the church watched as Gary reached into his pockets and started to hand money over to the large woman. She had her hand out and wiggled her pudgy ring-less fingers as Gary laid an unknown amount of cash into her hand. After a few seconds, it was all over.

Gary sprinted up the aisle and said, "You may continue padre." Then he leaned in close to the priest ear and said, "We'll just give the rings back when were done."

The bride and groom as well as the priest kept staring at him. In fact, the entire church was staring at him. Gary started to feel uncomfortable. He reached up to loosen his tuxedo collar. The pressure was building so he finally blurted out. "What? I rented them from her. I'm a cop for crying out loud, do you think I'd steal them?" All eyes were still on Gary who felt very uncomfortable. In a rushed voice and with hand gestures which suggested for the ceremony to continue he said. "Jez, were almost there. All that's left is man and wife; if you say man and wife we're outta here and I can make everything right again."

The priest turned to the couple and said. "I now pronounce you man and wife. You may kiss the bride"

The couple kissed in the quiet of the church. The silence and the kiss were broken when Jack yelled out, "Son of a bitch, I found them, they were in this stupid vest pocket all along." Then Jack pulled out the two golden bands, and the church erupted in applause. Outside the fire trucks started to sound their sirens.

Joe closed the book; he had a smile on his face and a tear running down his cheek. The couple started life together with such high hopes. It was a great first few years. Then, The Monster appeared. She just couldn't live with it. Joe never blamed her; he hated The Monster too. He sat for a few moments and thought. He was still so in love with her. He pushed the album back to the corner of the table, and in a low audible tone said, she'll he'll be free of me Tuesday."

Joe awoke Tuesday morning and kissed his wife as she lay asleep on the couch. Michelle felt the tender touch of his lips and thought it was unusual, then quickly fell back asleep. She didn't need to be at work until ten and wanted to sleep in. Joe took a quick shower and grabbed a cup of coffee; he wanted to be out of the house before Michelle got up. Today there would be no note. He envisioned a police officer coming to the door to tell his wife of the tragedy.

He placed the empty coffee cup into the sink. Then he tiptoed past the sleeping beauty on the couch. He slowly opened the front door hoping not to wake her. He stood inthe doorway and took one last look around his house. Then his eyes fell on Michelle asleep on the couch. He took one last long look and slowly and silently closed the door.

He walked the few blocks to the railroad station. It was a pleasant walk. He took note of all the houses and neighbors he would never see again. When he arrived at the railroad station, he walked over to the ticket counter to purchase his one-way ticket. Joe saw the irony in this as well. Soon the train conductor would be punching his ticket. He walked up to the window, and in strong confident voice said to the elderly ticket man, "One way to Penn. Station."

The balding man with thick glasses looked up at him and with a heavy Jewish accent said. "Vhat, you're not coming home? You've got some fancy schmancy business to do?"

Joe looked back confused and replied, "No sir, no business, I just need a one-way ticket."

"Vhat, you are made of money? You know the prices go up at peak times. Be smart my friend buy a round trip now."

"But I am only going one way. I do not need a round trip," Joe said, starting to lose his patience with the elderly clerk.

"Of course, you're going one vay, I know you're going one vay, everybody starts one vay. But you have to come back so you buy a round trip."

Joe glanced up at the large clock on the wall. The train was due in two minutes. "Okay, give me the round trip to Penn. Station." Joe said in frustration.

"Now you're thinking young man, you saved seven dollars." The clerk started to punch the information into his keyboard. Joe stood on the other side tapping his foot as the seconds counted down to the arrival of the train.

Finally, the clerk passed the tickets out to Joe. "This ticket is for your trip from here to New York. This one you keep. It's for when you come back." The clerk said.

Joe grabbed the tickets and started to run towards the steps. "But I'm not coming back," he yelled to the clerk.

"Vhy didn't you say so. You don't need a round trip for that, you dumb schmuck!" The clerk yelled back.

He climbed the steps up to the platform; he and Gary had spent many nights running up and down these steps getting in shape for their high school football team. When he reached, the top Joe took notice. The platform was not that crowded. Most of the people up here either worked off-hour shifts, or were just going in to spend the day in the Big Apple.

He walked over to the edge of the platform and thought. "I could just step in front of the train when it gets here. It would be quick and easy but it would also be rude; all these people would be late for work. Then they'll call the cops and the fire department and close the station. That would make more people late. Don't forget about the poor engineer. How would he feel if he killed someone?" Joe shuddered. It was horrible to even think about. Just stick with the plan, he thought.

It was a warm, overcast day as Joe walked up the steps of the New York subway into Downtown Manhattan. He needed to walk just a few blocks through the crowded city to get to the Palmer building. When he reached the front of the building he stopped and looked up. He counted up the ten floors where the windows were opened and was satisfied; it would be more than enough to finish him off. He walked through the revolving door with confidence, and with his head held high walked past the security desk. He wasn't sure if it was his swagger that showed he belonged in the building, or the fact that the guard was trying to pick up one of the beautiful girls who worked there. Either way, he was in the building and standing in front of a bank of elevators that went to the tenth floor.

Joe stood in front of the shiny gold bank of elevators. He waited with a few other people for the lift to arrive and the doors to slide open. Suddenly a thirtyish gentleman in a tremendous rush bumped into Joe as he stood waiting. Joe slowly turned to face the man, waiting for an apology.

After a few seconds, Joe said with a sarcastic tone, "Excuse me." The shiny gold doors opened and several people stepped out. As the elevator emptied Joe and the other people waiting stepped in. Again, the rude man pushed past everyone else knocking into Joe. Joe looked at him as the doors closed with a ding.

The elevator rose with a jerk. "Excuse me, that's the second time you bumped into me." Joe said in a polite voice.

"Screw you!" Was the short gruff answer he received.

"You're a jackass, mister," Joe shot back.

The man replied immediately, "Go kill yourself asshole!"

The elevator dinged again as it reached the tenth floor.

Again, the man pushed past everyone to be the first one out. Joe followed him with a polite, "excuse me." He pushed past everyone and followed the rude man as he hurried down the hall. "Hey! hey, you. Turn around!" Joe yelled at the man. His pleas were completely ignored. Just as Joe caught up to him the man opened an office door and slammed it behind him. He stood in front of the door debating if he should go in after the rude son of a bitch. Then he looked ahead of him and saw an open office door. Like a cat burglar he snuck over to the office and peaked in. It was empty and the extra wide window was already half open.

Joe forgot all about the asshole in the elevator. He entered the room and closed the door behind him. He walked around the big wooden desk and noticed a name plate that said Mr. Ramsay. As he got behind the desk he saw a picture. It was a classic family portrait of a loving family: Mr. Ramsay, a pretty woman seated to his right and two children, a boy and a girl both looked to be in their teenaged years.

As he opened the window he felt envious of what Mr. Ramsay had achieved in his life, a hardworking man with a loving family. It seemed he knew the secret of a loving marriage, a secret Joe wished he knew.

"Hey, you blew it, open the window and let's get this over with," came a voice from inside Joe's head.

"I've been wondering where you've been, you monster?" Joe replied.

The window slid open smoothly. Joe stopped to think; this was going too easily. He bent down to peek his head out of the window; he looked right and left then looked down. He took a deep breath and started to crawl through the opening. He stepped out onto the ledge. It was about twelve inches wide. He crawled about halfway, until he was between the window he went out, and the window of the next office. Still on his knees he slowly started to get on to his feet.

"What are you doing you don't need to stand, just roll off." The Monster said to Joe.

"You know that's your problem you have no flair for the dramatic. I need to stand up, look down and make my peace before I jump. So just shut the hell up and let me handle this," Joe answered sternly.

His years as a fireman taught him great balance. He had little problem getting to his feet. He braced his back against the red brick wall. He slowly tilted his down. Looking over his white sneakers he saw a crowded street below. It looked like a busy ant farm. Little people walking back and forth. Tiny cars not moving at all on the city streets. Like an ant farm everyone going about their business, not caring what is happing above them. He took a breath and started to pray asking God to forgive him for what he was about to do. He was sure that God would see this as a selfless act to destroy a monster and make a better life for a more deserving person.

The time had come, he made his peace with his maker and himself and was ready to die. He started to push his weight forward and lifted his right foot. Then he heard a sound.

"Hey, you on the ledge." Joe pushed back against the wall and turned to his left to see Mr. Ramsay leaning his head out talking to him.

"Listen, don't try to talk me down, I know what I'm doing," Joe said to him. "By the way you have a lovely family, cherish them," he continued. Mr. Ramsay looked scared which surprised Joe since he was the one in the building.

"Hey Mac, I don't care if you jump. And thanks, they're good kids. I'm very proud of them. No, I was hoping you could help me out first?"

"Hey guy, I'm about to jump here how could I possibly help you out?"

"I'm in a bind. There's a guy in the next office. He came up to confront his wife. She works here. He thinks she is having an affair and he's going to kill the son of a bitch when he finds out. I know this girl, she's gonna squeal. She'll tell him everything, she's no good under pressure. I think he has a gun!"

"How does that affect you?"

"Well she is having an affair, and when she tells him who the son of a bitch is, it will affect me because he's going to kill me!"

Joe thought about the picture on Mr. Ramsay's desk. It seems everyone lives a lie. Then he spoke, "What the hell am I gonna do?"

"Well, you want to kill yourself, right? And the guy in the next office wants to kill someone, so I figure you slide over to the next window and talk to the guy. Maybe you tell him you're the one having an affair with his wife, and he kills you. It's perfect. He kills you, which is what, you want and I'm still alive which is what I want. Then he goes to jail and I still have his wife, which is what she wants. It's like an equi-lateral triangle, it's perfect." He said with a smile.

Joe could not believe what he was hearing; he knew his plan was going too easily. "Look, Mister, I'll go in and talk to him because I don't care if he shoots me, but I'm not admitting to your indiscretion. I have a wife myself and I couldn't live with myself if she thought I was having an affair."

"But yet it's okay to kill yourself? That's a bit ironic," Ramsay said.

"Don't piss me off, pal or I'll jump, you'll get shot, and we can continue this discussion in front of the Pearly Gates of Heaven."

Ramsey answered, "Fine, fine it was a long shot anyway. Just get in there and calm him down. I'll call the cops."

Joe carefully slid his feet along the ledge to the next window; it was open about six inches. He peeked inside and saw a man waving a gun. It was the asshole from the elevator. He was pacing back and forth; the woman inside was crying, trying to tell him how wrong he was and how much she loved him. Joe put his hands under the window and tried to raise it. The window would not budge. He tried again, but to no avail. He didn't have the correct leverage. The two people inside were so engrossed with each other they didn't even notice Joe outside. Finally, Joe started to knock on the window. The girl turned around and let out a scream seeing the strange man on the ledge outside. "A little help, please," Joe said.

She walked over to the window and asked. "What do you want?"

Joe answered, "Well, I'm out here on a ledge ten floors up; so, I'll take a parachute or I guess you could let me in."

The beautiful lady looked at Joe and with confusion on her face said. "This is an insurance office; we don't have parachutes."

Joe just sighed and asked, "Can you open the window then please?" Together Joe and the woman were able to open the window and Joe climbed into the office.

The man holding the gun looked annoyed as Joe climbed through the window. "Hey, what the hell is going on here? You, you're the asshole from the elevator." Joe looked at him and replied, "No, you're the asshole from the elevator."

"I should shoot you right now."

Joe stood in front of the man with his arms held out to his side. "Why? What is that going to do? What's going on? Maybe I can help."

"I'll tell ya," said the man with gun. "This ungrateful whore is sleeping around on me and I think it's with that fat bastard next door."

"Well can you blame her? You just called her a whore," Joe shot back, then he spoke again, "Look put the gun down. If you kill anyone your life will be good as over too. If she's not happy any more than let her go. Nothing you do will change her."

The man with the gun started to well up with tears and slowly lowered his gun. The woman took this opportunity to slide behind him and out the office door into the arms of a rushing policeman. Joe walked over and took the weapon from the man just as the office door flew open and a New York City SWAT team rushed in. In an instant, they had Joe tackled on the floor and took the gun from him. Joe tried to explain but the cops would have none of it. In the confusion, the original gunman thanked the officers for saving him and walked calmly out of the office.

Joe was face down on the floor with his hands cuffed behind his back. Two huge New York City police officers were sitting on his back. He kept trying to raise his head and tell them what was happening. Every time he lifted his head a policeman would smack it back down to the floor. Then Ramsey popped his fat head into the room and said, "That's not him! He saved the girl."

The cops lifted Joe to his feet. "That's what I've been trying to tell you." Joe ran to the window still cuffed. "That's him! That's the guy!"

Below as casual as can be, the jealous husband sauntered out of the building. The sergeant in the office immediately radioed down to the cars in front of the building. The suspect was arrested on the spot without any fanfare or struggle.

The police as well as the workers in the Palmer building praised Joe as a hero. Against his wishes, he was taken to police headquarters to file a report. When the news media found out, Joe's face was all over the television and newspapers. The story was told in vivid detail of how Joe saw a man with a gun enter the Palmer Building. He followed him up to the tenth floor and saw him go into an office. Working only on instinct and with no regard for his life (they got that part right.) He climbed out onto the window ledge ten floor above the busy city street and into the office to save the poor defenseless girl being held hostage by the crazed gunman.

Joe must have given a dozen interviews between television and newspapers. When he arrived home that night he found Michelle sitting on the couch, the computer on her lap. She was playing her social media games.

"Where have you been all day?" Michelle asked. It was obvious to Joe that Michelle had not seen any news yet so he started his story.

In a nervous but excited voice Joe spoke. "Well if you put the eleven o'clock news on…"

"I'm sorry, I don't have time to watch the news. I need to finish this game and get to bed. We have an inspection tomorrow," Michelle shot back tired and disinterested.

"Oh, okay. Maybe you can check the paper tomorrow?"

Michelle just waved her hand at him as if to shoo him away. Joe took another look at his wife playing her game and walked up the steps to the bedroom. He wanted to tell her but the way she dismissed him made him feel hurt. He continued slowly up the steps still hoping at the last second Michelle would call to him and ask about his day. The closer he got to the top of the staircase the more the anger built up inside him. As he got to the top of the landing he saw the hangman's noose above his head. He reached up and gave it a slap with his hand. The noose started to swing back and forth; he turned to walk to his lonely bedroom.

"That one, was not my fault," a voice in Joe's head said.

"Yeah, I guess I should have rolled," Joe replied. Now his thoughts were of another way to end his life.

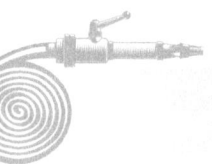

CHAPTER FOUR

OFFICER MURPHY

On Wednesday morning, Joe was up early. Since he botched his jump off the Palmer building, he had a commitment to keep. He had an extra shift to work today. On occasion, the paramedics were assigned a forced overtime shift. It was usually to cover another of the medics who might be on vacation, or sick leave. Today Joe would be working in Manhattan to cover a day shift for an old-timer named Butch. Joe had known about the shift for a few weeks. At the time of the assignment he was excited. Gary was also working in Manhattan and they might be able to meet up and perhaps have lunch. Gary had been working downtown near Wall Street for the last few years. When Joe awoke yesterday morning he was sure he would never see Gary again. But circumstances being what they were, he would be able to meet his friend today. If everything fell into place and their schedules meshed they would meet at the World Trade Center around noon, and have lunch.

It had been awhile since they last saw each other, although they talked to each other as often as possible on the phone. They had a special bond with each other. It was like a kind of telepathy. It was a feeling, an instinct, if one needed the other's help. In his college days Gary had a beat up old jalopy. It was mint green and had bullet holes running along the driver's side. It fit into his budget and ran well enough to get him to school. The car did have other issues though. The one that affected him most was the broken gas gauge. He would stall out on the side of the road, gas tank empty. A few minutes later Joe would be driving up the road in his beat up old Plymouth. Traffic would be slowing, and horns would be honking. As Joe slowly approached the backup, he would see the ugly mint green car with the bullet holes in it, stalled, sticking halfway out on the side of the road. The angry motorist's trying to get around it. Gary leaning against it, sarcastically waving to the irate drivers as they yelled all kinds of obscenities at him. Joe could only laugh, then pull his wreck over and help his friend.

Those who knew them best described it as though they have known each other since the beginning of time. They would say that somewhere during the history of time those two boys met. In his infinite wisdom, God decided this is a good combination. It's as good as any explanation. They were good for each other and the people around them.

Joe sat at his kitchen table drinking a cup of coffee with his wife. Neither one made eye contact with the other. They sat silently, only their small sips of hot coffee could be heard. She had her laptop open and was working on a presentation for the inspection today. She still did not mention the incident at the Palmer Building in which her husband was labeled a hero. It had become a typical breakfast for the couple; Michelle engrossed in her computer and Joe struggling for something to say. He was too angry or stupid to give in and mention the fifteen minutes of fame he achieved yesterday. Finally, he stood up and said in a purposeful, cold, unfeeling tone. "Bye. Good luck with your inspection today. See you later."

Michelle never looked up and gave her husband a wave as he left for work. As Joe walked to the train station his neighbors greeted him. It seems they watched the news last night. He was still fuming over the breakfast conversation, or lack of one. He could barely hear the voices calling out to him.

"Hey, Joe, great job yesterday. You're a hero," Mr. Jake yelled out from across the street. It fell on deaf ears. All he heard was The Monster in his head berating him for not rolling off the ledge. He continued his power walk to the train station. His head moving back and forth, his hands waving like a traffic cop.

The Monster continued, tormenting him. "What is her problem? Why is that damn computer so important to her? Oh, fuck it, we won't have to put up with it much longer."

When he got to work, his coworkers gave him a bit of the silent treatment. They all enjoyed doing that when someone did something special. If one of the medics delivered a baby, that was an occasion for the silent treatment. Saving a person from cardiac arrest and bring them back to life, earned a silent treatment. It was all done in good fun. It went on for a little while but soon his friends broke down and celebrated his adventure from the day before.

Joe signed out his ambulance and went to work on his checklist. It was the important part of the job. Making sure the ambulance was running properly and was stocked with all the medical equipment he needed for his shift. He checked all the lights, the siren, and then went into the back of the rig to go over his supplies. He sat down on the bench seat and systematically started to check and count his medical supplies. After that, he went over his to his drug box and checked the expiration dates on the medicines. If any of his meds were expired or about to expire he could trade them in for new ones. The last item to check was his telemetry system, a sophisticated EKG machine which transmitted cardiac rhythms to the doctors at the hospital via radio waves. The medic could dial in on his radio and speak to the doctor at the hospital. This allowed the doctors to help Joe interpret EKG rhythms and give the correct medication and dosage. When everything checked out he grabbed his medic kit. All the medics brought their own bags with them. It gave them the ability to set it up the way that worked best for them. Some of them wanted their IV supplies on top. Some liked to have their trauma supplies quickly available. It was personal preference.

Joe jumped into the driver's seat and started his rig. He pulled out of the garage and headed downtown. It was a hot day and the traffic and congestion in the city made it feel much hotter. The radio was somewhat quiet as far as emergences. It was a slow morning, just one transport to the hospital. Joe got a call at Battery Park for a young man having severe difficulty breathing. When he arrived, he found the man sitting under a tree. He was surrounded by half a dozen or so spectators. Joe ran up with his medic bag slung over his left shoulder. He pushed his way through and found a young man between eighteen and twenty-five years old struggling for every breath he could squeeze into his lungs.

Joe needed to quickly assess the cause of the man's distress. He could see the obvious respiratory trouble the man was having. He also noticed that his skin was cold and clammy, and his lips and face were swelling by the second. He already had an idea of what was going on and started to go through his bag. With his head, down fumbling through his kit Joe asked. "Hey bud, what happened?"

Still gasping for breath, the man said, "Bee sting!"

Just as the words came out Joe had found what he was looking for. He pulled out a long skinny object about the size of a pen. He quickly unwrapped it. Without hesitation took the device, which had a needle on the end of it, and plunged it into the man's exposed thigh.

By this time a few cops started to show up. In a calm voice, Joe spoke to one of them. "I just gave him an Epi shot. Can you bring me the oxygen and the trundle, please?" Shortly the cop returned with a green O2 cylinder and the rolling stretcher. The swelling in the man's face seemed to be going down, and his breathing seemed more relaxed. They loaded him into the ambulance and headed to Beekman Downtown Hospital. Joe took a deep breath as he sat in the back of the ambulance monitoring his patient. An acute anaphylactic reaction is a true life or death emergency. This guy would be okay but if help was delayed a few more minutes the outcome may have been much different.

It was close to lunch time when Joe left the emergency room. He was ready to meet his buddy. The downtown traffic was a beast at this hour. He was always annoyed at all the double-parked cars that held up the flow of traffic. He hated double parkers. "Arrest their asses and tow the damn car," he would often say. These crazy New York drivers would just stop anyplace they damn well pleased. Tourists who were coming to the city for the first time in their cars, have no idea what they're in for. Regular driving rules go out the window in Manhattan. All the double parking. Trucks just stopping anywhere to make deliveries. Pedestrians walking against the traffic light, between cars. It's the Wild West. Now add these novice tourists. They drive along and stop behind double-parked cars. Then sit, not moving, not going around the car, just honking their damn horn. There's no one in the car asshole! What is your horn going to do? This made it more difficult for the experienced Manhattan drivers to go around them. There is nothing more annoying than trying to go around a guy, honking his horn, at an empty double-parked car. It makes the traffic crawl.

Joe finally made it over to the Trade Center. As usual the streets were packed with cars and pedestrians. He was running late, so he double parked his rig, grabbed his portable radio, and locked the ambulance. He ran across the street dodging cars and people crossing. As he approached the front door, he could hear someone blasting their horn at his empty ambulance. He muttered under his breath. "Go around, asshole," and went inside. He ran to the burger joint where he planned to meet Gary. The restaurant was crowded. Joe scanned the room: there sitting alone in the corner by the window, looking regal in his police uniform was his friend, Gary.

Gary was a regular guy. He was average height with a solid build. With his short sleeve uniform on you could see his huge forearms and biceps. His hair was short and neat, a sandy blond color. His facial features were anything but regular. After all the fights, he was in he didn't have a mark on his face. His blue eyes were hypnotizing. His smile was infectious and he knew it. It was his best weapon in the battle of the sexes.

Joe bobbed and weaved his way through the crowd. He approached Gary from behind and clamped his hands down on his muscular shoulders.

"How's your father?" Joe said.

Gary of course gave the appropriate response. "How's your father?"

Joe passed in front of the table and sat. Before the boys could start a conversation a pretty, dark-haired waitress walked over to take their order.

She walked right past Joe, and looking directly at Gary she said, "Hi, my name is Amy, I'll be your server. Are you ready to order?"

Gary looked up and smiled. "Hello, Amy," he said oozing charm.

"Hi yourself, handsome," was her giggly reply. "What can I get you?" She continued. Looking directly at her, his blue eyes casting a spell.

Gary broadened his smile and said, "I'll have the turtle soup, and make it snappy."

Amy laughed and said, "Cute and funny, I like it."

"That's how I came out of the box," Gary replied.

By now Joe had enough of watching the Gary and Amy show. He purposefully and with a loud grunt cleared his throat. Amy turned to look at him. She rolled her eyes in a definite fuck you tone and turned back to Gary.

"He's annoying, but he's right. We need to order luscious," Gary said. Then he continued. "I'll have the Caesar salad and a Coke." Amy took her order pad out of her apron and wrote down the order.

"Hail Caesar!" Amy said in a sexy tone. Then her entire facial expression changed as she turned to take Joe's order. "What do you want?" she said in a deep workman like voice.

Joe stared down at the menu. He never looked up or made eye contact and said, "I'll have the duck soup with plenty of quackers, and bring him the bill." He pointed at Gary and laughed.

"Sir, do you know it's peak lunch time in downtown Manhattan. The busiest place on the planet. I really don't have time for nonsense. Do you want something or not?"

Gary broke in and said. "He'll have the chili burger and a coke.

Amy turned back to Gary and said. "Thanks, handsome I'll be back soon."

"I'll be here," he replied.

"You better be," she shot back.

"Oh, my, God, can you get the damn order?" Joe interjected with anger and frustration. Amy stormed off in a huff. Gary watched as she shook her ass back and forth while walking away. Gary brought his gaze back to the table and said, "I think she likes me."

"Ya think!" was Joe's response.

"So, what the hell was all that about yesterday?" Gary asked.

Joe looked embarrassed he did want to tell his hero, that he was trying to jump out of a window and stumbled into a hostage situation. "That was nothing. It was dumb. Right place, right time, that's all."

"Everyone says you're a hero. You showed true bravery. I agree."

"I'm not a hero. The funny thing is, if I were brave I wouldn't have even been there."

Gary had the sense he didn't want to talk about it. Still, he decided to try one more time to push him. "Joe, you climbed out a ten-story window and wrestled a loaded gun from a crazy man. That's quite an act of bravery I'd say."

"That guy was just an asshole. Brave? I wish I were brave. You're the brave one. Please don't use the word brave with me. I'm ashamed of how I've lived my life."

Gary truly looked puzzled. He said, "I'm not sure we have the same definition of brave."

Joe stared back and without blinking said, "You're the bravest guy I've ever met. You don't take shit from anyone, even going back to when we were kids."

Gary shook his head in disbelief and said, "You're confusing bravery with anger. I get angry and get myself and anyone I'm with into bad situation. That don't make me brave. The brave one is the guy who wants to run but stays anyway so his friend won't get his head bashed in. That's you; it's because of you I never got my head bashed."

Joe paused and reflected on what he had just heard. In some crazy, mixed-up way it made sense to him. He never thought of it in those terms. He looked up and said, "so I'm the bad ass here?"

Gary laughed and replied, "Yeah, the secrets out." As the boys laughed Amy returned with their drinks. She passed by Joe and with her right hand slammed his soda down. Joe watched as half his glass emptied onto the table. With her left hand, she carefully placed Gary's drink. A beautiful dark beverage with a nice foam on top and a lemon wedge. "Thank you, luscious," he said.

"Anytime handsome." She giggled back. "I'll be back in a minute with your food," she continued. Then she turned and wiggled away.

"What is it with you? How do you get all the girls?" Joe asked. Gary just shrugged his shoulders.

"So, how's Michelle?" Gary asked.

"She's good," was Joe's short, curt, answer.

"What does that mean? She's good."

"You know things haven't been great for a while. She likes her computer. We don't talk too much. She doesn't even know what happened yesterday. She even sleeps downstairs now. I don't blame her. It's more my fault and The Monster but I'm working on fixing it."

Gary looked confused. "I don't understand how did it get like this?"

"You know," Joe placed his hands in the air to make air quotation marks with his fingers. "The Monster."

Their conversation was interrupted by a plate smashing down in front of Joe. Amy had returned with their lunch. As the plate slammed down a few of the French fries fell to the floor. Then Amy with loving care placed Gary's salad in front of him. Gary looked down to see that Amy had taken the croutons and made a heart shape on the top of his salad. He looked up and smiled. Joe sat on the opposite side, his head and arms moving back and forth looking for a bottle of ketchup.

"Excuse me!" he said. "Excuse me!" He tried again, but he could not break the spell Gary cast on her. Keeping with his mood lately, Joe gave up. He picked up his messy chili burger and started to eat. Finally, Gary and Amy had stopped talking. Amy turned and started to wiggle away.

Gary looked across at Joe eating his messy burger and said. "Oh, you poor thing, eating that burger with no ketchup. Hold on." He turned to look for Amy and shouted, "Luscious, can you bring my friend a bottle of ketchup please?" She turned and gave an approving wave.

Joe sat, chili sauce covering his face and said, "Thanks a lot."

As lunch continued the boys started to talk about The Monster again.

"You, know, Joe I'm not sure it's The Monster that bothers you. I think you never got over leaving the Fire Department."

"Oh, thank you doctor Freud," Joe said sarcastically.

"No, really. That's when you were most happy."

"Look those days are over. I'm past it. My problem is I'm like a Disney character."

"What the hell does that mean?"

"Well look at their movies. Pinocchio, Beauty and the Beast, The Little Mermaid, and a bunch more. What do they have in common?"

"I don't know, they're cartoons."

"No, they all want to be human. That's what I want. I can't stand to be looked at. I just want to be human."

Gary let out a sigh and said, "That statement alone makes you the most human person I know." Joe looked down and finished his lunch.

Gary broke the silence, he looked up at Joe and said, "I don't understand. She married you for better or worse. I've never once heard her complain. She never left your side in the hospital. I sat with her and watched her cry and pray for you. I think you're wrong and she still loves you very much."

"No, it's over, I'm sure. I will never love another person as much as I love her. That's why I want to see that she is always happy. I never thought anyone could ever love me. I'm happy for the few years we had. She gave me water." Joe said in a low meaningful voice.

Gary stared at him as if he knew exactly what he meant. Then he said, "What the hell does that mean?"

"In The Hunchback of Notre Dame, Quasimodo is being whipped on the pillory. When his lashes are done, he must stay on the pillory for public exhibition for another hour. He's beaten, and in pain, people are mocking him, spitting at him, and all he wants is a drink of water. He asks over: and over, water, water. He begs for a sip of water. But he is so hideous that the people watching just stare at him, and continue to mock him. Finally, the beautiful gypsy girl

Esmeralda sees him begging for a drink. She shows some compassion for the poor deformed man. She walks up the pillory and tries to give him a drink. He doesn't want to take it at first. Maybe he's embarrassed because she is so strikingly beautiful and he is so ugly. She keeps trying. He finally, gives in and accepts a drink. Even trapped in that misshapen body she sees a human being. When he is released from his punishment, he runs to his home in the great Cathedral Notre Dame. He's just been whipped and publicly humiliated yet he is happy. His life has changed, someone took a little pity on him. Treated him like a man, not a monster. He sees his caretaker and says to him in a gleeful tone, 'She gave me water'. It was like having a reason to live. That's what Michelle did for me. She gave me water."

Joe put his head back down. Gary looked at him and said, "I think I understand." They finished off their drinks and Gary said. "Hey, before we go I've got a riddle for you." Joe looked up a bit surprised and said. "I'm all ears, what is it?"

"Well, you have thirty pennies."

"Why pennies? Why not nickels?" Joe interrupted.

"You want nickels, you can have nickels. It doesn't matter." Gary shook his head in frustration and continued. "You have thirty nickels, they are all face down, or tails, except for two which are heads up. Now, the object of the riddle is to make two piles with the same number of heads up nickels in each pile. Obviously, there are some rules. You cannot see the coins. You cannot feel the coins to see if they are heads or tails. You can touch the coins, and move them, and flip them. The piles do not have to have the same number of coins in them. They only need the same number of heads up coins. Ya got all that?"

Joe was staring at Gary very intently. He was concentrating on every word he heard. "I have a few questions," Joe said.

Gary motioned with both his hands. "Let's hear them."

"Okay I can move and touch the nickels."

"Correct."

"I can flip the nickels."

"Correct again. Two for two."

"When I touch, them I can't tell if it's face up or down?"

"Right you can only move them or flip them. Also, the piles don't have to have the same number of pennies, I mean nickels. You can have a pile with ten nickels and two of them are heads up and a pile with twenty and two are heads up. The only thing that matters is the number of heads up coins are the same."

"Okay I understand, I need some time to work on it."

Lunch was just about over and the boys waited for the check. Suddenly, the air was filled with the sexy aroma of Amy's perfume. Joe looked over his shoulder and saw the beautiful waitress walking toward them. She stopped by the table and tore the check out of her order book.

She held it in the air and Joe said, I'll take that please."

Amy looked at Gary and said, "I think the policeman should pay."

"Well I could never refuse a beautiful woman," Gary answered She passed him the check and he unfolded it and read the bill.

He looked at the big loopy writing on the check; it read, "Compliments of the house. Call me."

Under that was written a phone number. In the lower corner of the check was drawn a pair of handcuffs. It was signed Luscious! Gary looked at the phone number and recognized the area code as being from Queens. He held the paper in his hand and started for the cash register. Joe followed behind. Gary stopped short, peered over his right shoulder and said, "I'm paying the bill. The least you could do is leave the tip."

"You're right, I'm sorry," Joe replied. He turned and walked back to the table to leave a couple of bucks. Gary quickly stashed the paper in his pocket.

As Gary walked by Amy, he cupped her chin with his hand and said, "I'll talk to you tonight, Luscious."

She leaned into him and whispered, "Don't forget the handcuffs." Joe put his head down and smiled.

As they walked out of the restaurant he said, "How do you do that?"

Gary shrugged his shoulders and answered, "It's do or die."

They walked out of the cool restaurant into the hot summer city. Gary chuckled when he saw Joe's ambulance double parked with a block of noisy traffic behind it. "I should give you a ticket for double parking," Gary joked.

"Yeah, I hate those double parkers," Joe replied and he walked to his rig waving his hands at the cars honking their horns at him.

Gary turned and walked to his squad car double parked on the other side of the building. Nobody was honking at his car. He unlocked it and sat down. He needed to radio in that he was back from his lunch break. He drove off and started thinking about the conversation he had with Joe about bravery. He honestly never thought of himself as brave just short tempered. He didn't like to be taken advantage of; when he was in high school his summer, job was watching the bicycles for the summer school students. One hot day he noticed a car at the far end of the field driving slowly past the bikes. He stood up and started to walk down to where the car was. Usually that would be enough to make a thief leave. As he closed in on the car he was surprised. The car wasn't leaving. Then he saw the trunk pop open and someone trying to put a bike into it.

Gary started running to catch up with the thugs stealing the bike; he tried to keep as silent as possible. It always bothered him when he watched the cop shows on T.V. how they always seemed to yell at the suspects to "stop", or "halt" before they were even close to catching them. All that ever did was give the crooks a warning that trouble was coming, and a head start on the cops. He was about fifteen yards away before the thieves spotted him. They quickly closed the trunk and ran to the car and sped away. Gary started to full sprint and was able to catch up to the car before it could peel out. He leaned his upper body into the driver's side window. The two bike thieves were startled; of all the bikes, they stole in their lives no one had ever gone this far to stop them. Gary was able to grab the keys out of the ignition and turn the car off. He took the keys out of car and threw them on the ground behind him.

The passenger door swung open and out ran one of the thieves: the other wasn't so lucky. Gary grabbed him by the neck and pulled him out of the car and threw him to the ground. Gary pinned him face down on the pavement. By now half of the summer school was hanging out of the classroom windows watching and one of the teachers called the police. Soon the police arrived to arrest the thief. To Gary that's not being brave that's just not being taken advantage of. It was that attitude that Gary took with him to the police academy in 1988 when his dream was fulfilled and he became a police officer.

He learned a lot about dealing with people from the academy, and he did his best to that put into practice. If anyone needed to learn how to take verbal abuse from ignorant people it was him. Some techniques he learned from his training, like how to control his temper. Sometimes the abuse was too much, so he came up with his own techniques. One day on patrol in Brooklyn, he pulled over a speeder. It was a nasty section of town. The buildings were in various states of disrepair. Steel bars covered the windows, garbage cans and trash bags lined the sidewalks. The streets were mostly deserted with the exception of small clusters of young men and women huddled in doorways smoking cigarettes or God knows what. A cluster of four or five were wearing the same color jackets. It was the middle of summer, but the jackets identified the gang they belonged to. It also helped to hide their weapons. Crime had been on the rise in this area, most of it gang related.

It was close to sundown as he approached the car. It seemed to be a routine traffic stop. As he approached the car, he started to size up the situation. The driver was a well-dressed middle-aged, white male. As he got closer to the car he could see the gentleman was somewhat overweight. As he sat with the lap belt across his waist Gary could see the buttons on his white shirt straining to hold his belly back. The driver also had a very dark, black, bushy mustache. It looked like a thick, dirty broom under his nose. With the courtesy and professionalism, he was taught in the police academy, the officer leaned into the driver's side window and said, "Okay sir we'll try to make this fast. May I have your license and registration please?" Then to Gary's surprise the man just snapped.

The driver turned his shoulders toward the left and his fat head followed. He stuck his right arm out of the window. He was swinging it back and forth. He started yelling at Gary. His voice was extremely high pitched; he sounded like an Orca. As he screamed spit came flying out of his mouth. Gary had to step back to keep out of the splash zone. Most of the juice was caught in the driver's bushy mustache. The crazy man also had another peculiar habit. As he continued to squeal Gary felt a poking on his arm. That crazy bastard had his middle finger sticking out and was poking the police officer with it.

He launched into an outrageous tirade at Gary and the police department in general. Gary could feel his blood pressure rising as the man was relentless with his verbal assault. This had to be the busiest man in the world Gary thought. He said he was a lawyer. Then he said he was a judge. Then he said he was a former Navy Seal. Then he went on to yell about the people he knew. He knew the

Mayor, the Police Commissioner and ended with the classic I'll have your badge for this. The entire time spit was flying from his mouth and his middle finger was poking at Gary. To his credit, Gary kept his cool. He stood silently listening as the man droned on and on. When it seemed, the man had nothing left to say the police officer took the license and registration. Then he made an unusual request and asked the driver for his car keys. When he had what, he needed Gary walked to his squad car. As he walked away the driver started yelling more insults to the police officer. Gary sat and radioed the information to the dispatcher.

As expected the man had no warrants against him. It would have been just a warning but the driver dug his own grave with his disrespectful demeanor and insults. Gary sat in his car and wrote the ticket. When he finished writing the ticket, he took a few extra moments to look at the car keys. He took the ignition key and started to bend it back and forth. It was difficult at first but the more he wiggled it back and forth the easier it became. Soon the metal was so fatigued it was ready to break; that was when he stopped. He got out of his police car and walked over to the nasty man to give him his ticket. He bent down and leaned into the car. "Here, sir, your ticket and your keys. Please try to drive safely."

"Oh, fuck you jerk, my taxes pay your salary. Why don't you try and find someone breaking the law, you piece of shit!" the man said, and he grabbed his ticket and keys. He found his ignition key and put it into the slot off to the side of the steering wheel.

Gary backed off and said, "Have a nice day, sir."

The man stuck his head out of his window and responded. "Screw you I hope you get shot!"

With a cheeky smile on his face Gary responded, "I'm sure you do." Then he turned and slowly walked to his squad car listening and waiting for it. Just before he got to the car door, he heard it. It was a loud, painful, anguishing, girly scream. Gary heard the man shout "OH SHIT! OH, MY GOD. NOT NOW, NOT HERE!"

Gary turned, and with a smile on his face slowly walked back to the car where the nasty man was in a sheer panic. "Problem, sir?" he asked.

"The key broke in the ignition! I can't get it out and I can't start the car."

"Wow, that's bad luck. It's gonna be dark soon and this isn't the best neighborhood to be stuck in."

"Well you're here, and you're a cop. You can help me."

"Sorry, I have to earn your tax dollars and find a criminal. But I'll tell you what. Here's a quarter." Gary flipped the coin into the car. It hit the man's big belly and landed on his lap. Then Gary stuck out his middle finger and started to poke the fat nasty man in the chest. "Why don't you try calling your friend the Mayor, or the Commissioner?" Gary backed away from the car and slowly turned his back on the panicked man. He stood listening to the raving asshole. A smile crossed his face and he turned and again leaned into the driver's window. When the frantic man saw, the cop lean in a second time he felt a wave of relief come over him.

He said. "Oh that's more like it. Now get me a tow truck lickety split."

Gary shook his head in disbelief at the man's arrogance. "Sir, I wish I could, but I have criminals to catch. I just wanted to give you some friendly advice. You should roll up your windows. They'll steal the eyeballs out of your head in this neighborhood! Good luck." Then he backed away and walked to his car. He opened the door got in and drove away. Surprisingly, the man sat in his car silently, maybe reflecting on his poor attitude towards the police department.

The city seemed quiet for a Wednesday. Joe's shift was very quiet, he had one more call in the afternoon a quick run to the hospital with a jogger who fell and twisted his ankle. He was in a good mood the rest of the day after seeing his friend at lunch. He turned in his ambulance after his shift and headed home. He looked forward to seeing Michelle and telling her about his lunch with Gary. He hoped she would not be immersed in her computer. Maybe he would ask her if she wanted to go out tonight.

Joe was walking down the block to his house and he saw Michelle's car in the driveway. "Good," he thought, "She's home". Maybe tonight will be different. They'll go out for a nice dinner and maybe a movie. He entered the house and yelled out. "Baby, I'm home!" He turned the corner to the living room and saw her sitting on the couch without her computer. He got excited as he started to tell her about his lunch with Gary. "Guess who I saw today?"

She abruptly cut him off in mid-sentence and in a very stern tone started speaking. "Excuse me, but I have had the most humiliating, embarrassing, day of my life today. Can you tell me why I have to hear from almost total strangers about my husband saving someone's life yesterday?"

Joe stood with a dumbfounded expression on his face as Michelle continued. "Yeah, that was my day, people telling me about my husband and how great he is, and what he did. I have to stand there like an idiot because I don't know what they're talking about. When are, you going to learn how to communicate? Your problem is you don't talk to me and I'm getting sick and tired of it. You're killing this marriage, Joe."

He stood motionless, almost not believing what his ears were hearing. Then he started to speak "I tried to…"

"I don't want to hear it. I'm just going upstairs; I'm too upset even to eat!" Michelle rose off the sofa, walked past the dining room table, picked up her computer and walked up the steps to the bedroom. When she reached the top, she stopped, turned, and yelled down to Joe still standing stunned in the middle of the living room. "Another thing, I decided that I hate this piece of rope hanging over the stairs. GET RID OF IT!" and she stormed off, slamming the bedroom door behind her.

Joe stood alone in the living room. He slowly turned and sat on the couch shaking his head. In a low audible voice, he said. "What the hell happened? I was in such a good mood three minutes ago."

CHAPTER FIVE

THE BIRTH OF THE MONSTER

The next morning Joe awoke earlier than usual; his back was sore from a night of tossing and turning on the sofa. He slept on his left side as much as possible to protect The Monster. Once he was off the sofa it took a few minutes for him to get going. His back was sore and achy. He stood in front of the couch, his body anything but aligned. He looked like a twisted question mark. With his hands on his hips, he slowly tried to straighten out. The object was to get as erect as possible. When he finally straighten himself out it was time to do his usual morning stretches. This helped to relieve the tightness of the skin on his right side. After a few minutes of painful stretching, he felt well enough to start his day. He began to make breakfast and brew the coffee hoping the blowup from last night was over

Joe finished his breakfast. He heard Michelle walking upstairs. "The princess is finally up," he thought to himself.

He sat quite a few more minutes until The Monster disturbed his peace, "Just go up there. You don't need to be afraid of her."

"You're right!" Joe responded. He pushed his chair out from the table. Stood up proud and defiant and started towards the stairs. As he reached the bottom of the steps he saw Michelle just coming out of the bedroom. At about the midway point of the staircase they passed each other. They turned their bodies so each could pass and without a word they continued. He felt no guilt and would not take any responsibly for the fight or the mood Michelle was in. In nature, this would be akin to two rams butting heads, neither one knowing when to quit.

Joe was off from work today. The last thing he wanted was to hang around the house alone. He thought about going down to the firehouse to check in with some of his buddies. Although he was discharged as an active fireman, he kept in touch and was always welcomed by his brother firefighters. Many of them felt he got a raw deal when he was relieved of duty. He started to clean the kitchen, and then walked upstairs to grab a quick shower. As he entered the bedroom to get some clothes. He started to take in a familiar scent. He closed his eyes and took a deep breath. It was sweet, and sexy, and Joe loved it. It was Michelle's perfume. He couldn't remember the name of it but he loved the aroma and the memories it brought back.

He started to undress, and as he pulled his shirt off he caught a glimpse of himself in the mirror. He quickly tried to turn away so he wouldn't have to look at his right side. It was too late; he shuddered when he saw those scars running down from his arm pit to the top of knee. He stood with his arm above his head, now unable to turn away. His skin looked like the side of a melted candle, like rippled wax it covered almost all his right side. He felt a wave of sorrow and self-pity rush over him. This grotesque disfigurement ruined his life. It would have been so much easier if he just died that day. His mind raced back through time, to that winter day in 1996, the last fire he ever responded to. The day the monster was born.

It was a bitter cold, late December evening. The crew at Rescue One was cleaning up after dinner. Some of the firemen were talking about their Christmas shopping. Others hadn't even started to shop yet. Joe was on the phone with Michelle. They had decided the time had come to start a family. They were talking about names and godparents. Like most young couples, they had big dreams. They were also very busy building their careers. One of the topics they were discussing was when they would be together long enough to make a baby.

The alarm came over at 1835 hours. The jovial conversation about the fast-approaching Christmas holiday stopped, as they listened to the dispatcher call out the alarm. Historically, this is a cautious time for firefighters. Every alarm a firefighter responds to could be his last. The firemen embrace the risk but nobody wants their family to remember the Christmas that daddy died at work. It was reported as a working kitchen fire. The crew stopped their cleaning and conversations. Joe told Michelle he loved her and hung up the phone. They quickly put on their turnout gear and ran for the trucks.

The chief jumped into his bright red chief's car and drove ahead to size up the job and prepare a plan. Joe climbed into his seat in the rescue truck. As Captain, he sat next to the driver. The firemen call that the officer's seat. As the huge bay doors opened the big shiny black tires slowly rolled off the apparatus floor, squeaking as they moved on the freshly waxed floor. The Captain started to formulate a plan, keeping in mind the personnel he had with him. Today would be a little tricky as he had two probationary firefighters with him. This sometimes happened when the men would switch a day off with someone. It wasn't ideal, but it wasn't against the rules either so on the few occasions it happened they dealt with it. It was his job to teach the probies and keep them safe. As the trucks got closer to the scene a call came over the radio from the chief. "To all responding units, be advised we have a signal ten!"

All the firemen got an instant shot of adrenaline; they were familiar with signal ten. They were now responding to a fully involved working house fire. The radio chatter quieted down as the responding units awaited the next orders from the chief. He knew what units he had responding and needed to plan where they would enter the street, and which fire hydrants they should hook up to or wrap as the firemen called it. The Chief needed to size up the situation as fast as possible. Did he have enough units responding or should he send out another alarm? These were life and death decisions not only for the firefighters but for the victims of the fire as well.

Joe's unit, the heavy rescue truck, was ordered to the front of the structure. They would prepare for search and rescue. The rescue truck did not carry water or ladders but it did have many of the rescue tools the firefighters needed to combat any emergency. The truck had huge telescoping halogen lights and a generator so powerful they could turn night into day. The truck also carried medical and rescue equipment. They had various types of rope used for repelling from buildings, as well as rescue operations. Many of these rescues involved a stokes basket, which were light weight fancy stretchers used for lowering victims from high places. They also had all kinds of extrication equipment to use at motor vehicle accidents.

As the huge red rescue truck pulled in front of the glowing and smoking house, Joe had made his plan. He would have his driver put the truck into generator mode and set the lights at the scene. Then he would take the two probies, Schmidt and Kirsh, into the building with him for search and rescue. This was an unusual move; the Captain rarely went into burning buildings. His responsibility was the safety of his crew. He needed to report to the chief at the scene. Together with the other unit's officers they would help execute the orders of the chief in an effort to bring the fire under control as quickly as possible. Joe knew going into a burning building with two probationary firefighters was not ideal. As a result, he didn't feel comfortable letting someone of less experience go in with them. They were good men, but they hadn't been tested yet. He also felt they would be more inclined to show the Captain how brave they were. His mind was made up. He would take them in. Today, Lieutenant Huber would be reporting to the command post.

The driver parked the truck and immediately started his duties as chauffeur of the rig. He revved the truck up to generate, and jumped down out of his seat to arrange the tower lights on the burning structure. Even from across the street on a cold December night, he could feel the heat of the fire. The Captain gave his orders to the rest of his crew. The men rushed to execute their duties. The Captain and the probies went to the rear of the truck to grab their irons. The irons are the bread and butter of firefighting, an axe and a halligan. The halligan is a multipurpose tool with a pry bar on one end and a pointed pick on the other. The tools are about three feet long and together weigh about seven pounds; they fit together in one hand and are easy to carry. Then they walked around to the other side of the truck, the side facing the fire and put on their self-contained oxygen tank or SCOT bottle. The SCOT weighs about 17 pounds; it has a black mesh designed to cover your head and still fit under your helmet. That is connected to a full clear face mask that the oxygen collects in so you can breathe fresh air. A black hose runs off the mask and connects to a regulator where the oxygen from the bottle is pressurized to a breathable form. If you keep your composure you can get about fifteen minutes of air out of the bottle. If you panic and breathe fast you could exhaust your tank in mere minutes. The regulator has a vibrating bell to let you know when you have about a minute of air left.

The three men put on all their gear and approached the building. The fire was very hot, so the three men got as low to the ground as possible to enter the building. Kirsh stuck the forked end of his halligan into the door. Before he could pry it the Captain tapped him on the shoulder. "Try, before you pry," he said. It was a fire department saying.

It was to remind the men that doors may not always be locked. It could be a huge time saver to open a door rather than knock one down. In this case the door was open. The rescue team put their breathing masks on and entered the burning building.

As they pushed opened the door the thick black smoke made it impossible to see. Joe signaled the probies to get lower to the ground. Now they were crawling on their bellies. The men crawled along the wall keeping their left hand against it. In a search and rescue scenario it's important to have a system when searching a room. Keep against a wall and continue to use the same pattern you started with. If you went to the left keep going to the left. Eventually you'll come out the way you got in. They each had a flashlight strapped to their fire helmets but the smoke was so thick and black it made no difference. The heat from the fire was almost unbearable. The only way to escape the intense heat is to stay as close to the ground as possible. It is simple physics; heat rises. The search team got as low as they could and pushed forward. Occasionally they felt some relief from the water of the fire hoses spraying into the house from the outside. When the water hit, the turnout coat it would become a vapor of steam.

The first-floor search came up empty. The search team then came across a staircase. Joe wanted to search the upstairs, that's where children usually try to hide from smoke and fire. They run to their bedroom because it's the place they feel safe. The Captain quickly checked the meter on his SCOT pack to check how much air he had left. Before he could focus on it he felt a tap on his leg. Schmitt and Kirsh both had their alarms going off. Joe immediately ordered them out of the building. They turned and crawled out the way they came in. As they exited the burning house their alarms were still going off. Kirsh came out first and he helped his buddy Schmidt. They stayed kneeling at the door waiting for their Captain. He should have been right behind them.

It was a total breach of fire department protocol but Joe stayed in the burning house alone. He still had air in his tank and without the probies he could search the upstairs faster. He crawled up the staircase to continue the search. Once he made that decision he knew he was past the point of no return. He would not have enough air to get out the way he came in. His plan was to make it to a window before his pack ran out. From the window, he could signal one of the truckies to get him a ladder.

When he got to the top of the steps the heat felt more intense, he was sliding along on his stomach and went to his left again. He kept his left hand on the wall and used his halligan to sweep the floor to the right feeling for bodies that he could not see. The heat was intense on the upper floor and he started to feel the vibration on his alarm going off. As his left hand followed the path of the wall he started to think of a way to exit the building. If his tank ran out and he didn't get out of the building he would be dead in minutes. The smoke was too thick to remove his face mask. It would be like drowning, holding your breath as long as you can knowing that if you try to inhale you'd be gulping water. You can only hold your breath so long before you're forced to gasp for fresh air. Instead of water Joe would breathe in toxic thick black smoke. It would choke him to death long before the fire would burn him.

His left hand pushed on the wall and a door opened. Joe entered and went to the left but he was in trouble; his air tank was empty. He was sucking his own co2 from his mask. Joe kept calm; he scanned the room looking for options. It didn't seem many were available; the room was full of thick black smoke. He couldn't see his hand in front of his face. He couldn't tell if he was in a bedroom. a bathroom, or maybe even a closet. Then it came to him. When he was a probie, he trained with an old-time fireman. He never knew his real name they just called him Duke. It was a trick Duke showed him one day at fire school. If it worked it might buy him a few more minutes of air. He unscrewed the hose from the regulator and placed it inside of his turnout coat. He hoped whatever clean air was trapped between his body, and his turnout coat, would buy him enough time to get out.

He continued to follow the wall into the room; it was still too smoky to see anything. Then he felt a body, that was much smaller than an adult. A child or maybe a dog he thought, he hoped it was still alive. Quickly, without regard for his own life he took off his SCOT pack and then his turnout coat. The thick heavy smoke started to choke him right away. He coughed uncontrollably, unable to get his breath, his eyes started burning; tears were streaming down his face. His arms and upper torso started to blister from the heat. Totally by feel and instinct, he wrapped the victim in his coat, trying to protect it from the intense heat. As he held the small bundle he could tell it was a child and it was still alive. He tried to make an area for the victim to breathe. He was coughing and choking on the poisonous smoke. Thick, black, snot was pouring out of his nose. His eyes watered and he was feeling light headed; he was running out of time. He took another a quick scan of the room and saw some light coming from the other side of it. It was the bright lights of the rescue truck shining through a window. Their only hope was to get to that window. The child would not survive much longer without fresh air. Joe put his helmet back on and picked up the child. He looked over his right shoulder at the wall of fire blocking his escape to the window.

Joe knew his life was coming down to seconds; he took his helmet off, and like a Frisbee flung it through the wall of flames and towards the window. The window smashed, as his yellow helmet broke through it. Broken glass fell outside onto the cold ground. The cold air rushed into the room and blew some of the toxic smoke away; Joe was able to get a small breath of air into his smoked filled burning lungs. The air also fed the wall of fire between him and the window, it grew taller and hotter. Joe took his little victim, still wrapped in his turnout coat. He ran through the wall of fire shielding the child with his own body. Joe could feel the intense heat against the right side of his body. His first sensation was a tingling feeling, but within an instant it changed over to excruciating pain. The right side of his body started to catch fire.

The helmet landed on the side of the house about fifteen feet from the command post. The chief saw the yellow helmet with the captain shield land and knew he had a man in trouble. He turned to the captain of the truck company and said, "I want a ladder on that window now!"

The truck captain replied, "Chief my men are taking the last ladder now to vent the roof."

"I don't care! I want two ladders on that window now!"

The truck captain immediately got on his radio and called for the two ladders. As the chief looked up he could see a face covered in soot, hanging out of the broken window. It was coughing and gasping for air. It looked like a little girl. He could see the thick heavy smoke pouring out through the smashed-out window over her head and noticed she was wrapped in a fireman's turnout coat. The first ladder went up and the truck company men climbed to the window to get the little girl. They brought her down; she looked to be about seven years old. Miraculously, she wasn't burned. The coat must have protected her, but she was struggling to breathe. Her face was black with soot and she coughed up black sputum. The paramedics at the scene took her from the firemen and placed oxygen on her, and she was rushed to the ambulance. One medic went into the back of the ambulance to tend to her the other ran to the driver's seat. The ambulance sped away with lights and sirens blasting to the hospital. Her parents rushed over to the chief with tears streaming down their faces. It's awful to watch your house burning down and not know where your child is. Through all this tragedy their little girl had a chance. They thanked the Chief and his brave men for saving their little girl. The chief ordered one of the men to take his car and drive them to the hospital so they could be with her.

The truck company firemen went back up the ladder and entered the room through the broken window. They found Joe lying face down; he was unconscious and his right side was singed and burning. His shirt appeared to be melted to his body. They passed him out through the window. He was still breathing, but it was very shallow and he was badly burned. As he was lowered closer to the ground the area was overcome with the horrible nasty odor of burning flesh. His right side was completely burned from under his arm to about his upper thigh. More paramedics were called over to treat him. There's not too much you can do in the field to treat a burn patient. They placed oxygen on him and several wet sterile dressings to his badly burned right side. The paramedics started a large bore IV and gave him as much fluid as they could. He was then quickly loaded into the ambulance. The Chief went over to the firemen who brought Joe and the little girl down from the window. He thanked them for their bravery. They thought the little girl would survive thanks to their timely rescue of her. Unfortunately, Joe was in much more serious condition but thanks to them, he had a fighting chance. The firemen turned and watched as the sirens blared and the ambulance left with Joe.

By now the firemen had the fire under control. They went about their business of overhauling and checking for burning embers and rekindles. Most of the men's turnout coats were frozen as a result of the water from the hoses freezing on their coats. It made a hard job that much harder. It wasn't uncommon to see one of the firemen walk over to his partner and have him chip the ice off his coat. Slowly the word started to spread of the heroic rescue the truck company made of the little girl from the bedroom window. Then that good news was overshadowed by news of the young captain of the rescue company being rushed to the hospital with severe burns.

Joe doesn't remember much after that. His body shivers when he thinks back to that night. He thinks back in anger at how much it changed his life. The firefighters from the truck company got credit for the rescue of Joe and the little girl. The fire department refused to cover any of Joe's medical expenses while he fought for his life in the hospital. They claimed he broke department protocol by being alone in the building. They said his right side was so severely burned that it limited his range of motion, and he was in constant pain. Due to his injuries, he was declared unfit to fulfill his duties as a fireman. All the years of hard work and sacrifice were taken away. Lost was the fact that the little girl would have died if he had not found her and got her to the safety of the window. Worst of all was the disfigurement itself. He wasn't vain enough to think as himself as handsome or good looking. Now with the horrible, melted, scarring running down the right side of his body, he didn't consider himself human any more. He went into a deep depression wondering why he lived and became a monster.

Joe walked downstairs; Michelle was long gone. He placed the breakfast dishes into the sink; he knew his wife hated to come home to a mess. He washed his hands and grabbed his car keys off the hook on the wall. He turned and walked out the back door making one more visual check to see if the kitchen was clean. He locked the door behind him and hopped into his car. He pulled out of the driveway and turned left. Today he was feeling nostalgic and needed a friend. It was time to visit his friends at the firehouse.

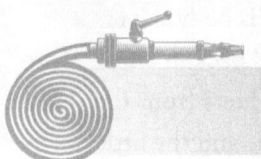

CHAPTER SIX

OLIVIA

Joe passed the firehouse and made a left turn at the corner. He drove down the street and made another left into the parking lot where the on-duty firemen park. The first cars he saw were those of his old probies, Schmidt and Kirsh. Joe parked his car and walked up the path to the back-door entrance. A familiar old figure was working in the back room. It was Sully. Sully was an old-timer who retired a few years back. He was a forty-year fire department veteran. It was safe to say the fire service was his first love. His second love was his wife, Sally Ann. Sadly, she passed away ten years earlier after a long painful battle with cancer. Sully had a hard time coping without her. His time away from home increased. As did his drinking. His children suffered also. They had already lost their mother and, over time they lost their father too.

When his girls were old enough they moved away. He never sees them and rarely hears from them. Sully holds no grudge. He knows it was his inability to cope without his wife is what drove them away. He wasn't home when he should have been. When he wasn't working, he'd stay at the firehouse. It was the only place where he didn't feel alone. It was the only place he could cope with life. On the rare occasions when he attended one of his daughter's school events, or birthdays he was often drunk and obnoxious. His heavy drinking forced him to retire from the fire service. Now during the few hours of the day when he is sober he reflects back on the days when his kids were growing up. He feels genuine remorse and often sobs. It took him a lifetime to learn you only have one chance to be a father, and his was gone.

Sully is a big man, six-foot-three and almost three hundred pounds. He never lifted a weight in his life, but was naturally strong. His hands were huge and the skin calloused and hard. Shaking hands with him was like putting your hand in a leather vise. He had a full head of snow white hair and his face was dark, almost dirty looking due to the years of soot and smoke imbedded in the lines of his face. Over the years, he lost most of his teeth. This gave him a peculiar way of speaking. His B's sounded like F's. Instead of fire truck, he would say byer truck. Most of the firemen understood him but when a new fireman was assigned to the station, his speech took some getting used to. To keep him busy and out of trouble they set him up with a part time job. Sully works off the books, taking care of the firehouse. He sweeps up on the apparatus floor. He does some light maintenance on the trucks, and some other odds and ends. Mostly, he just keeps the boys company.

Sully was working in the back room cleaning off some tables. The room was dark, no lights were on and all the shades were drawn. As Joe opened the back door to enter, a burst of sunlight followed him. It briefly lit up the room like a bolt of lightning. As the door closed behind him the darkness over took the light. The room was quiet with the exception of Sully's dirty rag rubbing over the tables. Like a vampire, Sully quickly turned away from the warm sunlight. The shadow of a man filled the doorway and Sully turned back. As the door slammed shut and the room went dark again the man said, "Hey Sully, what's the good word?"

"Ay Cap, long time no see. What's up?" Sully answered.

Joe smiled as he heard the distinctive way Sully spoke. Then he answered. "Just my blood pressure. Is anyone around?"

"News is on the apparatus floor werking on the bucking trucks," Sully answered, pointing to the door leading to the apparatus floor.

"Thanks, Sully." Joe gave him a wave and walked through the back room towards the apparatus floor where the fire trucks were parked.

He approached the heavy wooden and glass door. It was a beautiful door; the top was frosted glass with a blue and white Maltese cross painted on it. The entire door was outlined in gold leaf. On the bottom half of the door the fire department logo was painted, and outlined in gold leaf. Joe pushed the heavy door open and entered the apparatus floor. The first thing that hit him was the smell. He loved the smell of the trucks and turnout gear. It had a smoky aroma that only a fireman could appreciate. Next, he saw the beautiful red fire trucks. He walked over to his old rescue unit and laid his hand upon it. It was like saying hello to an old friend. As he crossed across to the next truck he spotted a fireman bent over a piece of equipment. He recognized him immediately and said, "Hey, News what's going on?" News of course was a nickname. His real name was Charlie, but if you spent any amount of time with him, it wasn't hard to see how he got his nickname.

When he heard Joe's voice he turned around and replied, "I got news for you, Cap. No one else cares about these trucks. I'm the only one who checks them."

"Aw News, you do it because ya love to, and ya don't trust anyone else to do it."

"Maybe, but I got news for you; Sully never comes out to check anything. That leaves Jackass or Smartass to check these trucks. I got news for you; I wouldn't let those assholes put a straw in my sippy cup."

Over the years, Joe's old probies Schmidt and Kirsh became good firefighters but they also received a reputation as wise guys. Apart from each other they could function well. Together they were trouble. Kirsh would dream up these outrageous schemes. His brain had no filter. Whatever screwy idea that popped into his head, he would spit out. That boy had some weird thoughts. He was the brains of the pair. He became known as a smartass. Schmidt on the other hand no fear of repercussion. The crazier the thought, the more he wanted to do it. It was obvious he was a jackass. He loved to push the envelope. When he got hold of one of Kirsh's ideas it became a challenge to make it happen. He once stole a firetruck from another company.

"Where are the assholes? I saw their cars in the parking lot?" Joe asked.

"They're on this new kick now. They went to do something they called ramping, I think. I got news for you; I don't think it looks good for the department."

"What the hell is ramping?"

"I'm not so sure, but one day Smartass told Jackass he looked pale and should get some sun. The next day Jackass comes in with two beach chairs. They grab a pizza box from the garbage and rip it in half. One of them takes the top half and one takes the bottom half. They walk out to the front bay, open the door, set up the chairs. Then they strip down to nothing but boxers. They sit in the chairs with the pizza box halves under their chins and soak up the sun like they're on some beach somewhere."

Joe had to laugh. It was typical of the kind of things they always seemed to do.

"I got news for you; it's not funny. Those two assholes smelled like pizza the rest of the shift!"

"News, I'm gonna go out and say hello. I'll catch up with you later." Joe started to walk away when he heard News; voice.

"I got news for you Cap; things haven't been the same since you left."

Joe turned, and said, "Thanks News, but I didn't leave."

"I know," News said in a low voice as he turned and went back to work.

Joe walked out to the front ramp of the firehouse and saw two figures sitting in beach chairs. He walked in front of them blocking the sun and said, "What's up boys?" The men lowered their makeshift reflectors and saw their old Captain.

"Hey Cap, how the hell are ya?" Schmidt said.

Then Kirsh added. "Long time no see."

Joe held no grudges against his old probies. They just followed orders that night. Aside from their quirky behavior they turned into excellent firefighters. Joe noticed something under the right eye of Kirsh. It was yellow, and brown, and a light shade of purple. It looked like an old bruise that had been fading.

He asked, "Kirsh, where'd you get that shiner?"

Schmidt started to crack up laughing then said, "Yeah tell him, I love this story."

A serious expression crossed Kirsh's face as he reached up to rub his eye. Then he started. "Well last week was the fire convention upstate. So, me and this jackass," he quickly made a hand gesture towards Schmitt and continued, "decided to go up for a few days. One day we're riding down in the elevator with these two big guys from some engine company in Texas." Kirsh looked over to Schmidt who was trying to control his laughter and continued, "Then this Jackass says nice and loud, there are only two kinds of people in this elevator, tap dancers, and cocksuckers. Then the two guys turn around and look at me, so what do I do,…I start tap dancing. BOOM! He slugs me and the lights go out, and down I go. That's how I got this." He pointed to his eye.

Joe was hiding a smile and just about to ask a follow up question when the fire alarm sounded. Schmidt and Kirsh quickly sat up from their beach chairs and put their clothes on. They took the chairs and stored them back in the firehouse. Joe felt a shot of adrenaline course through his body. As fast as he felt it, it passed when his body realized he was not going. The rest of the men came running from all parts of the firehouse to put on their gear and report to their respective trucks. Some of the faces Joe knew; many were people he hadn't seen before. It reminded him of how long he had been away from the fire service. The trucks rolled out of the firehouse on their way to a car fire. Joe walked back into the empty firehouse. He crossed the apparatus floor now void of fire trucks. Slowly he made his way to the back room. He saw Sully still working, but mostly watching television. Joe patted the counter to get his attention and Sully looked over, "I'm headin out, Sully. Take care of yourself."

"Yeah, Cap, you do the same."

As Joe opened the back door to the parking
lot he looked up at the framed
citation over top of it.
FOR OUTSTANDING SERVICE
TO THE COMMUNITY
FOR BRAVERY ABOVE AND
BEYOND THE CALL OF DUTY
ON TWENTY ONE DECEMBER NINETEEN
HUNDRED AND NINETY-SIX
WITHOUT THOUGHT FOR YOUR OWN SAFETY
YOU RESCUED A CHILD AND BROTHER
FIERFIGHTER FROM A BURNING BUILDING
IT IS WITH GREAT PRIDE AND DISTINCTON
THAT WE AWARD FIREFIGHTERS WELLS
AND VAN KOOTEN OUR HIGEST
AWARD THE MEDAL OF BRAVERY
SEVEN JANUARY NINTEEN
HUNDRED AND NINETY-SEVEN

Joe shook his head as exited the building.

Michelle was at work. It was lunch time and, as usual, she was sitting with her friend, Olivia. Olivia was a few years younger than Michelle. She was a very petite woman. Short and shapely. She had short, brown hair and was very pretty. Oliva and Michelle became friends a few years ago when Olivia started working at the hospital. It was just a few months after Olivia's husband was murdered. Michelle was one of the nurses who trained her. At that time Olivia spoke often of her husband's murder and Michelle lent a sympathetic ear. She had confessed that before her husband was killed, her marriage was also going very sour. Then came the fateful night. Someone broke into her house. They were startled by her husband. Apparently, he tried to fight the intruder off but he killed him. Shot him in cold blood. She remembers telling the police how lucky she was that she was working that night. It was a rare overnight shift for her or maybe she would be dead too. That was two years ago and the police haven't made any arrest.

Today it was Michelle's day to vent. She was still very angry about the fight she had with her husband. As they sat and ate she found herself still going over the details of the events that led up to it. Olivia listened intently and empathized with Michelle. When Michelle calmed down from her tirade Olivia asked Michelle how she met Joe. Michelle's demeanor seemed to change and a calmness seemed to cross her face. In a softer, comforting voice Michelle started to speak.

"I was working in the E.R. one night. In those days, I was a float nurse. I remember it like it was yesterday. It was

January 1989, just after the New Year. It was a bitter cold night. Joe came in with some of the firemen. They were bringing in a homeless woman they found huddled in some doorway. The poor thing was so cold. It was my turn to take a patient so I walked over to get report from them. He was at the head of the stretcher talking to the woman. You could tell by the way he carried himself that he was in charge. The other men with him looked up to him with confidence and respect. I asked what was going on with the poor woman. He heard me ask and he looked up. For the first time, his eyes looked right into mine. We stared for what seemed an eternity. It was really less than a second. Then he smiled at me. I was spellbound. For a few seconds, I couldn't think or speak. My body temperature seemed to spike. I started to sweat."

Michelle stopped for a second a smile crossed her face. Then she continued. "Well they dropped the woman off and Joe told his crew to gather up the supplies they needed. He looked down at my name tag and said,"

"Hi Michelle, are you new here?"

"I think I stammered something about being a float nurse. I don't know what came over me. I lost all my senses. Then one of his crew came back to him and said they had another call."

"It was nice to meet you Michelle," he said." I hope I see you soon."

"He smiled again and they all left. I was on cloud nine all night waiting for them to come back. I knew exactly what I would say. I would be the coolest, sexiest, nurse he ever saw. From that point on I checked my make-up every half hour. They never came back that night." Michelle reach down to take a sip of her coffee. She put her cup down, took a breath and continued her story.

"The next night Joe came into the E.R. again with another patient. He looked all over for me but I was not working the E.R. that night. He asked the charge nurse, an old biddy named Helen, if I was working that night. She told him I had been floated that night to the maternity wing. Joe asked his men to stay by the rig; he was going to run and visit me. Helen put a quick stop to that." Michelle put a stern look on her face and in a deep voice she continued, imitating Helen.

"Oh, no you don't mister. That is a mother and baby unit. Visiting hours are strictly enforced."

"Joe tried to explain that he just needed a minute to talk to me. He turned on his charm, flashed his smile, and told Helen he wanted to ask me out, for a date. Helen looked back at him. A big smile crossed her face and she answered."

"Well, when you say it like that I'm sure I will NOT let you up there. This is not the Dating Game. Take your crew and get out of my E.R."

Michelle reached up and started to twirl her long black hair. She started to gaze past Olivia and continued her story. "It could have all ended there but Joe was persistent. What happed next went down in the annals of fire department history. Not to mention what hospital administration had to say about it. About an hour after getting kicked out by Helen the crew was back. They came rolling into the E.R. with a woman in active labor. That's what everyone thought. It was actually a fireman named Schmitt. They had him all bundled up on their gurney with blankets covering him from head to toe, which they needed to cover his thick black, bushy, moustache.

"We need to take this woman up to L and D right now."

"Joe said to Helen. She tried to stop them but Joe would not be denied. With Schmitt moaning and screaming on the rolling gurney Joe said in his most stern and authoritative voice."

"Helen let us through or I'll pick out six tiles on the floor and she will go there."

"Helen stopped for a split second then waved them through. The boys rushed out of the E.R. and to the elevators. They were laughing and proud of themselves as they waited. The worst was over. So, they thought, until Joe felt a tap on his shoulder. He slowly turned and heard a deep voice say to him."

"What have we here boys?"

"Joe turned and to his surprise he saw an elderly man with thin graying hair. He was dressed all in black except for a stiff white color around his neck. Joe was surprised and tried to hide his expression. In a, less than confident voice he spoke to the priest. As he spoke his Irish Catholic guilt overtook him. He did his best to sell it but it wasn't easy for him to lie to the priest."

"Well Father we're bringing this nice lady up to Labor and Delivery to have her baby." Olivia interrupted Michelle's story.

"Are you kidding? They ran into a priest?"

"Hand to God," Michelle answered as she raised her right hand. "Well what happened?" Olivia asked in anticipation.

"So, the priest wants to bless the expectant mother. He says."

"Would you mind if I say quick prayer for her and the baby?"

"No Father please give us a prayer."

"Joe tells him. All the guys took off their hats and bowed their heads. Joe quickly pulled the blankets up to cover Schmitt's face better. Just as the priest said Amen the bell rang and the elevator appeared. They all jumped in, including the priest. Joe quickly ushered him out and asked him to wait for the next one. If she gave birth in the elevator they would need all the room they could get. Once the doors closed Schmitt jumped off the gurney and the firemen made it up to look as if it was never used. When they hit L and D Joe ran out and found me. I will always remember how he asked me out. He said."

"If you know what I just went through to get up here to ask you out you would say yes."

"I didn't need to know, I said yes anyway."

"It sounds wonderful! "What the hell happened?" Olivia asked.

"December 1996," she answered. "Joe almost died in a fire. He spent months in the hospital. That poor man was in so much pain. He saved a little girl that night but they don't care. His body may have survived but the Joe I knew died that night. Those bastards at the fire commission fired him. They say he broke regulations. They even stopped paying his medical bills. Between that and the hideous scar running down the side of his body he's not the same person I married. We were going to have children. Now he says no. He doesn't want his kids to have a freak as a father. I really tried to make things work but he's just not happy anymore." Michelle now had tears running down her face.

Her voice now weaker and occasionally cracking as she spoke. She continued, "they took everything away from him. Eight years he gave to them. He was so dedicated to them. He became the youngest Captain they ever had. He saved that little girl and almost died in that fire." The tears were now streaming down her face. She reached up to wipe the tears away.

"Joe became depressed," she continued. "It took him a few months to find another job. He became a New York City EMT. He seemed happy, but things were never the same. We started to drift apart. We stopped talking. I thought maybe starting a family would help but he wanted no part of it. I started to resent him for that. He kept saying he was a monster. That's why they kicked him out of the fire department. When we did talk it would turn into an argument over having children. I tried to tell him that scars are not heredity. He would yell back at me and say all the kids at school would make fun of them. Torment them about their hideous father. He became obsessed."

Michelle took a few seconds to pull herself together. Then she continued. "Well, I didn't know what to do. We stopped talking to each other. I became angry at him. I started feeling that he took away my chance to be a mom and I hated that. I occupied myself with the computer. He went to work and occasionally went to visit his friends at the fire house." Michelle's voice grew angry. She slammed her hand on the table and said, "I can't live like this anymore.

Olivia could see how upset her friend was. She had known how unhappy Michelle had become over the years. She glanced over to see Michelle with her arms folded on the cafeteria table and her head hanging down. Olivia reached across the table and placed her hand on Michelle's arm to comfort her. In a soft but deadly serious voice Olivia whispered to her, "should we kill him?"

Michelle looked up and with tears staining her face and said "What?"

"It's been done before. I personally know of husbands who outlive their usefulness. They need to go."

"Do you know what you're saying?"

"Yeah, Michelle I do. You're miserable! He took the best years of your life. It's not a big deal. He's not happy either. It's almost like killing him would be a favor to him. I know a guy; for two thousand bucks, he'll take care of everything. He does good work. Believe me, no one will ever know." Michelle was in shock. When she left for work this morning there was nothing she wanted more than to see Joe dead. Now after speaking to Olivia, it could happen.

"Olivia, give me some time to think about it."

"Not too long. We need to strike while the iron is hot, so to speak. I'll make some phone calls and see who is available." Lunch was over and Michelle and Olivia rose from the table and headed back to work. Murder was not the type of thing that Michelle thought much about. She was not happy though, and she knew Joe wasn't either. Most couples might sit down at this point and talk about divorce. That talk would never happen with Joe and Michelle; because they were people of great faith and practicing Catholics. Catholics don't divorce, it's a sin. Michelle felt trapped and out of options. Suddenly Olivia's idea didn't seem too bad.

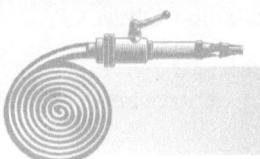

CHAPTER SEVEN

ENTER THE GOVERNOR

The Fourth of July had passed, the summer was getting hotter, but Joe and Michelle's relationship remained icy cold They walked around the house not speaking to each other. She appeared preoccupied with her computer, but Joe noticed she wasn't playing the games she liked. Now she seemed to be using e-mail. Michelle was also talking more on the phone to her friend, Olivia. Joe had never heard Michelle speak much about her. He knew she was a work acquaintance, he never thought they were such good friends. Perhaps they have the same computer interest. He didn't really care, at this point in their relationship, he was sure there were plenty of things he didn't know about his wife. Michelle was indifferent as well. She was waiting for a phone call. If the call went well, after tomorrow she would be out of her misery.

When the phone rang she ran to it. Joe didn't even make an effort to answer it. Michelle picked up the receiver and brought it to her ear. She took a quick look around to see where Joe was and in a low voice said "Hello."

Joe stood and watched the mysterious phone call. Michelle didn't seem to be doing much talking. The call was less than a minute then Michelle gently placed the receiver down. Her last words were, "Okay, I'll see you in a few hours."

Then she grabbed her computer and looked up directions to Allentown, Pennsylvania. She quickly jotted them down and left the house. It took about two and a half hours to drive to Allentown. She was meeting Olivia in a coffee shop outside of Dorney Park. It was a hot, humid, mid-July day and traffic around the park was heavy, but Michelle managed to find the meeting place with little difficulty.

She parked her car and walked into the coffee shop. Olivia was sitting alone at a table. Michelle breezed by the table touching Olivia on the arm and said, "I need to find the ladies' room." Olivia smiled and pointed behind her. After a few minutes Michelle emerged and sat across from her friend. Olivia said hello and called the waitress over to their table.

An older woman came over. She was wearing a black dress with a white apron, and was holding a pad and a pencil. In a strange almost German accent she asked, "What can I get you hon?"

"I'll just have a coffee," Michelle answered. Without writing it down the waitress turned and walked away.

"So, Michelle," Olivia started, "I'm sorry we couldn't drive in together but it's probably safer this way."

"I understand," Michelle shot back. "When do we meet this friend of yours?"

"Well that's another thing we need to discuss. Ya see he's not going to be able to make it today." Michelle stared in silence at Olivia. Olivia watched as Michelle's face slowly morphed into a panicked expression. Before Michelle could form a sentence, Olivia spoke again. "Michael, the person we contracted to do the job, is not ... oh I guess you would say, not available."

"Why, where the hell is he?"

"He's in jail," Olivia said calmly.

"Oh, that's great. He's probably telling the police right now about us. I knew this was a bad idea. How could I let you talk me into this? Now I'm gonna wind up in jail, become some bull dyke's bitch, have to wear orange every day. Ya know orange just completely washes out my hair color." Michelle said as she puffed her hair up with her hands.

"Calm down, he got arrested for not paying child support. Turns out he's a deadbeat dad; it has nothing to do with his profession." The girls stopped talking and took a breath just as the waitress returned with Michelle's order. She leaned over and took a hot cup off her tray, and carefully placed it in front of Michelle.

"Here ya go, hon. Anything else?"

Michelle looked at the hot cup in front of her and said, "Yes, actually. I ordered coffee and you brought me tea."

"No dear, I wrote down what you ordered and it was tea."

"You didn't write anything down."

"Perhaps you're right but you'll enjoy the tea more. Let me know if ya need anything else, dear." Then the older lady turned and walked away.

Michelle stared at her cup and said to Olivia. "Pass the sugar, please."

Olivia passed the small packets to Michelle and started to talk again. "Anyway, when I got ahold of Michael he told me his uncle Jerry, A.K.A. The Governor, is taking care of his clients."

"Ohh, the Governor. Why do you think they call him that?"

"I guess because he likes to execute people." The girls broke into a sinister laugh. Olivia continued, "Michael said the Governor would met us here. He'll be wearing a brown hat with a red feather in it."

"He must be very professional, wanting to meet so far from the job," Michelle said, reaching over, and touching Olivia's arm. "So, I guess we wait." Michelle picked up the hot cup in front of her and took a sip. "By the way, the waitress was right. This tea is delicious."

The ladies sat for a few more minutes in silence, both waiting for The Governor to make his appearance. Every time the door would open a bell would jingle and they would stare waiting for a man with a red feather in his hat to walk in. After about ten minutes they got their wish, as the door to the coffee shop opened and in came a man with a brown hat and a red feather tucked into the right side of it.

The girls faces went blank as the man entered the coffee shop. He was much older than they thought he would be. He had thick black glasses sitting on the bridge of his enormous nose. The lenses looked like two magnifying glasses. Under his nose was a thick, bushy, mustache; it looked like a paint brush dipped into a pail of white ceiling paint. He was somewhat overweight but not obese. As he walked to the table he bumped into every chair and person who was in his path. It was as though he was unable to navigate any obstacles in his direct path. As he came closer the girls noticed his uneven gait. He would take a small step with his left foot and swing out his right leg to catch up with it. This gave him a distinct wobbling motion. When he arrived at the table the girls didn't know what to say; they just stared in silence.

In a low, almost inaudible voice he said, "You the broads waiting for Michael's Uncle Jerry?"

Olivia nodded and pointed for him to sit. He stood next to the empty chair at the round table the girls were sitting at. Slowly he started to shuffle his body between the table and the empty chair. He placed his huge hands on the table. He rolled his fingers under his hands like a gorilla. With all his weight leaning on the table he started to lower his rear end down to the chair. You could have timed him with a calendar before his butt made contact with the wooden seat. When Jerry got settled he said, "Okay, ladies, let's get down to business. My nephew said you need someone eliminated."

The girls looked at each other; Olivia was the first to speak. "Yes, we do. It's her," Olivia's voice went into a whisper, "Husband."

"Pardon?" Jerry replied.

"I say it's Michelle's husband we would like you to take care of."

"Yeah, sure, simple. You dames bring the money?"

Michele was starting to get nervous with Jerry and said, "Hold on. Before we start exchanging money what's the plan?"

"Pardon?" Jerry replied

"I'm beginning to see why they call him The Governor, and it's not about execution," Olivia whispered to Michelle.

Jerry leaned in to hear what the girls were saying, and said, "Pardon?"

"Jerry, I need a minute to speak to my friend about this before we proceed any further," Michelle said.

"Sure, sure, I understand. It's a life altering decision so to speak. Take your time."

Jerry leaned back into his chair and watched as the women stared at him. It took a few seconds before they realized Jerry wasn't leaving. The girls decided to talk it over in front of him; they figured he couldn't hear them anyway.

As Michelle started to whisper to Olivia they were interrupted by an outrageously loud sneeze that shook the entire table. Every head in the coffee shop turned to see what made such an outrageous sound.

"God bless you Jerry," Olivia said.

"Pardon?" was the reply she heard back. Michelle just went back to whispering to her friend.

Jerry started digging around in his pockets looking for a handkerchief. He started to empty his belongings onto the table as the women continued to whisper to each other. Jerry had his head down. His bushy mustache was now showing bright shades of yellow and green snots. He had a long string of boogies from his nose to the middle of his red tie. He pulled out his wallet and placed it on the table. He reached into a pocket with his opposite hand and pulled out a yoyo and placed it on the table. Then he reached in with his other hand and pulled out a half-eaten sandwich wrapped in cellophane. By now the girls had their total attention drawn to him. They watched in disbelief. As he placed the sandwich down.

"What, I'm a diabetic," Jerry said with dismay.

He reached into another pocket and took out a dull, blue, metallic object. The girls could not get a good look at until he released it from his huge, fat hand. Once it was on the table there was no mistaking it was a gun.

"Um, Jerry, maybe you shouldn't have that out on the table?" Michelle said.

"Pardon?"

Michelle raised her voice almost in a panicked mode and repeated louder, "I said you should put the gun away."

Olivia's face cringed. At that instant, almost the entire coffee shop was still watching as the gun lay on the table in plain view for all to see. Just then Jerry found the handkerchief he was looking for. He took it out and brought up to his face to blow his nose. As he was wiping the snot off his face he could feel all the eyes of the patrons staring at him.

He slowly turned in his chair and in a loud authoritative voice he addressed the customers of the small, now silent coffee shop. "Mind your business and finish your coffee! I'm a cop."

An audible sigh of relief ran through the coffee shop. Then the coffee shop started to buzz again as everyone turned and went about their own business.

The waitress walked over to the table and stood next to Jerry. "Excuse me officer, may I bring you something? As she spoke she swiveled her bony hips and batted her cataract-filled eyes. "On the house, of course."

"No thank you, miss. I'll be leaving shortly."

"Boy, you don't see many revolvers like that anymore," the waitress continued, now fussing with her blue and gray hair. "Most people nowadays have those semi-automatics."

"Yeah, I'm more of a Kojak type of cop. I like to use the old-school type methods. You know, rubber hoses, bribes, kickbacks, that kind of stuff."

"Wow, you are fascinating. Well let me know if you change your mind, Sugar," and she turned and walked away. She took her time, as she did so, trying not to dislocate her hips. While she tried to sway her boney ass back and forth.

Michelle turned and whispered to Olivia, "Who the hell was that Ma Barker?"

Still, the girls were both impressed with Jerry's calm demeanor and quick thinking. Perhaps he was the guy to handle their job. Michelle reached into her bag and took out a brown envelope and handed it to Jerry.

"This is half the money. You get the other thousand when the job is done."

"Of course," Jerry answered.

"What's the plan?" Michelle asked.

"When do you want to do this?"

"Tomorrow, if possible. My husband is off, but he plans to be out all day. He told me he's going to see his friends at the firehouse."

"Perfect. When is he due home?'

"He usually gets home between nine and ten o'clock."

Jerry thought for a moment and then said. "Give me your address. I'll show up about an hour before he gets home. When he comes in I put two in the back of his head.

Then I mess up the place a little bit; make it look like he came home to a burglary in progress. Simple."

"That's how they did my husband," Olivia said.

"It's always about you!" Michelle shot back. In an almost indignant tone.

Olivia ignored her comment and said, "Well if I were you I would make some arrangement to work late so you have an alibi."

"I already have. I'm going in at ten to do a mock inspection of the night shift nurses."

"Perfect!"

"Well, ladies, if we're done here then I will take my leave of you," Jerry said. He started to pick up his belongings and place them back in his pocket.

Just as he reached for the gun on the table Michelle stopped him. "Excuse me, Jerry, but I couldn't help but notice all the notches and grooves on the handle of your gun. You must have killed a lot of, I mean you must have done a lot of jobs."

"Pardon?"

Michelle was exasperated with Jerry's hearing deficiency by now but she was curious and said again, "I said I noticed all the notches on your gun."

"Oh, those aren't notches. I left the gun on the coffee table at home the other day and the dog got hold of it. Yeah, he chewed the hell out of. It was bitch to get it off him too. The worst part of it was the dog shot the stupid cat. Try explaining that to the vet."

Jerry put the gun back into his pocket and started the long process of trying to stand up. As he was getting to his feet he said, "Okay, ladies, I'll see you tomorrow night."

When he was on his feet and clear of the chair he started to turn to leave. He stood on his left foot and with small steps from his right leg he started to pivot. It wasn't more than twenty degrees at a time, his shoe squeaking on the floor as he turned. When he had, his body pointed towards the door he started to wobble and limp out, bumping into everything in his path. As the door closed behind him the girls sat and wondered if they were doing the right thing.

Olivia dropped a twenty-dollar bill on the table to pay the tab for the ladies. She said good-bye and walked out the door. Michelle stayed a few minutes longer and finished her tea. She had a lot to think about on her drive home to New York.

Michelle was making good time on her drive home. The traffic was much lighter than she expected. Her thoughts wandered, thinking about The Governor and his ability to take care of her husband. More importantly wondering how to stay out of jail. As she approached the Verrazano Bridge that crosses from Staten Island into Brooklyn she came up with an idea. When she got close to home, she would stop at the public library and use their computer to research Uncle Jerry. It seemed brilliant to her; if anything, ever came back to her the cops wouldn't find a trace of the research on her laptop. It was an uneasy feeling as well. Now she was thinking like a criminal. She took the upper level of the bridge and glanced over to her left at the Manhattan skyline. It was a beautiful sight. The cool blue water with some boaters out enjoying the day. As your eyes panned off the water into the sky you see the jagged outline of New York against the blue sky, and white puffy clouds above it. It was easy to spot the Twin Towers, the tallest point in the city. It was a landmark that signified to Michelle she was almost home.

When Michelle made it back to Long Island she headed for the public library. She turned down Main Street and made a left into the parking lot. She grabbed her purse and started to fumble, looking for her library card. She ran into the building with her head down. She stood at the front desk trying to fish her card out. With people behind her waiting patiently she continued to move items in her purse around.

The lady behind the desk gave Michelle a polite, "Ahem!" As if clearing her throat.

"Hold on, honey, it's in here somewhere," Michelle shot back. The librarian at the desk could not wait any longer. The line behind Michelle was building behind her.

She looked around Michelle and called out, "NEXT." A teenage boy started to walk around Michelle on her left. She quickly put out her left arm to stop him.

"Just a second kid. It's right here." She pulled out the card and flashed it to the librarian. She quickly turned and started to walk away.

The lady at the desk yelled to her, "Mam! Your card is expired!" Michelle ignored her and ran down the steps to the computer rooms. The librarian, completely exasperated with Michelle, just said, "Fuck it. Next!"

The library had four computers with internet capability. The desks were separated by tall dividers on each side, and each computer came with a set of head phones for privacy. All four computers were also occupied. Two women, one man, and a little boy about four or five years old were busy typing away on the key boards. Michelle was in no mood to wait. She surveyed the situation.

"How can I get on a computer?" She thought to herself. The man seemed to be listing to music. One of the women appeared to be working on some type of college paper. The other was typing perhaps an e-mail to someone. She walked over to the end of the row where the little blond boy was working. She peaked over his shoulder and saw he was playing a game that was teaching him about the alphabet. Ah, the weakest link, she thought.

Michelle placed her hand on her chin and started to think. After a few seconds, her face lit up. Like an evil genius she had the perfect idea to make the kid leave the computer. She slowly walked up closer to the little kid. She leaned in over his right shoulder and in a low, motherly voice said to him, "Excuse me, little fella, but the Librarian asked me to come down here to tell all the kids that Barney is upstairs to say hi to all the children."

"He is? No kiddin?"

"No kidding sweetheart. If you run up now you can say hi to him." The cute little boy pushed his chair away from the computer desk with his tiny arms and hands. When he had enough room, he slid off his chair and started to run down the hall to the staircase.

As he ran away he turned and waved to Michelle and said, "Thanks a lot lady, I wouldn't want to miss him!"

"Anytime, *you little brat,*" she muttered under her breath.

Michelle wasted no time taking over the computer station. As she sat in the chair and adjusted the keyboard, she was surprised and disgusted as her hands became covered in some sticky, jelly-like substance. She raised her hands to her face and sniffed them to see what she was dealing with.

"Mmmm grape." She was nervous that the kid may be back soon with his mother so she tried to ignore the grossness of the situation and continued to type in her search. She typed in Jerry's name and in just a few seconds a web site came up with information about him. She started to read, not realizing she was speaking aloud in a low voice.

"Gentleman Jerry Baker was very famous in the 1960's. He was known as an impeccable dresser and had the manners of an English butler. He was indicted in several murders for hire scams but was never convicted. Although the prosecution had enough evidence for conviction, it was believed that his courtroom manner and his polite testimony swayed the jury to acquit him. In 1969, he was convicted of passing a bad check and sent to Rahway State Prison in New Jersey. After less than two weeks in prison he escaped. Authorities believed he had some assistance from one of the ladies working in the cafeteria. He has been on the loose ever since."

Michelle sat back in her chair. She had a whole new perspective on The Governor. While she was lost in thought she felt a tap on her shoulder. She reached back and pushed the hand away without turning around and said. "Shove off, this one is taken." As she brought her hand back to the keyboard she noticed it felt very sticky. Then on the same shoulder she felt a more forceful tapping. Without turning she said in a very belligerent tone, "Look, kid, you can tap as hard as you want. I'm using this computer, so take your sticky fingers and get lost."

Suddenly her chair was pulled out from the desk and spun around to face a giant of a man with a little boy standing about waist high at his side. The boy had a dirty tear-stained face and sadness in his eyes. The man had a stone face and anger in his eyes. Michelle looked up at the man, and a creepy smile crossed her face: it was a combination of fear and surprise.

The man looked down at his son and said, "Caleb, cover your ears." The little boy placed his sticky hands over his ears. The man looked down at Michelle and spoke in a deep, menacing voice. "Are you the stink bitch who lied to my boy?"

"Well, stink bitch is a little harsh," Michelle started. "I can assure you it was a simple misunderstanding," she continued. The big man was in no mood to hear excuses.

He looked down at her and as she was speaking and said. "I don't want to hear your winey, made up, half-baked, lying, unbelievable, stupid, couldn't care less, bitch face, fuck you very much, excuses, Just. Get. Up."

Michelle slowly rose from her seat. She towered over the little boy, but was still a good foot shorter than his father. With the creepy smile still pasted on her face she carefully turned back to the computer key-board. As she faced the computer her smile vanished and she angrily muttered, "Spoiled little bastard!"

She reached down and carefully pressed control, alt, and delete. Slowly she turned back, the creepy smile appearing again, and said, "There, that should do it." She casually moved her right leg to the side and extricated herself from between the computer desk and the angry parent.

She patted the cute little boy on top of his blond head and her hand stuck to it. She tried to gently pull her hand away but she only brought up a bunch of blond hair with her. The little boy cocked his head and made a face as she tried to remove her hand again. Finally, Michelle gave a swift hard tug and her hand was free along with a nice clump of blond hair. The boy let out a loud yelp and Michelle quickly walked away. The boy tapped his father on the leg and pointed to Michelle's back. Sticking to her pants almost dead center to the crack of her ass was a huge wad of pink bubble gum. He looked up at his dad and asked, "Should we tell her?"

The father looked down at his son and said, "No son, let her walk around like that. It's called Karma."

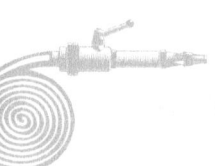

CHAPTER EIGHT

WILL IT BE MURDER OR SUICIDE?

The next day started out as another hot, sticky, late July day. The occupants of 721 Central Avenue were anything but cool. Michelle was up and about earlier than usual. Joe could hear her downstairs puttering around. She was banging pots and pans and slamming cabinet doors and drawers. It became so noisy down there he couldn't sleep anymore. He wasn't sleeping well anyway. He felt somewhat nervous and excited about his plans for the day. Over the past few days he had hatched a new scheme to free Michelle. By the end of the day his wife, whom he still loved very much, would be a rich widow.

He sat up on the side of his big, half empty bed, placed his feet on the floor, and hung his head. Slowly, he started to collect his thoughts and get ready to do his stretches. It was extremely painful every morning to loosen up the skin on his right side from the horrible disfiguring burns. He slowly stood up and twisted his torso from right to left. At first, he moved very carefully. The skin was tight and he could feel every tug on it. Then he raised his arms above his head and tried to touch his toes. This was his most painful stretch. He could feel all the folds of skin pulling apart. Each one felt like it was glued to the other. Pulling slowly apart with searing pain that reminded him of the day he received the terrible burn.

To keep his mind off the pain, he started to think about his drive into New Jersey. A smile crossed Joe's face. It was a flawless plan. He took solace in the fact that today would be the last day he would have to endure the voice in his head, the daily painful torture, The Monster, and the life it created for Michelle.

He brushed his teeth got dressed, and went downstairs to begin his last day on Earth. As he entered the kitchen, he saw Michelle. She was already dressed, and Joe thought she looked exceptionally beautiful today. Like Joe, Michelle seemed more preoccupied than usual. She was also more talkative than she had been over the past few weeks. She seemed almost nervous to him. "What are your plans for today?" she asked.

Joe was somewhat startled to hear her speak to him. It had been a while since they spoke to each other. He looked over at her; he felt confused and replied. "I mentioned the other day I was off. I'm going to the firehouse to see some of the guys. I guess you weren't listening." Then he muttered under his breath, "As usual."

Michelle heard the snide remark loud and clear just as Joe had planned her to. Ignoring his last comment, she replied with a smile. "That's right, dear, I forgot. Have fun."

Have fun. Joe could not believe his ears. Was this a conversation? After weeks of almost total silence they were talking. The longest conversation the couple had lately was asking each other to pass the butter. His mind started to race with crazy thoughts. Was she making an attempt to reconcile? Maybe if he tried a little harder, gave in a little more and stopped being so stubborn they could work this whole mess out. He took a long look at Michelle sitting across from him, looking all dolled up with her makeup on. The wonderful scent of her perfume, that he loved so much. As he gazed into her eyes his thoughts drifted off to days past. Then suddenly all those thoughts left his brain. He sat straight up and smiled; now he knew why she was so talkative this morning. Why she looked so pretty, and smelled so sexy. All those nights on the computer she's been e-mailing someone. It didn't take a genius to figure this puzzle out. She wanted him out so she could meet some guy. She was having an affair.

He looked at his beautiful wife and with a straight face and told her, "Don't worry about me. I'll be home late, probably around nine tonight, maybe later."

Without missing a beat Michelle said, "Well, you know I'm going into work late tonight. I probably won't be home when you get back. I need to do an inspection of the night shift nurses."

"Sure, I remember. Don't work too hard," was Joe's sarcastic reply. He finished his coffee, got up from the table, and put his mug in the sink. Michelle stayed seated at the kitchen table with her hands folded across her lap and her foot tapping on the kitchen floor. Joe started to get his things together. He used the fire house as an excuse but he did plan to stop there and see some old friends for the last time. As he gathered the things he needed his emotions started to build. How could she have an affair? Why would she be so obvious? He started to close doors a little harder. His footsteps were a little louder. He started to throw things out of his way as he looked for his belongings. He was doing what Michelle always referred to as the slow burn. He wasn't angry about her having an affair; after all she is a beautiful woman and deserves more than a monster like him. He was angry that she thought she could hide it from him. He didn't like the idea of her thinking she was smarter than him.

After about forty-five minutes Joe was ready to leave for his visit to the firehouse. He walked over to his wife still sitting at the kitchen table with her hands folded on her lap and her foot tapping away on the floor. He knew it would be the last time he would ever see her. He looked into her eyes and cupped her chin with his hand. He tilted her face up so he could take one last look at her beautiful features. Inside, he started to feel happy that she was having an affair. At least she found happiness so he wouldn't be missed. Joe turned to take his last look at her. He looked closely at her, with her face all made up and beautiful, just like when they first married. He stared at her, his eyes moving all over her body; he wanted to remember as much as he could about her. He was hoping when they meet again in Heaven he would have the chance to explain and say I'm sorry.

Michelle took a long look as well; she knew it would be the last time she would see him alive. Tonight, when he got home The Governor would be there waiting to murder him. It was certainly not what she wanted to do, but after listening to Olivia it was the best solution she could come up with. Joe took his hand off her chin and softly ran it along the side of her face. It was a tender moment. He always liked how soft and smooth her skin felt. In a low voice that almost seemed to crack as he spoke, he simply said. "Goodbye."

"Goodbye," Michelle said softly, tears welling up in her eyes. Joe turned and left. Michelle sat alone in the kitchen. She watched as the back door slammed shut. She heard the car door close and then the engine start. Then she heard the car pull out of the driveway and listened as it went down the block. When she could no longer hear the car, she rose from the kitchen table. As quickly as she could she went into the living room and picked up her laptop computer. She logged on and went directly to her e-mail. She quickly wrote a note to her friend Olivia. She hit the send button and it instantly went to Olivia's e-mail account. Olivia was sitting at her kitchen table with her computer open waiting for the message. Her computer made the familiar beep to alert her of a new message. She quickly clicked on the new mail from Michelle; she stared at it for a moment and smiled. It simply read, "He's gone."

Michelle sat, staring at the computer screen waiting for a response. It seemed like hours to her. In reality, it only took a few seconds. Her eyes were burning a hole in the computer until she heard it beeped back. It was from Olivia. It read, "I'll be over in a few hours." Michelle closed her laptop. Her hands were shaking. She bent her head down almost as if she were praying. Over her left shoulder, unknown to her, a face was peeking in through the window. Joe had parked his car at the end of the block, then he doubled back to see if he was right about his wife's marital indiscretion. He could see her reading the message, but he could not make out the words. It was still enough evidence to him, she was having an affair. With tears running down his face, he shook his head and whispered, "I knew it."

On the drive over to the firehouse, Joe continued his slow burn. "Why does she think she is so much smarter than me?" he thought to himself. "I'm the smart one; she has no idea what I'm doing." As he got closer to the firehouse, he started to calm himself down. He certainly did not want the guys to see him all riled up.

It was a relativity quick visit. He saw a lot of his old friends. They sat around the table in the back room. They told some old war stories. Many of the dates and times were correct. Many of the facts were embellished. They were still all true but much more exciting now. Listening to the stories and having a few laughs was Joe's way of saying goodbye. Around two o'clock a box pull alarm sounded at the station. The firemen rushed out of the back room and on to the apparatus floor. They grabbed their gear and hopped into their respective trucks. In less than three minutes Joe was alone in the back room with Sully. He quickly finished his soda and said goodbye to Sully. He pulled open the back door once more. Looking up at the citation hanging over it.

He turned to Sully and said, "You know, Sully, I hate this thing."

"I know, Cap. It was a bad day for all of us."

"Amen, Sully." Joe left the building, the door slamming shut behind him.

Today it would be a quick and creative death; electrocution. He was going to drive into Manhattan, then across town and through the tunnel and into Newark. Once there he would rent a hotel room. It was perfect; he had never been to Newark before so no one would know him. He would check in, go to his room, and grab the clock radio. All rooms come with clock radios. He would fill the bathtub with water, and sit in it with his clothes on. He wanted his clothes on so they wouldn't find him naked. It would be the last time he would have to hide the monster on his right side. Once in the tub he just needed to drop the clock radio in. But bathrooms have ground fault plugs. That means if you plug something in and it gets wet the breaker will blow before you can get shocked. That's where Joe's genius came into play. Sitting tucked in his pants pocket is an eight-foot extension cord. With that he could plug into any socket in the room. Nothing could go wrong today.

It was about four-thirty in the afternoon when Joe parked his car on the street in Newark. It was much hotter than the morning had been. The temperature had to be in the upper nineties with high humidity. He stepped out of his air-conditioned car and felt the heat hit him like a hot, wet blanket. He turned and looked across the river. Through the muggy air, he could clearly see the iconic outline of the Manhattan skyline, the World Trade Center and the Empire State Building. Then Joe turned and surveyed his new surroundings. It was a rundown section of town with lots of graffiti. All the businesses that were open had bars around their windows and the huge metal roll-down doors for when they closed for the night. The buildings that weren't doing business were either burned down or had been closed and looted a long time ago.

Joe looked down the street ahead of him and could see the heat radiating off the blacktop. He turned and looked down the street in the other direction. He saw a fire hydrant about a block and a half down spewing water onto the hot street. Kids were running through the high-pressure hydrant water trying to keep cool. He took note of an old black man sitting in a lawn chair with his back to the water as it spewed on him.

He closed and locked his car door although he didn't know why. It wasn't like he was going to need it again. He walked around to the front of his car to cross the street. He took in more of the sights of this depressed city. He noticed old men lying on thin, slabs, of cardboard, next to burned out buildings. Young men and women walking around the hot streets with bitterness in their eyes, most of them giving Joe a long hard stare. They knew he did not belong there. Joe crossed the street and walked to the hotel he was going to rent the room from. It was called the Plantation Motel and it had bars on the windows and entrance door. It seemed strange to Joe that a hotel would have bars like a prison. It was like a roach motel. You can check in, but you can't check out. It made no difference to him. He wasn't staying long.

Joe approached the entrance to the motel. He politely stepped over a man passed out lying on a piece of cardboard. He reached through the bars and pulled on the door handle. The door rattled but did not open. He pulled again with the same result. He stepped back to reassess his options. Then on the right side of the door, he saw a small plaque that read. "Press Buzzer for Access."

He looked below the plaque and saw the small black button and pressed it. The button had a slimy residue on it that disgusted him. He held his finger up in the air. His head rotating back and forth trying to find something to wipe his finger on. Just as panic was about to set in he looked down. The old man lying on the cardboard. He was sound asleep. Joe reached down and quickly wiped his finger on the poor soul's shoulder. The old man stirred and Joe let out a short quick scream. Instead of cleaning his finger he now picked up a new substance. The door buzzed. Joe put his hand to his side, and quickly wiped it on his pants. He pushed the door open and walked into the lobby. He was expecting to find the cool relief of air conditioning but instead it was hot as hell. A fat, middle- aged man, in a torn, dirty tee shirt sat behind the desk. His face was wet with beads of perspiration. He looked as though he hadn't shaved in about three or four days. There was an open container of Chinese food on the counter and more of it on the salt and pepper facial hair of the clerk. A small metal fan was blowing hot air into his face. Sitting behind him was a white cooler. Judging from the open can of beer sitting next to the clerk Joe figured it was filled with beer.

"What can I do for you, Jack?" The desk clerk asked in a raspy voice.

"Uh, yes, hello, um, well, I would like to rent a room for the night, please," was Joe's nervous response.

The clerk looked at him and said. "You're new at this Bub; No rooms for the night, just by the hour."

The conversation was halted temporarily by the buzz of the door. When the clerk responded with his buzzer, an old man walked in with a very scantily clad woman. Even for such a hot day Joe thought she should have some more clothes on. Her makeup was caked on her face, very thick, almost like she used a trowel to put it on. There was so much on her you couldn't tell if she was a nasty looking young girl or an old bag trying to fake out Father Time.

The old man had the woman by the hand and was leading her up the steps to the rooms. The woman breezed by the desk and said, "Hi, Lyle. I'm going to take room seven for an hour. I'll settle with you later."

"Sure, Sugar, I'll be here," the clerk responded, and up the steps they went. "Now back to you Bub. You want a room for an hour. It will cost you thirty-five bucks."

"Well. Mister, Lyle." Joe said nervously, "can I get a room for two hours?"

"Do you have seventy dollars?" Lyle said as if he were talking to a baby. Joe reached into his pocket and pulled out his wallet. He took out four twenty dollar bills and handed them to Lyle.

"Here, Mac, keep the change," Joe said in his best tough guy voice, which wasn't very convincing. Lyle took the cash and turned to the board holding the room keys. He reached out and grabbed number eight and handed it to Joe.

"Here, Bub take eight. It's next to Sugar. She doesn't make much noise."

"Thank you, sir." Joe took the key and stood in front of the clerk. Lyle looked across waiting for him to either say something or leave, but to his surprise there was no sound or movement. Finally, Joe spoke up and said, "So, do I sign the registry or something?"

"What the hell are you talking about? Is this your first visit to this planet? Get the hell outta here the clock is ticking on your seventy bucks."

Joe turned and walked away embarrassed and angry. He had planned to sign some type of book or registry. He was going to use an alias; it would be his final jab at the world. He was going to sign it Richard Kimble, the fugitive. As he started up the staircase, he heard the door buzz again. He ran up the steps so he wouldn't be seen by the next circus act walking through the door. He reached the top of the first floor and turned right. He walked down the hall and past room seven. Lyle was right. Sugar doesn't make much noise but that friggin bed sure squeaks like hell. Joe slid the key into the lock on room eight but the door was already open. "I guess that's why the girls don't have to stop at the desk," he thought to himself.

Joe walked into the room; it had a large beat-up bed. There was a night stand next to it where a black clock radio sat. The numbers on the screen were bright red. Joe checked the time on his watch and then looked again at the clock radio. The time on the clock was wrong.

"Of course," He thought.

On the other side of the room was the bathroom. The door was half open but it could not hold the stench in. He walked over and with and held his breath, as he pushed the door the rest of the way open. Behind the door was a toilet bowl. It appeared to be very old. At one time, it may have been white, now it was so stained and neglected you would need to sand blast it to get to its original color. Next to that was a small sink with hot and cold-water faucets that was covered with rust stains. Sitting on the floor of the bathroom against the back wall was what Joe needed. The bath tub. Still holding his breath, he pulled the dirty, moldy, shower curtain away and looked inside the tub. It was filthy. There was a ring of soap scum and multi colored hair around it. The drain was full of all kinds of disgusting debris. A quick glance showed hair, toe nails, soap scum, and plastic wrappers. The faucets looked like someone had just pissed on them. He had seen enough. He ran out of the bathroom and gasped to get some air back into his lungs.

Joe thought to himself, "What a way to go. I don't even have to fill the tub, I could just sit in it and die of disgust."

Then, another voice decided to chime in. It was The Monster, "Dude even I don't want to die this bad." he said.

Joe took another breath in and went back in. He reached over to grab one of the dirty towels hanging in the bathroom; he bent down and used it to turn the faucet on and start filling the tub. The quicker he could get this over with, the less time he'd have to spend in this hot, smelly, rancid room. He turned the one faucet as far as he could. His ears were greeted with a loud annoying squeal from the pipes followed by a loud knocking sound. His eyes were disappointed as no water came out. He reached over to open the other faucet. He turned it all the way, but again no water came out.

"ARE YOU FRIGGIN KIDDING ME!" he screamed out.

"Thank God," came the voice in his head.

He stood motionless staring down at the empty tub. He turned around and stood in front of the sink. A smile started to cross his face, his knack of keeping his cool had rescued him again. He reached down and turned the faucets on the sink and the water flowed like milk and honey. Honestly, it looked like milk and honey. It wasn't the clearest water he had ever seen, but it was wet and it would work.

Joe heard the voice of The Monster in his head say, "Oh no, you're not thinking about getting,…"

Before the voice could finish Joe said aloud, "I'm gonna get me some hose."

Joe walked out of the smelly bathroom and out of the motel room with purpose. He walked quickly past room seven with the squeaky bed and down the stairs. When he hit the lobby, he walked over to Lyle at the desk.

"Excuse me, Mr. Lyle," Joe started. "I have a problem upstairs in my room. I need to get some hose."

"Yeah, I thought you forgot something when you checked in," Lyle responded.

"You knew I would need hose when I checked in?" Joe asked.

"Listen, Bub. I've worked here for twelve years and believe me people come in everyday with hoes."

Joe looked a little confused, but didn't want to get into a discussion about the motel plumbing with Lyle. He just let it go and asked, "Do you know someplace around here I can get some hose?"

"Sure, just go out here and turn right. There's a very well dressed black man on the corner. He wears a white hat with a black band around it. Tell him what you want and he'll help you out."

"Out here and to the right?" Joe asked pointing at the door.

"Yeah you can't miss him; he's like six foot six."

Joe tapped the counter with his hand and said, "Thanks."

Again his hand seemed to touch some foreign, slimy substance. He walked out of the lobby towards the door, trying to inconspicuously rub the residue off the fingers of his hand. Joe opened the door into the hot summer day; and stepped over the man lying on the piece of cardboard. His eyes squinted as he took the full brunt of the sun's brightness. Across the street he saw something that bothered him. He placed his hand over his eyes to shade them from the sun. Then he focused in and saw what was bothering him. His car was up on cinder blocks; all the tires were taken. The hood and trunk of the car were also popped up. Joe threw his hands up in the air in disbelief.

"How did they do that in broad daylight so damn fast?" he thought. He stopped for a second should he walk over and see the damage. No, there was no need to; he didn't need the car anymore anyway. Besides he needed to find some hose.

He took a right and walked down the street. Standing on the corner was a tall black man with a white hat. "That must be him," Joe thought.

He walked over to him and looking up said, "Excuse me sir. The clerk at the Plantation Motel said you might be able to help me?"

"That depends, my brother are you a cop?"

Joe was confused at his response but replied, "No I'm not, although I use to be a fireman."

"That's coo', that's coo'. What can I do for you my brotha?"

"Well, I'm looking for some hose and Lyle said you could help me."

The tall black man tipped his hat up on his head and responded, "I think I can help you, brotha, but it will cost you."

"Oh, I have every intention of paying, and I have cash," Joe said with smile.

"That's coo, we's only accept cash. Just walk down this block here and go into the bodega. Tell the guy at the counter Thomas Jefferson sent you, and he'll send you to the back of the store. When you get back there you'll see a hip brotha with a big fro. That be my cousin Benny Franklin. He can get you all the hoes you need."

Joe listened carefully to the instructions. It seemed easy enough to him, although it was a lot of steps just to buy some hose. "Thank you, Mr. Jefferson." Joe said.

"No problem my brotha. My cousin Benny has the highest quality hoes in Newark."

"Does he have short hoes?" Joe asked?

Thomas Jefferson clapped his hands together and arched his back as he started to laugh. "Oh, my freaky brotha, he's got any kind of hoes you want."

"That's great, Mr. Jefferson. Thanks for your time."

Joe took off down the street with a hop in his step. As he approached the bodega he checked his watch. About a half an hour had passed so far, still plenty of time to get back, fill the tub and take care of business. As he approached the bodega Joe heard from The Monster again.

"I still don't like this plan," the voice said.

"I really don't care what you think. I just may get two hose to make sure I finish the job," Joe said in a loud voice.

The few people on the street stopped and looked at him with distain. He just shrugged his shoulders and entered the store. He walked up with confidence to the man at the counter.

"Hello, sir. I just spoke with Thomas Jefferson. He said you could help me."

The man looked up and without saying a word pointed to the back of the store. Joe walked back and saw the maroon curtains separating the front of the store from the back. Without breaking stride, he pulled the curtains apart and strode right in.

There wasn't much back there except for a black guy with a huge afro and a white guy puffing on a cigar. Lots of boxes were in the small room, some of them being used as tables.

Joe walked directly over to the man with the afro and said, "Are you Benny Franklin? Your cousin, Thomas Jefferson, sent me over. He said you had some hose."

The men in the room didn't speak. They just exchanged looks at each other. The silence was deafening, Joe felt compelled to say something.

"Gentleman, I'm in sort of a hurry. I have a room at the Plantation Motel but only for two hours. So, if you have any hose I would appreciate purchasing some. I'll take anything you got. I'll even buy used hose I'm kinda desperate. I really need to get back to my room and tack care of business."

The man with the afro spoke. "Okay, let me get this straight. You have a room at the Plantation and you want to buy hoes to bring back with you. Is that right."

"That is correct, Mr. Franklin. I'll buy sight unseen, I'm kind of in a hurry to get my hose and get busy." Joe said with authority.

The two men in the back room looked at each other and almost simultaneously reached into their back pockets. In an instant, they flashed police badges and announced, "You're under arrest, dirt bag!"

They jumped at Joe and tackled him to the floor. They were like a precision calf roping team. Before he knew it, Joe was frisked and handcuffed. Just then Thomas Jefferson walked into the back room.

"You got him, good. I'm sick of these rich white guys coming into our neighborhood to get prostitutes," he said. Jefferson looked directly into Joe's face and said, "Today's not your day perv. You messed with the Newark Police Department."

Joe was still in a state of shock and was trying to process what the hell was going on. Then it started to make sense to him. Prostitutes. They thought he wanted to buy sex.

Joe finally spoke up, "Guys, you got this all wrong. I was trying to buy hose."

"Yea, that's why you're under arrest, dirtball," Benny Franklin said.

"No, like to water stuff, kind of hose," Joe responded anguish.

"Sure, sure, you're starting a garden at the motel."

All the police men laughed at Franklin's comment, then the policeman puffing on the cigar said something.

"Hey guys, he might be telling the truth. Do you know who this is? This is the guy who saved that girl in the

Palmer building a few weeks ago. Remember? He went out the window on the tenth floor, snuck into the office and disarmed that crazy son of a bitch. Guys, this man's a hero."

Joe started to shake his head up and down. In a high squeaky voice, he said, "Yeah, yeah, that's me. The hero! This is all a big mistake."

Thomas Jefferson spoke up and said, "I think you're right. He did look familiar to me."

"It is me! I went on the ledge and saved that girl," Joe said with desperation in his voice. The policemen walked over to the far corner of the room. They huddled like football referees trying to decide what penalty to call. Joe tried to lean in to hear what they were saying. In less than a minute they broke their impromptu huddle and walked back over to Joe. Benny reached into his pocket and pulled out the handcuffs keys. They decided to let him go.

"Thank you, guys, this was all a big mistake," Joe said as he rubbed his wrist to get some circulation back. He did his best to explain why he wanted to buy hose. He thought fast and came up with a believable story. "Ya see, my car broke down outside this motel. I tried to fix it but it was so hot and I got so dirty I wanted to take a shower. When I checked into the room the bathtub water didn't work. So, I went to buy the hose so I could hook it to the bathroom sink and then take a quick bath."

The police officers sat and listened in silence. When Joe's explanation was over no one spoke. Joe just looked on hoping he sold his story. Then the police officers looked at each other and at the same time they all said in unison, "Oh the bathtub was broken."

Joe told the police how his car had been stripped in the middle of the street. Thomas Jefferson said, "Yeah I'm not surprised. This is a bad neighborhood."

Joe and the officers talked for hours. They exchanged war stories with each other. Joe talked about his days in the fire service. He told them about the fire that burned him so severely. How he rescued the little girl. The policemen were heartbroken to hear how Joe was discharged from the fire department.

The Newark policemen also shared some of their exploits with him. As nighttime fell Joe knew his plan had failed. It was time to head home and rethink his options. Joe's new friends, the Newark Policemen, were also coming off duty. With Joe no longer having a car to drive they offered to drive him home in their unmarked police car. Having few other options and enjoying the company of his new friends, he accepted. They police officers were on duty till eight o'clock. Joe would hang out with them until then. Then the four men would pile into the unmarked white Chrysler and head to Long Island.

CHAPTER NINE

MURDER

Michelle and Olivia were busy all day making preparations for when Joe arrived home from the firehouse. They sat down at lunch and went over the plan to make sure there were no loop holes. At approximately eight p.m. The Governor would arrive at Michelle's house. Olivia could tell her friend was nervous about the murder, and might even back out of it. If that happened the entire scheme could spill over to her. She decided it was in her best interest to stay with her, and make sure it happened. The girls continued to talk and plan. Every detail had to be ironed out. Most important was their alibis. Michelle had made plans to work the overnight shift at the hospital. Olivia, of course, thought she would be above suspicion. The murder was staged as a robbery in progress at Joe and Michelle's house. Olivia would just say she was home all night.

Michelle made tuna fish salad for lunch with a pitcher of cold iced tea to chase it down. The pitcher sat on the kitchen table. The clear brown liquid filled with ice cubes.

As the pitcher sat the outside of it started to sweat, beads of water running down the sides of it. The girls sat at the kitchen table staring at the bowl of tuna salad. They were both hungry but too nervous to eat. They sat silently staring at empty plates and glasses.

After several minutes Michelle left the kitchen table and walked into the living room. She walked straight towards the liquor cabinet. She bent down and opened the small double wooden doors. Staring back at her were a collection of mostly full bottles. Many of them were never even opened. She reached in and grabbed the first bottle she laid her hands on. She walked back to the kitchen and placed the bottle down. It was rye whisky. Michelle reached into the iced tea pitcher and pulled out a few ice cubes. She dropped them into her glass and opened the bottle of rye. As she poured herself a drink Olivia reached into the pitcher and pulled out some ice cubes for herself. When Michelle put the bottle back down Olivia reached for it and poured herself a drink. The girls picked up their glasses and with a silent toast they clinked them together.

It was about twelve o'clock when they took their first drink in silence. By two fifteen they were still going strong. The bottle was empty and they were nonstop gabbing. Michelle was a basket case; she was sobbing and filled with remorse over her marriage. Olivia was cold as the ice in her glass. She listened as Michelle droned on and on about how this was a bad idea.

"I still love Joe. He's made mistakes, I've made mistakes, but we can get past this. Maybe if we went on a trip together we could work it all out. I think he still loves me; You should have seen him this morning. He was so tender, almost like he knew he would never see me again." Michelle continued to sob as she took another sip of her drink.

Olivia reached for the empty bottle and started to speak. "Listen, honey, I know how you feel. I know what you're going through. Believe me you'll be much better off. When Michael killed my husband, I thought it was wrong. Then I realized it was the best thing I ever did. I was free; no more waiting for him to do something right. He was so useless I would have been better off married to a house plant. At least they give off oxygen."

Olivia held up the empty bottle and shook it in Michelle's face. "We need another, honey," She said with a distinctive slur. "After the investigation, I got all of his insurance money, which was nice. I can come and go as I please, and now, and best of all, I have my choice of lovers. Tell you the truth, right now I have my eye on that E.R. doctor that works in the morning, Alex Blaze. Oh, he's so cute!"

"My Joe is cute!" Michelle said as she staggered to her feet to find another bottle of liquor.

"Your Joe is a pig!" Olivia replied, leaning forward as if to make a point.

Michelle placed a bottle of Johnnie Walker down on the coffee table in front of Olivia. Then she fell into her chair and brushed her hair out of her face. She looked over at Olivia who appeared a little blurrier than before.

Olivia pointed at the staircase and continued, "Look at that monstrosity hanging over the staircase. Who hangs a noose in their living room?"

"He thought he was doing something good. He'll take it down soon."

"No, he won't. He'll be dead soon."

That ended their conversation. The room went silent. The girls were left with their own thoughts and the bottle of Johnnie Walker.

It was getting close to five o'clock. The bottle of Johnnie Walker was sitting half empty on the coffee table. Two glasses sat almost full next to it. The girls were fast asleep. Michelle started to stir when she heard the doorbell ringing nonstop. She tried to shake the cobwebs out of her head, and tried to focus her eyes on the big clock in the living room. Then they were startled by loud knocking on the front door. Michelle slowly came to her senses got up and to staggered to the door to answer it. As she opened the door, she was first blinded by the sun which was slowly starting to set. The next item that caught her attention was the shining badge of a handsome police officer standing in her doorway. It took several seconds for her inebriated brain to process what was happening.

"Oh shit, I slept through it," she thought, then she said, "Arrest her officer, it was all her idea, I tried to back out but she wouldn't let me."

Over on the sofa Olivia stirred. She saw Michelle standing at her front door speaking to a police officer and pointing at her. Panic raced through her body; the deed was done and the cops already caught them.

She sprang to her feet and although still wobbling pointed at Michelle. "Don't listen to that bitch, officer, I was a victim here also."

The policeman grabbed Michelle by the shoulders and shook her. "Michelle it's me, Gary. I came over to see Joe."

Michelle suddenly recognized her husband's good friend and said, "Oh, Gary, I'm sorry. I'm not myself today."

"I can see that," was his reply.

This is my friend, Olivia.

"Pleased to meet you handsome," she said as she daintily extended her hand to him.

"What's going on here?" Gary asked. Michelle and Olivia looked at each other neither one wanting to answer.

Then Michelle said, "Joe is not home. He went to the firehouse."

"I'm glad he's not home to see this. I'm going to put a pot of coffee on and sober you two up." Gary walked into the kitchen and started to rattle the pots and pans looking for a coffee pot.

Olivia stumbled over to Michelle, almost falling into her arms, and said, "He's dreamy."

"Hands off him, he's Joe's best friend. We'll both wind up in the clink."

Gary finished making the coffee and brought two hot black cups in for the girl's. They slowly sipped on the strong brew. After a few minutes, the girl's buzz started to fade. The importance of the evening started to creep into the back of their heads. Gary seemed very comfortable sitting in the reclining chair waiting for Joe to come home. Michelle knew she had to get rid of him before The Governor arrived at eight.

As the time passed Gary started to recognize Michelle was coming to her senses. He was now confident she could string a few thoughts together.

He started to tell her why he stopped by. "Michelle, I'm worried about Joe. I don't think he's long for this world."

Olivia gasped. Michelle looked over to her. "Sorry, just a hiccup," she said.

Gary continued. "He seems very depressed to me; I don't want to say he's suicidal, but you do have a hangman's noose over your staircase."

"Oh, that's nothing. He just trying to redecorate." Michelle shot back.

Gary was not fazed, he continued to give some examples of the strange behavior Joe had been exhibiting. Meanwhile the clock on the wall continued to tick closer to eight o'clock.

The Governor was close to Michelle's house. He had just turned off the main street and was driving down Central Avenue. It was passed seven thirty and the street was packed with cars parked on both sides. He slowly drove down the street looking on either side for a place to park his car. He passed by Michelle's house and still could not find parking. He slowly circled the block again. Still no spots were available. He became frustrated and started to mumble to himself. He did not want to be late to a job. It was unprofessional. As his level of frustration grew he spoke louder.

"God, please help me find a parking spot. I know I've done wrong in the past,… present, yeah, the future too, but if you help me find a parking spot I'll turn over a new leaf. I'll be a model citizen. I'll give up the profession. I'll work in a soup kitchen. I'll volunteer and become a Big Brother, and you know I hate kids. As soon as this job is over, just send me a sign. Anything you want. Please, please, Lord just help me find a spot."

No sooner had he finished his little prayer, he looked to his right. There in waning minutes of sunlight, was a huge, beautiful, empty, parking spot. It was truly a miracle, it wasn't there a few minutes ago when he first circled the block.

With a huge sigh of relief, The Governor looked up to the sky and said, "Oh, never mind God, I found one."

At seven forty-five with Michelle now fully recovered from her afternoon binge, she decided it was time to give Gary the bum's rush. "Gary, I don't expect Joe home until very late tonight and I am also working tonight. I hope you don't mind if I tell him you stopped by and he can call you tomorrow."

"Oh shit, look at the time. I'm so sorry, I just wanted to tell him about something I found out, that he may be interested in. Some of the guys down at the station are taking the fire department test in Fairfax, Virginia. The pay is pretty good and the cost of living is much lower than New York. I wrote the web site down for him. I think he might enjoy working in the fire service again and the change of scenery may do the both of you some good."

"Oh, that's great! He'll just die when he hears it.

"Just have him fill out the online application; the test is in October. He should pass that with flying colors and in a few months, he can be doing what he loves again. It's perfect with you being a nurse; you'll have no problem finding a job at one of the local hospitals."

"Sounds great! Really, really, great! I'll him tell as soon as I see him. Thank you."

Gary stood up from his reclining chair. The girls stood also. He leaned in and gave Michelle a kiss on the cheek. Olivia took a quick peek at the clock; it was almost eight.

"It was very nice to meet you Olivia." Gary said as he offered his hand to her. She reached for his arm and grabbed it. With unexpected strength, she pulled him into her and gave him a big, wet, sloppy kiss on the lips.

"Don't be a stranger handsome," she said.

Gary blushed and turned towards the door. He turned the knob and opened it. He took one last look at the women in the living room and waved goodbye. He exited the house and walked down the driveway. It was just about dusk. The sun was down and night was falling. He didn't realize it, but he just sobered up the women who were going to murder his friend. As he walked down the block to his car he saw an elderly gentleman stumbling down the street. As they walked closer to each other Gary could make out a brown fedora hat with a red feather on the side of it. He was wearing a brown rain coat and seemed to have a very difficult time walking. He seemed to walk forward and sideways at the same time but at a very slow pace.

When the older man looked up and saw a policeman about to walk past him, he quickly put his head down and pulled his hat lower across his brow. As they approached each other no words were spoken. Gary took a long, hard look at the odd man. Something about him seemed familiar. The Governor did all he could not to look directly at the police officer. As he stumbled down the street he tried with all his might not to bump into Gary. It was no use. Like a magnet his odd gait took him directly into Gary's path.

Even as Gary tried to lean away The Governor fell right into him.

"Excuse me, officer," The Governor said apologetically without looking up.

"No problem sir," was Gary's shocked reply. Gary walked a few more feet and unlocked his car. He walked around to the driver's side and opened the door. As he was about to slide into it he took one last look at the odd man hobbling down the street. He hadn't gotten much further.

As Gary's car sped down the block The Governor did his patented three-point turn. Using his good foot to pivot, he slowly started to turn about twenty degrees at a time. By the time he got his big head around the car was long gone. He slowly turned back and continued towards Michelle's house. He stopped in front of the house and pulled a piece of paper out of his pocket. He double checked the address on the paper. He did not want to relive the incident in Asbury Park.

His assignment there was to kill the wife of a business man. She had been cheating on him with someone from her work place. In that instance, he did not write down the address, he committed it to memory. Unfortunately, his memory wasn't so good. He wound up on the wrong block. When he opened the gate, and hobbled down the driveway, he was met with a vicious dog barking and growling at him. When the owner of the house came to the door, The Governor noticed it was not the same man who had hired him. The Governor tried to leave but the dog jumped at him. Without hesitation, guilt, or remorse, he took out his gun and shot the animal. To his credit he only winged the dog. After all, he was an animal lover and would never kill a loyal dog protecting his master. As the canine hobbled away the Governor look up at the man standing at the screen door. He tipped his brown hat and said, "Sorry, wrong house." Then he limped away.

He stopped in front of Michelle's house and double checked the address with his paper. He limped up the driveway and rang the bell. Michelle answered and hurriedly said, "Come in we're all ready."

As The Governor entered the house Michelle peeked her head out the door to check which nosey neighbors were out. She was relieved; the coast looked clear.

The Governor hobbled over to the living room. "You have a nice house here, miss," he said. Then he looked up above the staircase and saw the hangman's noose slowly swinging back and forth. "Nice touch. I like the noose. It adds class to the joint," The Governor said in a low voice. Michelle just grabbed his arm and walked him into the kitchen. She wanted to go over the plan again.

Back in Newark, Joe and the Newark police were getting ready to wrap up their sting operation. By now Joe had learned the real names of the officers. Thomas Jefferson was really Eddie Foster, the plainclothes officer chewing on his cigar was Lenny Kiner, and Benjamin Franklin was William Brown. It was after eight o'clock and the team was relieved by a fresh group of officers. The four men piled into the Newark unmarked police car parked out behind the bodega. Brownie did the driving. The police wanted to stop off and have a beer with Joe but he begged off. He was anxious to get home. He was curious to see if Michelle was back from her date with her new boyfriend. He counter offered his three new friends. He would sit and have a beer with them at his house.

It was after nine thirty and Joe still wasn't home. Michelle was losing her nerve with every tick of the clock. She wanted to call the whole thing off, pay The Governor the rest of his money, and never see him again. A few minutes later a car pulled up in front of the house. Michelle pulled the curtain slightly.

The street was dark, but she saw the silhouette of a car stopped in front. "It's him," she whispered in a low nervous voice.

Quickly and silently the trio changed positions. The girls went deeper inside the house. The Governor took his place behind the door.

Joe was the first one to open the car door and exit the car. As he stood in front of the car stretching he was surprised at how dark the house was. Not a light on in the place. Usually, Michelle would leave the kitchen light on when no one was home. The men did not talk as they opened their doors and prepared to accompany him inside. Inside the house, no one spoke. It was so quiet you could hear their hearts beating. Then they heard the car door slam shut. Michelle let out a small gasp. Then surprisingly another car door slammed. Followed by two more car doors closing. The killers' hearts stopped. The trio turned and looked at each other. Olivia looked at Michelle. She held up four fingers and whispered the word four? They were mystified.

Something was wrong; why was Joe opening and closing four doors? He was supposed to be alone. The Governor slowly reached up and using his fat fingers parted the curtains. He let out an audible gasp! It was the first time since the girls had known him that they saw him sweat. His eyes had a heart attack when he saw four people walking up the driveway. Three of them had police badges swing from their necks.

"You didn't tell me your husband was a Newark cop," he said in an angry tone.

"He's not. What are you talking about?" Then Michelle peeked out the window and saw four men approaching the front door.

The Governor jumped back from the window and dropped his old chewed up gun on the shag carpet of the living room. Just then the front door opened and the light switch clicked on. The room was filled with light and people. Joe was surprised to see his wife and two people he did not know standing in his living room. In the background, a man with a brown hat and brown rain coat was stooped over trying to pick up something from the floor. The police took a great interest in what was on the floor. The Governor looked like one of those claw machines you see in an arcade. Every time his fat fingers got a grip on the gun and he would start to lift it, it would slip from his grasp. Again, and again he would reach down for it and get it a little bit further from the ground, only to let it slip again.

"FREEZE!" The cops yelled out in unison as they drew their weapons.

The girls' arms shot up into the air and The Governor slowly looked up at the police officers. Foster stepped forward and kicked the gun on the carpet away from The

Governor. It bounced on the carpet skipping under the coffee table and sliding under the couch.

"What the hell is your problem Foster? You didn't have to kick it so hard. Now we got to crawl under the damn sofa and get it," Brownie said in frustration.

"Take it easy, Brownie. You know he thinks he's a T.V. cop," Kiner replied.

As The Governor slowly got his body into a more erect position his face became more visible to the police officers. Brownie looked directly at him and said, "I think I know you."

With a blank stare on his face the Governor said, "Pardon?"

"You're The Governor, aka Gentleman Jerry Baker."

"Pardon,… oh shit!"

Suddenly Joe spoke, "What the hell is going on here?"

"I'll tell ya what's going on," Foster said, "This is Jerry Baker, a notorious murder for hire hit man. It looks like you were coming home and they were going to kill you. Look, there's a hangman's noose over the staircase. Probably going to hang you and make it look like a suicide."

Suddenly, Joe felt very uncomfortable. The cops figured out about his attempts to kill himself. He kept calm and quickly thought of a way to distract them. He broke into a loud laughter and said. "You guys are way off. I put that noose up last month."

The Governor, still standing with his hands in the air said. "Yeah it's a mistake."

"Oh no, Jerry, it's no mistake. You're done and you're coming with us." Foster said.

Kiner walked around and took Jerry's hands down and started to handcuff him.

Olivia broke her silence and said, "Good work, officers. I feel so much safer with a madman like him off the streets."

Jerry didn't appreciate Olivia's contribution to his predicament. As the cops were ushering him out the door he stopped short and said, "Hold on, guys. You better arrest her too. She had her husband killed a few years ago. I know, my nephew did the job."

"That's outrageous!" Olivia said, trying to sound indigent.

"Better cuff her too Kiner. We can take her in for questioning." Foster said. Kiner took out another pair of handcuffs and slapped them on her.

"We'll have to take a rain check on those beers, Joe," Brownie said.

Joe went back over to the front door and let the police and their suspects out of the house. "No problem, boys. Anytime. You know where I live," he said.

As the door closed behind him Joe turned and looked to Michelle, waiting for an explanation. Michelle stood silent with her arms folded across her chest. She had a blank look on her face as her mind raced for something Joe would believe.

She took a breath, and in an understated tone said, "That was my Uncle Jerry." The couple stood staring at each other in silence. Michelle broke the silence again and said. "Well, I have to go to work now. See you in the morning." She kissed Joe on the cheek and left the house.

Joe stood alone in the empty house and in a barely audible and confused voice said, "I didn't know she had an Uncle Jerry."

Joe placed his right hand on the back of his neck and turned away from the door. He started to walk toward the living room. Just as he crossed into the room the front door burst open. Foster came running back into the house.

He pushed past Joe saying. "Excuse me!" as he passed. He dove onto the floor in front of the couch and reached under with his right arm. He lay spread-eagle on the floor, his arm swinging back and forth under the couch. "Got it!" He yelled. Then, he jumped back to his feet with The Governor's chewed up gun in his hand. "Almost forgot this. It's evidence you know," he said as he ran past Joe and out the door.

Now Joe was standing in the middle of his living room, his hand on his hips. He shook his head and threw his hands in the air. "How do I meet these people?"

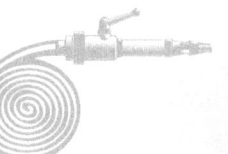

CHAPTER TEN

"YOU" ARE INVITED TO AN ANNIVERSARY PARTY

When Michelle arrived at work that night she was still very shaken up about what had gone down at her house less than an hour earlier. Her hands were trembling and she felt a little hung over and nauseous. As she walked through the halls of the hospital several coworkers greeted her. It took all the composure she could summon just to make eye contact with them and say hello. All she had on her mind was getting to the safety of her office and clearing her head. It seemed like the longest walk of her life. Guilt can do that to a person, it's difficult to escape.

Finally, she reached her office. She stood in front of the door fumbling through her purse for the key. When she found the key ring, she removed it from her purse. The sound of the keys chiming echoed in the empty hallway. She needed to use two hands to muffle the sound and keep her hand steady enough to unlock her door. Entering the room, she slammed the door behind her. She again fumbled with the lock but was finally able to latch it. Then she threw her things on the desk and sat in her chair. She slowly lowered her head onto the desk and cried.

After a few minutes of feeling sorry for herself it was time to try to pull herself together. Whatever happened, she would accept the consequences. If Jerry and Olivia spilled the beans and brought Michelle into the scheme then she would confess. After all, it would be her first offense. It's not like they would throw the book at her. In the meantime, she needed to make this right for Joe. He didn't deserve to be murdered. She was glad it fell apart. The truth of the matter is she was going to warn him before The Governor could do anything anyway. She knew deep down she acted out of anger. She let her friend get into her head. Olivia blew her feelings for her husband out of proportions. Truth be told she still loved Joe very much.

At police headquarters Foster, Kiner, and Brownie were greeted as heroes. It was one of the biggest busts in the history of the Newark Police Department. They brought in a known and dangerous fugitive who may have been responsible for countless murder for hire schemes. On top of that they may have solved another cold case with the capture of Olivia. She was to be extradited to New York for insurance fraud and the possible murder of her husband.

Routine police procedure is to immediately separate the suspects and question them independently. Jerry was brought to Interrogation Room One. Olivia was taken to Room Two. Both rooms were small and well lit. Each room had a table and two chairs placed on opposite ends. On the table was some type of voice recorder. The suspect sat against the far wall, away from the door and facing an obvious two-way mirror. Foster was assigned to room one to question Jerry. Jerry sat quietly with his hands folded on the table, waiting to be grilled by the police officers.

Jerry sat alone in the room for about forty-five minutes. Suddenly the door swung open and Foster entered the well-lit room. His entrance had a swagger that would have made Steve McGarret proud. He immediately made eye contact with Jerry as he approached the table. He grabbed the unoccupied chair and with little effort picked it up and placed it next to The Governor. He turned the chair so the back of it was facing his suspect; he straddled it and sat down.

"You're in a lot of trouble, mister," he started, and then he reached into his shirt pocket and took out a pack of cigarettes. Like his cop heroes on television, he smacked the pack on his hand and a cigarette popped up from the pack. He reached over and offered one to Jerry. The Governor reached out with his huge hand and fat fingers and took the cigarette.

"You see, dirtball, I'm not a bad guy; I'm here to help you," Foster said in a kind, trusting voice. Just like on T.V. he wanted to gain the trust of his suspect.

Then he reached into the pack and took a butt out for himself. He wanted to create the atmosphere of two old pals having a cigarette and talking about the old times. He placed the cigarette between his lips and without losing eye contact reached into his shirt pocket for a match. His fingers came out empty, so he tapped his shirt and reached into the pocket again. He moved down to his pants, tapping the sides of his legs and around to the back. He stood up and started to place his hands into every pocket on his person. He looked frantically but could not find a match.

Jerry sat patiently, the cigarette dangling from his lips. It suddenly occurred to Foster, that he forgot to ask for matches when he borrowed the pack of cigarettes from the sergeant. Jerry sat across not saying anything; he raised his huge hands into the air as if to ask what's the problem. Anger and embarrassment ran through Foster's veins as he reached across and swiped the cancer stick from Jerry's mouth.

Foster changed his tactics and in an angry voice yelled. "No more games, pal! I want some answers and you're going to give them to me!"

The questioning went on for over two hours Foster was starting to lose his voice from yelling so much. The Governor was as cool as the other side of the pillow. He never uttered a word. He sat in total silence, and never even asked to lawyer up. He seemed to have a super power of turning off things he did not want to listen to. On the other side of the two-way mirror the Captain and Sergeant watched in shame as Foster fumbled through the interrogation.

The Sergeant could see the anger on his Captain's face and felt compelled to say something. "Maybe the rooms are too bright?" he said, hoping to defuse the situation.

The Captain's head never moved. He continued to stare at the two-way glass, his arms folded across his chest. In a loud sarcastic voice, he replied, "Are you kiddin', the only bright thing in that room is the light."

Finally, the Captain's pain was over, the interrogation was done, and Foster left the room. He was tired and dripping in sweat. He walked over to his Captain and said. "Sorry, Cap. He's a tough old rotten egg. He just clammed up on me."

"It's okay, kid, we'll nail this son of a bitch. Please, go home now." The Sergeant looked over and gave his commanding officer a quick tap on his arm. The Captain looked over and then continued his sentence "and get some rest." The Captain gave Foster a pat on the shoulder as he walked by.

In Interrogation Room One an old man sat alone. He reached into his shirt pocket and took out a small device. It had a tiny dial in the middle of it. Very gently, Jerry used his huge, fat fingers and turned the dial up. Then he carefully placed the hearing aid attachment into his right ear. He sat motionless and smiled.

In Room Two it was a totally different story; they couldn't shut Olivia up. The police officers were amazed at the harebrained, far out, wild story she was concocting. She was telling the police that Michelle was going to have The Governor murder her husband, Joe. She was trying to convince them that she was there to talk her out of it. It didn't matter how hard she tried, or pleaded, she could not convince them. They had spent the entire day with Joe. He was a great guy, a hero who risked his own life to save a girl in an office building. The police were convinced that Michelle was a lucky woman to have him. There was no way she would have him murdered.

The police put their own story together. It was their suspicion that Olivia hired The Governor to come over to Joe's house to kill Michelle. Then with Michelle out of the way Olivia could swoop in and take Joe for herself. It was a nasty, diabolical plan, but she had done it before to her own husband. The police booked her for murder and attempted murder.

By now Michelle had pulled herself together. She felt guilty and filled with remorse. All she wanted to do now was make it right again. In a few days it would be August, summer was coming to a close. August was the month Joe and Michelle were married. This year would mark their ten-year anniversary. Michelle thought that maybe a nice anniversary party at the house would help put things right again. Yes, that was the answer; "It will help us both get our minds off of things," she thought. With a new energy, she pulled her chair in closer to her desk, and logged onto her computer. Soon the room was filled with the sound of the tapping of the keyboard as she typed out emails to her family and friends. YOU ARE INVITED TO AN ANIVERSARY PARTY.

After Michelle left for work Joe sat and watched television for a while. He was just killing time until he felt sleepy enough to go to bed. It had been a long day. Before he knew it, his eyes started to feel heavy. Soon the sound of the television faded away and Joe fell off to sleep. Joe liked his sleep. His life was much better in his dreams. His pain was gone and he became human. The monster that ruined his life no longer plagued him. In his dreams, he was brave and bold. He ran fearlessly into fires, rescuing women and children. His life was perfect; his wife was deeply in love with him. She understood him; she knew when he needed to be left alone, and when to comfort him. Growing up, he was always told that the early bird gets the worm. Good for the early bird. But, does the early bird enjoy the worm as much as the late bird enjoys his sleep? Joe was a late bird.

Joe was startled by the sound of the back-door slamming shut. He stirred on the couch slowly gathering his wits from a deep sleep. Michelle walked into the living room surprised to see Joe lying on the couch. Joe started to pull himself into a sitting position. Michelle just stared at him, his hair a mess and a line of drool sliding down from the corner of his mouth to his undershirt. He looked at her but didn't say a word. She looked at him and said. "Don't forget to get next weekend off for our party."

"What party?" Joe answered confused.

"Ugh, you do this to me all time. I told you we're having an anniversary party next weekend. I told you this last month. You said it was a great idea. You picked the weekend for crying out loud. You said it would be the easiest for you get off. We discussed this; don't look at me as if I'm making this up and you never heard it."

"Oh yeah, that's right, I remember. Give me a break. I just woke up." The room went silent again as Joe internally searched his brain for any evidence that he had heard this idea before.

Michelle walked over to her husband still sitting on the couch. She bent down as if she was going to give him a kiss. As she got closer to him she changed her mind and just cupped his face with her hands.

As she pulled away she said. "I'm going to bed now, I had a rough night." She turned and headed up the steps to the bed-room. As she climbed the steps she chuckled, thinking to herself. "I can make him believe anything." When she reached the top of the landing she turned and yelled down, "Joe, take this damn noose down!"

Joe sat alone on the couch, confused about a conversation he couldn't remember but said he did. Slowly he started to wake up. His side was hurting him again and his clothes were all bunched and tangled about his body. He sat and tried to loosen up the burned skin on his side. Then he reached down and pushed his hand down his pants and readjusted his private parts. With his other hand he took the television remote and searched for another show to watch. He sat on the couch, balls in one hand, remote in the other, trying to remember a conversation that never happened.

It took some wheeling and dealing but Joe was able to get the weekend of August eleventh off for his anniversary party. He was proud that Michelle never found out he had to make some switches to get off. As far as she was concerned he never forgot about the party. It was a beautiful summer Saturday. The sun was shining and the humidity was low. Joe and Michelle were up early to set up their backyard with tables, chairs, and several canopies' they borrowed from friends and neighbors. They had the party catered with hot and cold food. Although he wasn't a big drinker, Joe spent several hundred dollars on beer, wine, and hard liquor.

The party was scheduled to start at two p.m. sharp. At one thirty the caterer showed up with delicious trays of food that Michele had them set up in the kitchen. Joe was out in the yard filling up the coolers with beer and soda. At two o'clock on the dot the doorbell rang. Joe started to walk from the back yard to answer it. He walked through the kitchen and into the living room. As he passed the large mirror on the wall, he stopped to fix his hair and check his shirt for stains. He looked good so he continued, to answer the door.

He swung the door open and greeted the first guests to the party. Joe did not recognize them; perhaps they were friends from Michelle's work. Or maybe he thought sarcastically they were her internet friends.

With a smile on his face he said, "Hello, and welcome. So, glad you could make it." He guided them through the house. They were just about to enter the living-room when the door-bell rang again. Joe stopped short and apologetically said. "I'm sorry, excuse me. But I have to get the door. Michelle is right straight through in the kitchen. Make yourselves at home."

He left and went to answer the door. The group continued into the living-room and suddenly stopped in front of the grand wooden staircase. In unison, they looked straight up.

A voice in the small huddle spoke, "Their it is the noose. It looks just like I pictured it."

"I knew he wouldn't take it down," another one said.

"I bet he hangs that S.O.B. that's sleeping with Michelle, when he catches him," said another of the mysterious guests. They all chuckled. Michelle looked up and saw the guests congregating at the staircase. She did not recognize any of them. Ever the gracious hostess and without missing a beat, she put a big smile on her face and yelled into them, "Hello I'm Michelle, Joe's wife." She started to wave her arms at them to guide them into the kitchen. "Welcome to our house. We have plenty of food and drinks. Please help yourself." She pointed to the food and then to the coolers out in the back yard.

"It's nice to meet you Michelle, I feel like I've known you since chapter one," one of them said.

Michelle stood confused, "Where's chapter one?" She wondered to herself.

"Look at the kitchen table. That's where he left the note!" Someone else said, pointing to a spot on the table by the wooden napkin holder.

Then they walked past her and out to the yard. Michelle stood confused and silent. Who were those people? She had never met them, yet it seems like they had been in the house before. What the hell did they mean about chapter one and what note were they talking about?

She stood up straight shrugged her shoulders and said. "I guess they're friends of Joe. I'll have to ask him later?"

Her concentration was broken by Joe escorting the next guest into the house. "Michelle, honey look who's here," Joe yelled in a less than enthusiastic voice. Michelle looked up and saw a young man about thirtyish carrying a huge brown box. "Your cousin Tony," Joe continued.

Tony walked into the kitchen and placed down the box, which made a sound like bottles rattling. When Michelle peeked into the box she could see why, it was full of bottles of booze and mixers. Then Tony dropped his right shoulder and a cooler bag slid down his arm. He left that on the floor and said, "I brought you some beer too."

He was also wearing a black back pack so Joe asked him. "What's in the back pack?"

"It's a blender in case anyone wants a Margarita."

"Of course, silly me! I should have known," Joe replied.

"Yeah, let me grab a beer and I'll set up the bar." Tony said. Tony popped open a cold one and went to work on his version of a bar. Joe threw his hands into the air and walked outside; he left Michelle to visit with her cousin.

By three-thirty the party was in full swing. People were eating, drinking, talking, and most importantly having a good time. Joe did a quick scan of the back yard and noticed something odd. No one from his side of the family was there. None of his friends were there. No one from his work, his firemen friends, not even Gary. That seemed odd for a party that he and Michelle spoke about. You would think that she would have asked him who he wanted to invite. He was starting to doubt how much he knew about this party.

He continued survey the back yard. His gaze spotted the first guests that arrived today. They were sitting at a table talking amongst themselves. No one sat with them. They just talked and pointed at certain people, mostly Michelle and Joe. He grabbed a beer out of the cooler and walked over to sit with them. Just as he arrived there The Major stopped to talk to him. The Major was a cousin in-law to Michelle. He was a career military man who now worked at the Pentagon in Washington D.C. He was holding a can of beer in his right hand and his left hand had a vise like grip on Joe's upper arm. "Joe, how the hell are you? It's good to see you again." He said in a deep voice almost like it was an order.

"I'm really good Jack," (that was The Major's given name) "thanks for coming." Joe said.

"Are you shittin' me? I wouldn't miss this! You and Michelle are my favorites on this side of the family."

"Yeah, lucky us. We like you too. How's the Pentagon?"

"Aw you know, eight sides' lots of secrets."

"Awesome, eight sides now, thanks for the update, always nice talking to you." Joe tried to walk away. "He's so drunk already, he doesn't know how many sides the building he works in has."

"Hold on." Joe could feel the grip on his arm tighten. All he wanted was to get away from this guy. He was okay when he was sober but after a few drinks he was an obnoxious mess. The Major continued. "We need to talk buddy, tell me about that hero shit they said you did."

Joe's face started to feel flushed with embarrassment. He was still uncomfortable talking about that. If everything would have gone the way he planned, he wouldn't be here at this party. His mind started to race, trying to find a graceful way to get away from the Major. Luckily, he was blessed with a knack for getting out of situations he didn't like. In his most sincere tone he said. "Oh, yeah Jack, but let me get you a beer first. Then we can sit and shoot the breeze."

"Now you're talking my language!" The Major replied. Joe pulled away and hurried to the beer cooler. The Major lifted his beer can up to his mouth and gulped down the last half a can. He looked around for a place to sit. A few feet away was a table with a few empty chairs. He lumbered over to sit with the guests there. He scanned the table and realized he didn't know these people. The Major never had a problem with shyness so he blurted out, "Who the hell are you guys?"

"We're friends of Joe and Michelle. You're new to the story. Who are you?" One of them asked.

"Who am I? I'm Major Jack Kincaid, on loan to the Pentagon, Washington D.C." The guests at the table shook their head in unison. The Major slammed his beer can down on the table. It made that horrible tinny, echo sound that all beer drinkers hate. It was empty. "Now, if you nice people will excuse me I need to get a beer," The Major said as he stood up from the table. He turned and walked away, looking for the beer cooler.

With no one from his family their Joe decided to lay low. He sat in a shady spot by the rear of the yard watching and counting the minutes for the party to end. Joe sat quietly, watching the dynamic of the party unfold. He did his best to keep all the action in front of him. If someone spotted him and started to walk over it gave him a chance to bail out. It was a good strategy unless you lose track of someone. It was a rookie mistake, but Joe made it. From out of nowhere Joe felt an arm go around his shoulder. He looked to his right and let out an audible sigh. Somehow, Cousin Tony was able to sneak up on Joe. Tony was a pro, in that he even had his own chair with him, and he plopped it right next to Joe's.

He sat on Joe's right side as close as he could. He leaned in and said. "Joe, you don't know how much I love you and Michelle." It was obvious that Tony had been drinking nonstop since he walked in the door. "Thank you so much for inviting me to your house." He leaned in closer and cinched his arm tighter around Joe's shoulders. With the stale smell of alcohol on his breath he continued, "I may have had a little too much to drink, I don't want to embarrass you or Michelle." Joe was amazed at how sincere he sounded, Tony even had tears welling up in his eyes as he spoke. But Joe wasn't buying it. Why would a guy bring three hundred dollars' worth of liquor to a party that was already stocked with alcohol? No, that's a guy who wants to get hammered. What the hell was his plan bring the alcohol and not drink it? For crying out loud he brought his own blender!

Deep down Tony was a good guy. But his problem was that he drank too much. Joe called him a reluctant drunk. A poor soul who can't control what he does and lives with the guilt of it. Maybe we all have a monster. "Listen, Tony, you're fine. As a matter of fact, I want you to stay over. We can go out tomorrow and get a nice breakfast at the diner. Why don't you give me your keys and enjoy the party?"

"God, bless you, Cousin Joe. But if I get out of hand feel free to throw me out."

"Consider it done." Joe took Tony's keys and started to walk away. He could hear Tony still thanking him as he walked, so he walked faster.

The party had been rolling for several hours now and the sun was getting ready to set. All of the regular drinkers had their buzz on and better. Uncle Mike was sitting in a lawn chair. His head was bent down and his arms were resting on the arms of the chair. When you looked at him you could see him spasm and jump every few seconds. It looked like someone was giving him electric shocks. His head would shoot up and his arms would jerk in and out. He was sitting all alone. Not a soul was near him, yet he never stopped talking. He was mumbling and carrying on a conversation with no one listing.

Then the spasms would kick in and he would start yelling, "Charlie, Charlie." He kept saying it over and over. Then he would start screaming, "Charlie Begelman hit the deck!" The guests at the party would just ignore him as if it was normal behavior.

Every once in a while, his wife Doris would walk over, smack him on the head, and say, "Charlie Begelman has been dead for fifteen years, Mike! wake up!" Then he would fall back into a short slumber.

The Major, who was never spotted without a beer in his hand the entire party, was now himself drunk as a lord. He became so annoying to everyone that he had no one left to talk to until, he spotted people he hadn't met before. Unfortunately, David and Tyrone were sitting alone so The Major, beer in hand, parked his obnoxious rump next to them. David was a handsome white man about twenty-five or so. He had Jet black hair cut short and neat. Tyrone was also in his mid-twenties; he was African American with a body that looked like it was chiseled out of solid stone.

The Major started the conversation with a quick, slurred, "You guys related?" The two men looked at each other. Simultaneously they lifted their hands in front of their faces. Then they scanned them with their eyes as if to say, how can we be related were different colors? The Major picked up on their little joke and said, "No not to each other, asshole's. I mean are you related to anyone here?"

"Oh, I'm sorry; we were just having some fun. I'm Tyrone and this is David. We work with Michelle." Tyrone said in a surprisingly high falsetto voice. Then he reached out his hand to greet The Major. The Major put his beer in his left hand and extended his right. He was prepared for a strong grip given the size of Tyrone. But as they shook hands he was almost disgusted by the weakness of the grip and soft texture of his skin. Then Tyrone leaned back in his chair and crossed his legs over his knee. He took his left arm and placed it over the back of his chair. He took his right hand and slowly brought it up to his long ebony neck and said. "So, who do we have the pleasure of addressing?"

The Major clearly looked confused. He glanced down at the table and noticed the men were drinking wine coolers. As his eyes scanned lower he could see David's hand resting on Tyrone's knee. The Major's eyes shot back up to Tyrone's face. He was sure he figured out what was going on and he did not like it. His homophobic reflex kicked in and he said, "Don't ask, don't tell." He stood up, and hurriedly staggered away from the table.

As he was walking away he heard David and Tyrone giggling and saying. "Bye, bye, handsome. Come back and see us soon. We'll miss you."

Night fell and it was getting late. Finally, to Joe's relief, people started to say good bye. The last people to leave were the first who arrived. They were nice people who kept to themselves. Joe thought. These are the kind of people I could hang out with. Why doesn't Michelle invite them over more often?

Joe and Michelle stood at the door as they said goodbye. They thanked their hosts and said they had a nice time. Joe spoke first and said. "It was our pleasure! I hope we can do something like this again." As the guests reached their car Joe and Michelle yelled out simultaneously, "It was nice meeting you!" They turned and waved one more time.

One of them yelled back. "I can't wait to see how this ends." They sat in their car and slammed the door.

Joe closed the front door to the house. He turned and looked at his wife and said, "What does that mean? See how it ends."

"I have no idea. All I know is you have some weird friends."

"I don't know them. Aren't they your friends?"

"I don't know them."

Silently they closed the door and walked toward the kitchen. They walked through the living room being careful not to step on Cousin Tony who was passed out on the floor. When they reached the kitchen, they started to clean up some of the mess from the party.

Michelle was the first to say what was on both of their minds. "Are you sure you didn't invite those people Joe?"

"I'm sure; no one I invited even showed up."

"What are you talking about? Everyone showed up."

"What about my family and friends? I didn't see any of them, did you?"

Michelle stopped the conversation for a moment. She remembered, tricking Joe into thinking he knew about the party. It was always her job to send out the invitations. Joe must have thought he made out a list and gave it to her.

She needed to change the subject, so she asked again, "Who were those people?"

"I don't know them, or who could have invited them, but they did seem to know a lot about us and our house." was his definitive response.

Just past the kitchen out in the living room a body lying on the floor stirred. It was Cousin Tony. Even in his semi-comatose condition he could hear the conversation the couple were having. He raised his head and started to say something. His speech was very slurred from all the alcohol he had consumed.

He tried to make his words sound clear as he spoke. "They were mice, I mean nice. They said that the, otter, I mean, auter, invited them." Then Tony's head hit the floor again and he was out for the night.

"What did he say?" Michelle asked Joe.

"It sounded like he said, "Otter?" Joe answered. Michelle looked at her husband and said. "I thought he said Auter."

"What the hell kind of name is Auter?"

"I don't know that's what it sounded like."

One last time Tony raised his inebriated head off the floor. He concentrated as hard as he could. He thought about the word he wanted to say.

In a weak voice that no one heard he said, "The author invited them." Then his head fell with a thump to the floor. The room went silent as Joe and Michelle went about the task of cleaning the kitchen.

After a few minutes had passed, Joe said to no one in particular. "Still they were very nice people."

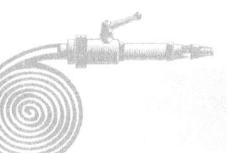

CHAPTER ELEVEN

JUMP

Joe woke up early the next morning. He was alone in his big bed. Slowly, he started to move his tired body out of the bed. His side was hurting and it was difficult to move. After a few grunts and moans, he was able to reposition himself and was sitting up on the side of the bed. He started to slowly move his right arm in small circular motions to loosen up his tightly scarred skin. Soon he felt well enough to stand and do his regular stretches. Once he had his range of motion back he walked to the bathroom and started to get ready for work.

The cool shower water helped clear the cobwebs out of his head. It was a late night between the anniversary party and the cleanup. Today would have been his day off, but he had made a last-minute switch to be off for the party. Which he still didn't remember planning, no matter what his wife said. He stood with his arms pressed against the shower wall, his head hanging down, the cool water spraying over him, lost in thought. He was wondering why he would even agree to plan the party with Michelle. He knows she does not love him; that's why she is having an affair. Suddenly Joe snapped back from his daydreaming. It was like a clock went off in his head telling him it was time to get ready for work. He quickly finished washing and stepped out of the shower to dry off.

While Joe was upstairs getting ready for work Michelle was already up. The house was still shambles from the party the night before. Ironically the mess did not seem to bother the meticulous woman. She was sitting on the couch with her laptop computer typing away. She was looking at an online application for a fire department in Fairfax, Virginia. Joe exited the bed room and walked to the top of the staircase. He looked down directly into the living room and saw his wife sitting on the couch engrossed in her computer. He rolled his eyes and realized nothing had changed. He reached out his right arm and tapped the hangman's noose still over the staircase. It swung back and forth as Joe walked down the steps.

Joe walked past the couch. His wife could sense his approach and lowered the screen of the laptop. At this point in their relationship, he didn't even care who she was hooking up with. Joe walked to the kitchen to get a cup of coffee. He stepped over Cousin Tony, still lying on the floor from the night before. He was still face down with his head turned to the left, a pool of saliva running under his mouth and chin. As Joe entered the kitchen he was disappointed the coffee was not made. How long had she been up and couldn't even start a damn pot of coffee? He walked back to the living room. His anger was slowly building up inside him. As he crossed over Cousin Tony his frustration got the best of him. He gave him a nice swift kick in the ribs.

Tony replied by lifting his head and muttering, "What the fu?" Then he lowered his head back into the gooey pool of saliva.

"Well there's no coffee made, so I'm leaving early for work so I can stop and get a cup." Joe said disappointed and angry.

"Okay, have a great day; I'll see you later," was Michelle's reply without even looking up.

Joe started marching towards the door, slow burning the entire time. As he reached out for the door knob he turned again and now with pure anger he said, "And I want him out of here before I get home!" He was pointing directly at Cousin Tony still passed out in his own drool on the floor.

Still engrossed with her laptop computer Michelle answered, "I'll take care of it." Joe threw open the front door and stormed out slamming the door behind him. Michelle never looked up.

Joe drove to work angry. He was starting to lose his drive to be the good husband and step aside so his wife could go on with her life. When Joe hatched this crazy scheme to kill himself, he felt it was a brave and noble thing to do. It was his way to show her how unselfish he was. He was going to release her from being married to the monster. The monster that cost him his job with the fire service and his marriage. Now he wasn't so sure. Since she had found a new world on social media, he became virtually nonexistent to her. Why did he have to be noble and make the supreme sacrifice for her? As he continued to drive to work the answer came to him. He was still deeply, madly, in love with her. In the end her happiness was all that mattered.

Joe pulled into the parking lot at work. He opened his car door, stepped out, and slammed it shut. He clipped his keys onto the belt loop of his pants and with his head down power walked to the office. He passed several of his coworkers who greeted him with a friendly good morning but they received no response. He just walked past them as if they weren't there, mumbling to himself the entire time. He went to his locker to put his uniform on. As he started to undress, he took a quick look around to see if anybody was nearby. He never liked taking his shirt off in front of people because he was so embarrassed by the monster. With no one around he quickly changed his clothes and reported to the ambulance bay to get his assignment.

Joe was one of the last medics to report and sign in for work. He walked over to the other paramedics gathered around the lieutenant. He was working today because he switched a day with someone so the chances are he would be working in a different borough than usual. As he suspected when the lieutenant called out his name he was assigned the Rockaways in Queens. Just another way the universe screwed with him. He was going to a location that during the summer was over populated with people going to the beach. He was not familiar with the area and its traffic patterns in the middle of summer. Joe's body language spoke volumes as he slowly walked over to the lieutenant with his shoulders hunched and took his assignment sheet. He never made eye contact or said a word. He turned his back and started to shuffle towards his ambulance to perform his check list.

As he finished checking out his rig's supplies and doing his mechanical check he tried to shake his miserable mood. Maybe it would be a slow day. Perhaps he could find a nice fresh fish restaurant for lunch. At the very least he could do some girl watching. There were bound to be some pretty girls strutting around in bikinis. He pulled his ambulance out of the garage and headed for the Belt Parkway. It was about a twenty-mile drive to the Rockaways from the medic headquarters in Fort Hamilton. Joe's journey would take him past the Verrazano Bridge through parts of Brooklyn and into Queens.

The Belt Parkway is a tight, bumpy road that is too small for the number of cars that travel on it. A twenty-mile trip could turn into an adventure in patience between the amount of accidents that occur on the road and the never-ending construction detours. Today Joe found the traffic to be slow but moving. He drove past Sheepshead bay and was heading towards Flatbush Ave. As he approached the exit for Kings Plaza traffic started to crawl. Joe suspected it may be an accident; he put his lights and siren on and started to weave in and out of the traffic to see if he could help. As he approached the Gil Hodges Memorial Bridge the cars were just stopped. He pulled his rig over to the side and stepped onto the running board. With the extra height of the ambulance he peered over the scene. To his surprise he did not see a car accident. He grabbed his medic bag off the jump seat and stepped down from his rig. He walked past several motor vehicles just stopped in the middle of the overused busy parkway. He wasn't sure what all the commotion was about but he was slow burning over the ignorance of people just thinking they could stop their cars anywhere they felt like. Just like the morons in Manhattan who double parked anywhere they wanted.

The Gil Hodges Memorial Bridge was a small draw bridge that connected Brooklyn and Queens. It was over a small bay that was a haven for sail boats in the summertime. Today the bridge had a visitor. As Joe approached, he could see an elderly man approximately seventy years old. He was tall and thin with a full head of white hair blowing around in the summer breeze. It did not take long to discover why the people had gathered and stopped traffic. The old man was on the wrong side of the bridge. He stood facing out toward the bay with his right hand behind him holding on to one of the steel beams of the bridge. Joe pushed his way through the crowd of people. Most of them would not stop to help a stranded fellow motorist. But to watch someone jump to his death off a bridge, that was a show worth seeing.

Joe started to push and order people back off the small bridge. Everyone seemed to respond to his orders. Perhaps it was his uniform or the confidence with which he gave his instructions to everyone. Whatever it was the people responded and started to back away.

Joe walked up the side of the bridge and yelled out to the distraught man. "Hey, old timer! What's going on? What are you doing out here?"

"Stay back, young fella! I'm serious about this and no one's gonna stop me," the elderly man replied in a shaky voice.

Joe slowly continued to walk up to the bridge speaking in a kind and reassuring tone. "Hey, old timer. There is nothing so bad that you could want to take your own life," Joe said ironically. "Are you sick?" He continued.

"I've never been sick in my life, I'm in perfect health."

By this time, Joe had made it almost up to where the man was standing. He was trying to create a rapport with the old man. He was inching closer, thinking of comforting things to say when something in the background caught his attention. It started out low, but was now getting loud enough for him to hear. It was the voices of the people gathered.

They started a chant, "JUMP, JUMP, JUMP!"

When Joe heard this he quickly turned and faced the obnoxious crowd. His face turned beet red with anger and he yelled at them. "Really, really, is this what you people want? What the hell is the matter with you, for God's sake. Yes, he's a jumper, but he's also a human being."

The chanting stopped as the mob of people started to absorb the life lesson Joe laid upon them. He started to back away his eyes still focused on the crowd. When a voice in his head started to speak, "Let them have their fun. So what if the old jumps, you could go next. What da you think of that plan?"

Joe stood puzzled for a moment then he answered The Monster. "I'm getting sick and tired of you. You have no right to say who lives and who dies. I really don't want to talk to you anymore."

He turned back toward the bridge and spoke to the old man. "Hey, Pop, I don't think it's a good idea for you to jump from here. I don't think it would do the trick. You'll probably just get hurt real bad and suffer in pain for months.

Then you'll start to rack up all kinds of medical bills. Why don't you come back over here and find another spot."

"Are you kidd'in sonny? Look at me! If I fart I could break a hip. Nice try though."

"Well do you at least want to tell me why you're doing this so I can tell your story? You're not sick, you don't seem crazy, what's the problem? Do you need money?"

"Money? Are you serious? I got more money than you and I could spend in six lifetimes."

"Well I'm confused then. What the hell could drive you to this?"

The breeze was starting to pick up and the old man seemed to be getting weaker holding onto the steel truss of the bridge. With tears starting to roll down his face and his voice choked back and weak, he spoke again. "Sonny, I've got everything a man could want. I live in a mansion that has so many rooms I haven't even been in all of them. I have servants that do everything for me; they'll wipe my ass if I ask them to. I have the most beautiful wife. She twenty-five years old, and a former Miss California. She is so beautiful, and she loves me. She really loves me. She's not after my money; she doesn't even want to be in the will. We have sex twice a day and she'll do any crazy fantasy I have."

Joe stood perplexed and asked, "Pop, I don't get it. You have a perfect life, you're living the dream, why are you doing this?"

The old man's eyes were red and puffy from crying. He hung his head down, looking at the water below. In a loud desperate scream, he blurted out his answer, "I CAN'T REMEMBER WHERE I LIVE."

Joe tried to suppress his laughter. He was now close enough to reach out and touch the old timer. He put his arm around his chest and pulled him back gently towards the bridge. The old man had his head bent down and was still sobbing.

Joe whispered to him, "I'll get you home." He helped the old man climb back on to the safe side of bridge. As they made their way off the bridge the crowd which had grown larger started to applaud.

Joe and the old man walked over to the ambulance. They sat next to each other in the front of the rig. Joe gave the man a bottle of water and tried to calm him down. As he started to compose himself Joe discovered his name was Mike. As the men were talking in the ambulance a police officer approached the driver's side door to speak with them. Joe did not know this officer which was no surprise since it was an area he rarely worked in. Joe started explaining what had transpired and the officer made out his report. It was decided to leave Mike in Joe's care. By now the other police officers at the scene had started traffic moving.

Joe picked up the microphone from his radio and called into his dispatcher. He explained what had happened to him on his way to the Rockaways. If it was one of the other paramedics the dispatcher may not have believed him. But these things just seem to find Joe. He asked permission to bring Mike back home and it was granted. The dispatcher would just have to juggle some assignments around and have another rig cover the Rockaways for a while. Joe clicked his microphone back on to its receiver and turned to Mike. By now the old man had composed himself and was happy he didn't go through with his stupid idea.

"So, Mike, do you have a wallet or any ID on you?" Joe asked?

"No, I left it all at home. I just remember grabbing my car keys to take a drive to the pharmacy. They have this new pill out that helps you, you know, perform."

Joe looked at him confused. Mike could see he wasn't understanding him. He took a breath and tried again. "You know perform in bed."

Joe still wasn't getting it and now Mike was frustrated. "Like when you're married to a twenty-five year old former Miss California who wants sex twice a day and you're a seventy-three year old man that pees eight times a night. Jeeze, what kind of paramedic are you?"

"Oh, that kind of pill," Joe answered shaking his head. "So then what happened?" Joe asked.

"Well I got a little lost and couldn't remember how to get home and wound up here."

"Well I'm sure the police can trace your car and come up with your address and I can take you home."

"Do you think you could stop by the pharmacy on the way?" Mike asked.

Joe called the cop over and asked him to check the car. As the policeman walked away Joe was startled when a bright light flashed into his face followed by a big black microphone. When he was able to focus his eyes and brain he saw a beautiful dark haired woman. She was standing at the side of his ambulance with a crew of men. One of the guys was holding a huge television camera on his shoulder.

It was pointed at the beautiful news reporter who started to speak. "This is Heather Ellen Rodgers Ortiz reporting live for Channel Five News. I'm standing at the Gil Hodges Memorial Bridge on the Belt Parkway in Brooklyn with paramedic Joe Ryan. Many of you may remember last month when Mr. Ryan saved a woman who was about to be murdered in cold blood at the Palmer Building in Manhattan. Today Mr. Ryan risked his life again to climb out onto this bridge behind me and rescue a former Navy Seal who had recently been hospitalized with mental illness. Mr. Ryan, can you tell us in your own words what went through your mind as you attempted this daring rescue?"

Joe looked at the reporter in total disbelief and said, "If I don't use my own words whose words would they be?"

Just then a policeman walked up to the ambulance and handed Joe a slip of paper. Joe opened the folded paper and glanced at it. The newswoman looked on in silence as Joe thanked the officer. He quickly rolled up his window and started his ambulance.

The news reporter pulled her microphone out of Joe's face and back in front of her own. "As you can see the police just passed a secret message to Joe Ryan and after a quick glance he's on his way to another person in need. It's this reporter's understanding that the note read a bus and subway collided in a freak accident. I could not read the location but rest assured that Joe Ryan is on the way." After a short dramatic pause, she continued, "Reporting live from Brooklyn this is Heather Ellen Rodgers Ortiz Channel Five News."

Joe put his lights and siren on and pulled back onto the Belt Parkway. He was on his way to deliver Mike back to his wife and family. Mike lived in a very exclusive area of Queens, not too far from where he tried to jump. Joe pulled his ambulance through the heavy metal gates and up the long driveway past the emerald green, finely manicured lawn. He pulled in front of the huge house. A young, beautiful woman was standing in front, her hands up by her face. It was obvious to him she had been worrying. The ambulance stopped and Joe and Mike stepped out. She ran to Mike and threw her arms around him saying, "I was so worried about you."

Mike answered in a soft reassuring voice. "It's okay, baby. I'm back."

Joe started to turn back to his ambulance, he still had to go to work. As he walked around the front of the rig to get to the driver's door he felt a tug on his arm. He turned to see the beautiful young wife staring at him, her gorgeous brown eyes still swollen with tears. In a soft shaky voice, she spoke.

"Thank you so much for bringing my Mickey home to me. I don't know what I would do if anything ever happened to him."

"You're welcome, Miss. He's a good guy. Take care of him."

"I will."

She put her arms around him and gave him a tight hug. Joe could feel the emotion in her; she really did love him. When the embrace ended Joe walked over and entered his ambulance. He glanced out the passenger window and watched as Mike and his wife walked arm in arm towards the big house. Then Joe looked down and saw a small white bag on the passenger seat. He quickly honked the horn to get Mike's attention.

Mike turned around and saw Joe holding up the bag from the pharmacy. He quickly jumped down the steps of the house and ran to the ambulance. He reached in and took the bag. "Thanks, Joe. I'd be dead without these little buggers."

"You're welcome, buddy. Have fun." Joe replied.

Mike turned and waved the bag in front of his wife's face.

She smiled and said, "I'll race you upstairs." She disappeared into the house with Mike close behind. Joe drove off with a big grin on his face.

It was close to lunch time when Joe made back into the Rockaways to finish his shift. He called into the dispatcher that he was available. The voice over the radio replied he would release the other unit covering so Joe could finish his shift. It didn't take long before Joe was put to work. An emergency call came over for a non-responsive male on Beach Fourteenth Street. Joe took a quick look at his map. The Rockaways was laid out on a grid which made it easy to get around. It turned out he was not far from the location. He flipped his lights and siren on and headed to the location. He turned down Fourteenth Street and drove down the narrow road looking for the address.

He noticed a few people milling around down the block. In his experience he found that to be a good indicator of where the call was. That was also the case in this instance as the people started to wave him down. He stopped his rig in front of the house. A frantic woman ran up to him shouting, "He's in the back. He was washing his car and he got all sweaty and sat down and hasn't moved since. You gotta help him."

"I'll try. Wait here for the police and send them back for me."

The lady returned to the street to wait for the cops. Joe took his medical kit and oxygen bottle and went to the back yard. He looked into the garage and spotted a mint condition nineteen sixty-seven Pontiac Firebird. It was gorgeous. It was an almost forest green with a white vinyl roof. Joe couldn't take his eyes off it. He walked over to the man sitting in the lawn chair. He was a very obese man. There was a large yellow sponge lying on the floor not too far from the car, and a bucket of soapy water next to the lawn chair. Joe walked around to see if he could feel a carotid pulse on the man. He placed his fingers on the man's cold, clammy, neck while he continued to look at the car. It was just as clean on the inside as it was outside. Inside, Joe could make out a shiny black interior. He could not make out a pulse though, and the man was not breathing.

This patient was in cardiac arrest. He needed to perform CPR. To do that he needed to get him out of the lawn chair. Joe reached around the huge man and tried to lift him. His arms could not reach around the rotund man. Slowly the he got the big fella moving. He was using all his strength but could not free the man from the chair. It only took a few seconds for Joe to realize the problem. The victim's big ass was stuck in the chair. As Joe lifted him the chair was coming with him. Now, Joe tried to support the big man while using his foot to try and push the chair off his ass. He kicked and kicked at it until it finally shot across the immaculate garage floor. Joe was losing his balance with the well over four-hundred-pound man and quickly spun around with him. As they spun, the lifeless man's foot hit the bucket of soapy water and it spilled all over the concrete floor. Joe laid the man down on the wet floor and knelt next to him. He took his ambu bag out of his kit and started to pump oxygen back into his empty lungs. Then he started to do CPR compressions.

It seemed like forever but in reality it wasn't long before a police officer entered the garage. He was confused at the site of Joe performing CPR on this huge man in a puddle of water.

He looked at Joe who was covered and dripping in sweat and said. "What do ya got?"

Huffing and puffing Joe answered, "This guy is a full arrest. We need another unit to help transport."

The cop answered, "Okay, I'll call for one. Where did all this water come from?"

"Oh," Joe replied between compressions, still huffing away. "He was sitting in that chair." Joe motioned with his head to lawn chair in the corner of the garage. "So I had to get him down on the floor to do CPR and when I lifted him he kicked the bucket."

The police officer started to laugh and turned his back. Between chuckles he said, "I'll call for the other unit."

A few minutes later the other paramedic arrived. Both medics were determined to move him into an ambulance before calling medical control to speak to a doctor. All the equipment they needed was in their ambulance. They could hook him to an EKG monitor, start an IV and administer drugs to stimulate his heart. The medics switched places. Joe ran out to his rig with the police officer to grab his trundle. He also went into the side compartment and grabbed his Reeves stretcher. The Reeves is a long, foldable, stretcher with long, thin, wooden slats sewn into it for support. Joe wheeled in his trundle with the Reeves on top of it. The medics and the police officer rolled the big man onto the Reeves. Then they lifted him onto the trundle and wheeled him to the ambulance.

In the ambulance, the medics worked on their patient while the police officer drove them to the hospital. The ambulance rocked back and forth. There was still a lot of work to do to try to save his life. Through the starts and sudden stops, through the bumpy roads and sharp turns, they worked in the back of the tiny ambulance. They managed to start an IV and hook him to the EKG machine. His EKG read flat line. There wasn't much they could do with that. The doctors at medical control agreed, he did not have a shockable cardiac rhythm. The medics continued to work. Joe tried to intubate him. He took a curved, plastic, tube and tried to insert it from his mouth down into his trachea. This would enable the medics to better ventilate the patient. Within seconds Joe yelled out, "It's in!" They quickly hooked the oxygen directly to the back of the tube and started to breathe for the patient. They continued CPR and oxygen therapy. All this time the doctors were ordering the medics to push some medication to help stimulate the heart and other medication to combat the lack of oxygen in his blood.

The hospital was not far and the nurses had a room ready for the patient when he arrived. The ambulance backed into the emergency room bay. The medics quickly unloaded their patient and wheeled him into the trauma room the nurses had prepared. They transferred him from the ambulance gurney onto the trauma table. Joe gave the doctors as much information about the patient as he could, then stepped back and watched them work. It did not take long before they knew this man had been down too long. All the drugs and all the skill they had would not be able to bring him back. In less than ten minutes the code was over; the man had died. His name was Patrick Henry and now the doctors had to tell Mrs. Henry her husband had passed away.

Joe and the other medic walked around the emergency room to gather supplies that needed to be replaced. When they had what they needed they restocked and cleaned the back of the ambulance. Now it was time to head back to Beach Fourteenth Street. Joe needed to drop off the police officer and the other medic at the scene so they could get their vehicles. On the ride back Joe turned to the cop and medic riding with him and asked, "What was that guy's name?"

"Patrick Henry," the officer replied.

Joe continued. "Wasn't he a famous American? Didn't he say give me liberty or give me death?"

The cop yelled back, "Yes."

"Well he got his second wish," Joe quickly said.

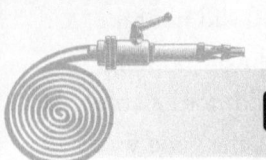

CHAPTER TWELVE

TUESDAY SEPTEMBER ELEVENTH

Over the next few weeks Michelle continued her love affair with her computer. It seemed like busy work to Joe, not the usual game playing he was used to seeing. Joe was off from work today and wanted to sleep in. But Michelle was up early and Joe could hear her tromping through the house. It was about six- thirty in the morning when Joe heard her. He laid in bed until seven, when he heard the side door slam shut and her car start. He tried to fall back asleep, but it was no use. He climbed out of the bed and decided to start his day early. He did his morning stretches to loosen up his monster. When he felt comfortable, he walked out of the bedroom and into the hallway. He looked up at the hangman's noose still perched above the staircase. He leaned far over the railing and gave the noose a tap. He walked down the steps as it swung back and forth above him.

As he hoped, the house was clean and empty. He walked into the kitchen and poured himself a cup of coffee. He sat at the kitchen table and noticed an envelope with his name on it. He rested his mug on the table and reached for the envelope. He recognized the handwriting on the crisp white envelope. The only person he knew that made that big, loopy J in Joe and ended his name with an E that slopes up then under his name was his wife. He opened the envelope and took out the note.

> Good Morning Baby,
>
> As you may have noticed I have been somewhat distant from you lately. Well the time has come to be totally honest with you, you deserve to know what's been going on. The truth is I've been talking to this guy on the internet. I need to tell you I haven't been this excited about something in all my life. I feel like I felt when I first met and fell in love with you. When I get home tonight we have a lot to talk about. Please keep an open mind.
>
> Michelle

It was beyond his control but Joe had tears running down his face as he read and reread the note. It was something he suspected was going on, but hoped he was wrong about. He kept looking between the lines hoping to find something that would ease his pain. It was no use; it was as plain as the ugly scars that ran down his body. He finally drove her away. Joe's eyes started to dry up and anger took over his emotions. He crumbled the note in his hand and threw it into the garbage pail. At that moment he decided he wasn't going to be around for that meeting. His mind went blank. He started to walk through the house. First he grabbed his car keys off the hook in kitchen. Then he headed for the laundry room. In a fit of rage, he pulled the clothes dryer out of its normal spot next to the washing machine. As if he had superhuman strength, it flew across the room. The huge three-pronged plug shot past his face as it tore from the wall. His mind was still a void as he reached behind the dryer and pulled the silver air vent off the back of it. The connection at the wall stretched to its limit until it snapped off. Joe continued walking from the room dragging the silver hose behind him.

He stormed out the side door, and dragging the silver hose, went directly to the garage. With amazing strength, he threw open the garage door. The first thing he saw was his motorcycle. It was perched on its kickstand, dead center of the garage. It was surrounded by tools, beer cans, soda cans, and other assorted junk on the floor. He entered the garage and went directly to the motorcycle. He picked it up off the kickstand and with his adrenalin still pumping lifted it up. He pivoted it on its back wheel and rolled it out of the garage. Once he had it outside and out of the way he turned his attention back to the junk on the floor. He started to pick up the junk laying around and throw it against the sides of the garage. Any object in his path was thrown or kicked to the side of the messy garage. He needed to make room for his car. In his fit of anger, it did not take long for him to clear a path wide enough for him to pull in. He walked out and got into his new car. It was only a week old and still had that new car smell. He sat down and stuck the key in the ignition. For the first time in the past few minutes his brain started to work again. He turned the key and the car engine turned over. As the motor hummed, Joe thought about driving his car right through the back of the garage. He pulled the shift lever into drive and slowly pulled into the space he cleared for his car. As he put the car into park he realized that driving through the back of the garage would not accomplish his mission today.

He left the car running as he got out and closed the garage door behind him. He then took the silver dryer hose and placed it over the tailpipe of his car. He took the other end and placed it through the back window on the driver's side. He got back into the car, then reached back and rolled the back window up as tight as he could with the vent in it. He checked all around to make sure all the car windows were up. Behind him deadly noxious fumes started to fill the car. Joe bent forward and turned his car radio on. He closed his eyes and listened to the music. He started to wonder what would be the last song he would hear in his life.

It did not take long for him to feel drowsy. He was at the point where he didn't even have the strength to keep his eyes open. Before he knew it, his eyes were too heavy to keep open. He fell into darkness. Even with all the strength he had earlier he could not open them.

He heard the voice of The Monster speak to him, "You thought you were rid of me. I just lay low waiting for your weakest point and strike. I make believe I'm your friend and talk you into things you know are wrong. I'm worse than a monster I'm a murderer. I take away all your options until I get what I want not what you want. I just wanted you to know before you're gone who made you do this."

With his eyes, still closed he saw a bright light. His mind started to race, as he thought to himself, "It's true, there is a bright light, I must go towards it."

As he approached the light he was able to make out a structure, he was sure it must be the pearly gates of Heaven. He was so excited, he started to run. When he arrived he was disappointed, the gates were not pearly white. It was a rather antique stone structure. The stones were two foot blocks stacked upon each other. They appeared to be very sturdy considering their apparent age. They stood over twenty feet high and wrapped around as far as the eye could see in both directions. In the middle, there was an opening. It was narrow at the bottom and started to flare out the higher it went. It looked like the eye of a needle.

Joe stood in front of the opening staring in awe. It was brighter on the inside than it was outside of the opening. Speaking loudly enough to be heard, but to no one in particular Joe said, "This must be the place." He raised his head and started to walk in. Suddenly he was startled and stopped short when he heard another voice.

"Tut-tut not so fast. Where do you think you're going?"

Joe's head spun around like the little girl in the Exorcist. "Excuse me who's there?" Joe said, in a timid reverent voice.

He heard the voice again. "Turn around and you shall see Joseph."

Stunned that this mysterious voice knew his name, he turned. Leaning against the stone on the inside of the gate was a man in a brown hooded robe.

He spoke again, "It is I Joseph, the Gate Greeter and keeper of records."

Joe immediately fell to his knees and said, "Oh, Saint Peter please forgive me, I did not recognize the pearly gates it's my first time up here and I am not sure of the rules."

The hooded figure pulled himself off the wall he was leaning against. He took his left hand and brushed off the dust that had collected on his robe.

As he brushed he said, "Pearly gates?" Then he addressed Joe directly, "First of all I am not Saint Peter; I'm a good six inches taller than he is. Besides he is much too busy with other tasks. He has no time to watch a gate. Therefore, I am here to greet all who wish to enter the kingdom of Heaven. I am still quite new here at the south gate. It is just my third century. You may call me GG. Not to be confused with my very distant cousin GR. You may have heard of him, the Grim Reaper. I know what you're thinking, we seem total opposites. Well that is true. Actually I don't think we are really related at all. Not by blood at least. He was more like a friend of the family. Somewhere along the line someone started to call him Uncle Grim, and before you know it he's in the family." The figure in the hooded robe stopped his long-winded tirade for an instant. He looked at Joe who was still kneeling. He had a blank expressionless stare on his face. Then GG spoke again. "Tell me why does everyone think we have pearly gates up here?"

"Well, the Bible says Saint Peter stands before the pearly gates of Heaven"

"Yeah, we gotta get that changed. So, my son, what brings you here?"

Joe, still kneeling, started to try and clear his head. He did not want to be disrespectful to GG but he did not fully understand the question. He looked up and in a thoughtful voice said, "Well, I'm pretty sure I'm dead."

The Greeter in his hooded robe reached out with his left hand and picked up a clip board that was hanging on the stone wall. He thumbed through the pages. When he finished he looked over at Joe who was still kneeling but now had his head bowed. It was as though he was waiting for his eternal sentence. GG put his head back down and started to mumble as he thumbed through the pages again. With a look of frustration on his face GG let the pages on the clipboard fall back into place. He reached with his left hand and hung the board back onto the stone wall.

"Stand up, my son," The Greeter said. Joe stood but still had a hard time making eye contact. "My son, you do not belong here."

Joe's eyes shot up at GG. His face went as white as powdered sugar. His voice trembled in fear as he started to speak. "Oh no, no, I think there's a mistake, I don't belong down there. I've tried my whole life to be good. I try to help people all the time. I never hurt anyone. I.."

"Slow down, that's not what I mean."

"It's not?"

"No, my son. What I mean is, it's not your time yet."

Joe looked confused. He'd been planning this for two months. "I'm sorry sir, but I'm pretty sure it's my time. I mean I am here."

GG reached into his robe and took out a small spiral note book. "Joseph," he said, "We have been watching you, and we are confused. You have been trying to take away God's greatest gift to you, your life. My son, you are a special creation by our Lord. He has given you special tools and gifts that no other person has. In your short lifetime, you have already had an impact on many lives. Did you not save a little girl from a horrible fire? Someday soon that little girl will become one of the most successful doctors in her field. She will champion new techniques and procedures to treat burn patients. With her help, someday people will not have horrific, painful scars like the one you live with." Joe reached down to his side to feel The Monster.

The Greeter continued, "It is because you found her, and saved her life she can do this. Because of your sacrifice thousands of lives will be touched. When you were in the hospital she came to visit and thank you. The doctors had you heavily sedated. When she saw you suffering, and realized all you did to save her she decided on the spot to learn how to help other people. She prayed day and night to God to save you. It was her devotion to God, and you, that our Lord blessed you."

"Wow! She is some special kid," Joe said in wonderment.

"All these years you have been angry at the firemen who got the credit for saving you and the little girl. That incident changed the life of Fireman Van Kooten. At that time in his life he was having trouble on the job. He was questioning his commitment to the job. He was scared that he would not have the strength to follow orders that could put him in danger. He was concerned that he would freeze at the wrong time and cost the life of himself, or worse, a brother firefighter. He was starting to drink heavily to hide his fear. This behavior took a toll on his personal life. He was on the verge of divorce and being relieved of duty. The day they got credit for saving the little girl changed his life. All of a sudden, he was a hero. It pushed all of his self-doubt away. He stopped drinking. He didn't need it any more to be brave. His wife was so proud of him they never talked of divorce again. Needless to say his job was never in question again."

"Honestly I did not know; how could I know?"

"It's Gods job to know. It's your job to have faith. God has a plan, sometimes your life is not just yours to live. God sometimes works through people. Never despair, Joseph. Keep the lord in your heart he will always rescue you."

GG flipped some more pages in his book. He looked at Joe who had an obvious look of shame on his face and said, "There are countless more examples here. Just recently you saved someone from jumping off a bridge. Do I need to continue?"

"No, I understand. But my wife doesn't love me anymore and it's so difficult to go on without her."

"Do not let your heart be troubled. Our time is growing short. Unfortunately, I am expecting a lot of souls very soon."

"I'll try to do better; I'll try harder to have faith."

"You're doing fine. Now it's time to go." GG turned and started to drift away.

Joe suddenly had a thought, he wanted to ask another question. "Excuse me before you leave can you help me with a problem?"

"That's our number one job up here, solving problems. What can I do for you?'

Joe took a breath and started. "Well, let's say you have thirty pennies."

"Why pennies? Why not nickels?"

"That's what I said. Nickels are better. Okay, you have thirty nickels twenty-eight of them are tails or face down. Two of them are heads or face up. You can't see them or feel them. You can move them and flip them. How do you make two even piles of heads up nickels?'

"Not the kind of problem I'm used to but still solvable. Just remove two nickels and turn them over. Chances are you take two of the tails coins. When you flip them, they will be heads. Then you will have two heads in each pile."

"Son of a bitch!" Joe shouted out. Then he quickly put both of his hands over his mouth. He looked in shame at GG who did not seem to react. Joe took his hand away from his mouth and softly spoke. "I hope you don't count that against me. It just slipped out. I forgot for a second where I was. Sorry. It's just that the answer is so simple. I've been working on this for weeks."

"I guess we can give you a mulligan on that. Don't worry about it, "GG said trying to hide a laugh.

Joe felt relief then said. "What if you don't grab two tails? What if you grab a head and a tail?"

"Same thing. If you flip both coins the tail becomes a head and the head becomes a tail. Again, you have one head in one pile and one head in another."

"Hm, well what if you took both head coins out and flipped them over?"

GG just grinned and said, "Then the piles would still be even. Each pile would have no heads in them."

"Oh yeah. Thanks, that was great."

GG turned again and said, "It's time to go back, Joseph. Follow God's plan. I must get ready, I will soon have many souls to comfort."

Joe stood and watched as mist seemed to envelope GG. and slowly he, disappeared into the fog. Joe started to cough. His eyes were watering and he had a hard time seeing. He started to move his arms and legs, and slowly he realized where he was. The radio was still playing but the car motor was not humming any more. Still coughing, Joe reached down and pulled the handle that opened the car door. The smoke and noxious gas fumes that filled the car started to vent out.

Joe looked down at the dashboard; the fuel gauge read empty. "Unbelievable! Out of gas!" Joe said in a semi-frustrated voice. "Well, I guess that's not the plan," he continued.

Then another voice was heard, "No, no, this was perfect. We should be dead by now. The Monster said.

Joe replied, "I done with you, you bastard! I was never a coward until I started listening to you. My whole life I've overcome obstacles I can easily beat you. You're done, finished. No one should ever live without hope."

As he started to gather his senses Joe could focus in on the voice on the radio.

"We interrupt this broadcast with an important news bulletin. At approximately eight-thirty this morning an American Airlines passenger jet crashed into the north tower of the World Trade Center. It is believed that all aboard have perished in the crash. At this time witness report that the north tower is on fire. Police, E.M.S, and the Fire Department have just arrived at the scene. Again, an

American Airlines passenger jet has crashed into the north tower of the World Trade Center. Keep tuned to this station for further updates."

Joe sat in disbelief for a moment. How could a jet plane veer off course and fly low enough to crash into a building? Well he knew he had to get there and help out in any rescue effort. He turned the key in the ignition and heard the engine, click…click…click. "Oh Motherfucker, out of gas!" he yelled in anger. He placed his arms over the steering wheel and put his head down to think. He lifted his head and turned to the right. The mirror on the right side of the car caught his eye. It was pointed at the side window of the garage. As he focused his vision, he saw the answer. His motorcycle was sitting on the side of the garage. He jumped out of his car and ran to the front of garage. With the strength of a super hero, he threw open the garage door and ran for his bike.

He straddled his bike and turned the key. Then he jumped on the starter a few times before the engine finally kicked over. He pulled out of his driveway and roared down the street. He was so focused, he forgot to grab his helmet. The streets were deserted. People were staying home, glued to their televisions and radios. The schools went into lock down.

He raced toward the city. He ran red lights and stop signs. As he got closer to Manhattan, he started to encounter police roadblocks. They stopped him and tried to turn him around. Joe was persistent; he flashed his badge to the officers, and they let him pass. Joe was stopped again at the Brooklyn Bridge. From the Brooklyn side it was easy to see the smoke and flames of the Towers. The police officers looked visibly upset. They had witnessed something that made them feel nauseous.

Joe was confused. The radio said a plane had crashed into one of the towers. It was obvious both towers were on fire. Then static filled the air as a voice came over the police radio. "It's confirmed, a second jet airliner has just crashed into the South Tower, over." One of the officers looked at his partner and said, "Were under attack!"

Joe felt the rage build inside him. He revved his motorcycle and got the cops attention again. "I'm E.M.S; they need all the help they can get. Let me through." With that he flipped his badge at them. The police knew that all emergency personnel available would be needed to handle the attack. They waved him on. Joe roared past them. As the officer's watched Joe cross the bridge one of them said, "God be with you."

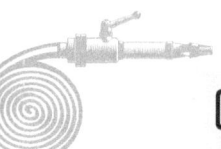

CHAPTER THIRTEEN

THE SKY IS FALLING

Driving through lower Manhattan was slow. Joe passed thousands of people fleeing the scene of the disaster. They were covered in smoke, blood, dirt, and fear. Joe wove his way through lower Manhattan. He was like a salmon swimming upstream. He arrived at the E.M.S. command post a few blocks from Ground Zero. It was still before ten a.m. The mood was all business, as plans were put into place to rescue and evacuate victims. He was overwhelmed at the sight he encountered in downtown New York City. In all the panic and chaos, the police had done an excellent job of evacuating the immediate area. Still smoke, dust, and fear of the unknown ruled the air. Chief Banks, who was in charge of the E.M.S. rescue effort was happy to see Joe. He knew Joe from when he was a fireman. He helped recruit him to E.M.S. when his fire service days ended. He knew Joe was a fine medic who could work well under pressure. Man, was there a lot of pressure today.

Joe walked across the street to an office building. The police had evacuated it earlier, and E.M.S. was using it as a staging area for personnel and to triage the wounded. He was greeted by several medics that he knew. Lieutenant Pete Hamilton was in charge of the area. Pete was a good friend of Joe's. When Joe was released from the fire service Pete helped him transition to E.M.S. They embraced as they greeted each other. Pete needed a hug; he looked frazzled but what else would you expect, with not only one jet, but two jets slamming into the World Trade Center.

"Joe, it's a mess. I've never seen anything like it," Pete said trying to maintain a calm exterior.

Joe looked around and thought to himself no one has ever seen this kind of carnage outside of a war. It was one of his strengths to keep that emotion bottled up and try to stay positive. Now more than ever he needed to stay in control, keep up a strong exterior and keep pushing.

"It's okay, Pete, we'll get through it," Joe said reassuringly.

"Joe, you can get a jumpsuit and helmet over in the next room," Pete said as he pointed over Joe's right shoulder. Joe nodded and jogged to the room to change. "I'll get your bag ready for you while you change;" Pete yelled out to him. Pete walked over to the supply area to stock a medic kit for Joe. He needed to be careful; without beds the victims were lying on makeshift stretchers on the floor of the building. Pete walked slowly zigzagging through the maze of bloody, moaning, patients, many of them reaching out to him as he passed, their arms connected to IV lines to help replace the fluids and blood that they were losing due to their injuries. There were a handful of other E.M.T.'s in the building helping Pete take care of the injured. Many of them were overwhelmed as well. In the far corner of the building's lobby was a makeshift morgue. It was full as well. "Lieu, when are those ambulances going to get here? This guy can't wait much longer," a shaky voice called out. In a calm but commanding tone Pete responded, "easy, Smitty, they're on the way. It will be soon."

As Pete continued to pack a medic bag for Joe one of the other medics walked over to him. His jumpsuit was coved in dirt and blood. He leaned in and whispered something into Pete's ear. When he finished the medic grabbed a one thousand CC bag of Ringers Lactate and walked away to tend to his patient. Pete just stood motionless and hung his head.

Joe passed the tired medic as he walked toward Pete. He gave him a pat on the shoulder. Joe's jumpsuit was a bit on the baggy side but it did not matter. He continued walking to meet up with Pete. As he approached he saw an orange medic bag, which appeared to be all packed and ready to go. Next to the bag Pete stood, arms on the table head hung down. Joe reached over and put his hand on Pete's shoulder. "Are you okay bud?" Joe asked.

"Another plane just crashed. This one in Washington D.C., into the Pentagon," Pete said in a low, shallow voice. "It's like the end of the world."

Joe lost the positive attitude that people admired in him. It was not despair he felt. It was anger. This is the greatest country the world has ever seen, and now some scum bags are trying to take it away from us. Not today! Not while I still have a breath in my lungs!

Joe looked Pete in the eye and almost as if scolding him said, "No, don't say that, don't even think like that. This is the time when people look to us. It's our turn to shine. We'll get through this, we have to. One step at a time. I have a friend, he's a cop. He's the bravest person I know. He never quits, he never gives up. He always says it's do or die. Today, Pete, it's do. Let's go out and do our thing."

Pete turned and faced Joe. "You're right my friend, here's your kit. It's all packed, be careful."

"Thanks." Then pointing at the countless victims lying on the floor of the lobby, Joe continued, "Make sure all these people live, they need you now!" Joe took the bag and ran to the command post to receive his orders.

As Joe arrived at the command post he passed many police and firefighters. They were covered in building ash and dirt. Some of them were having a real hard time breathing, but they knew they had a job to do and refused to stop to receive any medical help. Then his attention was diverted by a loud cracking sound. Everyone seemed to hear it. All the heads seemed to turn in unison. Suddenly activity on the fire and police radios went crazy. Orders were being shouted to all emergency personnel. "EVACUATE THE SOUTH TOWER!" As everyone watched helplessly the tower started to move, and the cracking sounds became more prevalent. Joe looked up as the tower seemed to start swaying back and forth. People who went to work on this beautiful Tuesday morning, just trying to eke out a living for themselves or their families were now so desperate to escape the raging inferno that their office building had become. They were now jumping out of the windows eighty or ninety stories up in the sky. In the last moments of their lives, they took control of their destiny. They chose how they were going to die.

Suddenly hearts started to beat much faster. The noise on the streets seemed to die down to a murmur. The only audible human voices seemed to come from the radios the rescuers had. All eyes were up at the South Tower, as floor after floor started to collapse onto each other. On the street below people were frantically running from the bottom of the doomed building. As the steel and concrete gathered speed falling towards the earth, a cloud of dust started rising. If it didn't really happen you might have thought it was a magic trick. First you had a one hundred and ten story building. Then abracadabra in a plum of dust and smoke it was gone. Unfortunately, it was no trick.

Once the building hit the ground the noise level started to rise again. Screams and tears filled the thick, smoky, dusty air. Hearts were still racing as witnesses calculated the loss of life that happen in the blink of an eye. Joe was snapped back into reality by a voice on the police radio. "Command post, I just received word. I have an officer in the lower level of the South Tower. He was leading victims out when the tower went down. They are still alive but need help, over!"

"Roger," the voice on the other end replied in an exasperated tone. Then silence. Joe waited for what seemed like an eternity but actually was a mere few seconds for further instructions from the voice on the radio. Who was going into search and rescue those people? If they needed volunteers he was ready and willing to go. Then the silence was broken with the sound of static. Again, everyone waited for the voice. "Roger on the South Tower, but we need to secure the North Tower in case it comes down. Have Captain Scotko report to me and we will work on that, over."

"Roger!" was the exasperated response, the radio went silent again. With his adrenaline pumping Joe looked at his chief. Before he could even open his mouth and give him an assignment, Joe said, "Chief give me a flashlight. I'm going in to find those people. They're alive and need help."

The Chief looked back at him. He knew there was too much going on to try and reel in a renegade. Joe reached behind him and grabbed a flashlight from the shelf. Then he reached into his medic bag and pulled out a rectangular box. He opened it and pulled out a folded piece of cloth. He started to open it and as he unfolded it the thin cloth got larger. When it was completely open it looked like a big triangle. The big, triangular bandage is called a cravat. It's a special bandage used mostly to make slings with. It can also be used to secure fractured limbs to splints. Some medics even use them to cover head wounds. Its use is only limited by the medic's imagination. Joe took it and tied it around his mouth and nose. On a normal day he might be suspected as a bank robber. Today he was going to use his wits on a search and rescue mission.

Joe took off for the South Tower. He ran as best he could lugging all his equipment. It started to get substantially darker the closer he got to the tower. He was coughing and choking even through his make shift filter mask. He spotted a small opening that seemed to be sturdy enough for him to enter through. It was about five feet at its widest point near the bottom. It ran up about six feet high and was about a foot wide at the top. He turned his body sideways and ducked his head slightly and entered the tower. His flashlight was on but it was still very dark and difficult to see much ahead of him. His mind did a quick flashback to that cold December day. His last search and rescue with the fire service. That one did not end well for him. It created the monster. It wasn't for pity that he thought of that. It was his way of drawing on all his experience to make the rescue as successful as possible.

It was very difficult crawling through all the debris and the dead bodies he encountered. It was still pitch black, but the dust did not seem as thick as he crawled further along. In the darkness, his hands became more important than his eyes. He reached out with his left hand to feel for a sturdy surface to crawl on. His right hand dragged his flashlight and medic kit. Little by little he pulled himself over the uneven surface, mostly feeling hard, rocky edges and broken glass. Occasionally his hand would cross over something soft and wet. When he shone the flashlight on his hand it was covered in red. He had been crawling over dead bodies. He tried to quicken his pace and started to call out, "Hello, hello, fire department, I mean E.M.S. Can anybody hear me?" Then up ahead he saw a faint light. Maybe a flashlight. He started to call louder, trying not to cough. "HELLO! ANYONE THERE?"

"Help, please help us." It was not very loud but it was certainly a woman's voice calling back to him.

"I'm here, I'm here, hang on." Joe started to crawl faster. When he arrived he was amazed. It was a miracle from God.

A small area about ten feet by ten feet did not collapse when the building fell. Behind it a huge piece of concrete wall or maybe the floor above had fallen. It looked like they just got to the miracle spot before it fell. "Is everyone okay?" Joe asked.

"We're alright but the policeman is hurt bad," the woman with the flashlight replied.

Joe crawled over the last of the rubble and squeezed through the small hole where the woman had been calling. Carefully, through sharp, broken, concrete, and pointy rebar, he entered the safe space where the victims were. By Joe's count there were fifteen people trapped in there. They were all standing huddled together. No one looked seriously injured. Joe turned to the woman and said, "Where is he?" The woman pointed to the wall that had fallen behind them.

Joe pointed his flashlight toward the back and started to search with it. He started to pan from east to west. The beam of light hit the wall and he pointed it down. All the dust and dirt could be seen passing through the light's beam as he moved it about. At the bottom of the wall toward the west side he saw a figure lying face up with a young man in a business suit kneeling beside him. He was using his tie to wipe the blood from the cop's face. Joe grabbed his medic bag and started to walk over to him. He kept his light on him the entire time. The young man in the suit wiped the blood off the cop's face. No sooner was he done than the blood would pool back again. It was running down his mouth and nose and blocking his airway. The cop was choking on it.

Joe went over and knelt next to the policeman. He lowered his make shift filter mask down around his neck so the officer could see a friendly face. He reached down and turned the policeman's head to the side so the blood could drain better. The cop started to breathe much easier. Then he took his cravat off his neck and started to wipe the cop's face clean. The cop looked up and could clearly see the medic's face. In a weak but friendly voice, he said to Joe, "How's your father?"

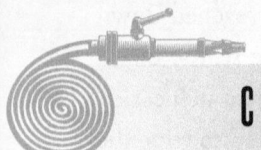

CHAPTER FOURTEEN

ONE NINE SEVEN EIGHT ONE

Gary was pinned badly. The wall was resting just above his waist. His lower torso and feet could not be seen. The blood was still running down his face. It was dripping so fast a puddle had started to form on the ground under Joe's hands. Joe knew it was bad. For the first time in his professional career, he was having a hard time staying calm.

"Gary, can you hear me?" Joe shouted in a loud, shaky voice.

"Hey Joe." Gary replied softly trying not to choke.

"Hey, it's gonna, be alright, I'll get you outta here." He kept the injured cop's head turned to keep the blood from accumulating in the back of his throat. He turned to survey the small dark area that miraculously had not caved in yet. He shone his flashlight in a circular pattern around the contained space. He saw the small group of men and women, mostly standing huddled together, their faces black with dirt. The air was dense with dust and fear.

"Leave him, we gotta get out of here!" a man exclaimed with a scared fury Joe had never heard before. Then more voices started to chime in.

"We have to go or we'll all die here!"

"We'll never get him out from that wall, we have to save ourselves!"

"Please you came to help us, please help us!" The voices of the frightened men and women trapped started to swell, with one common thread. Get us out of here.

Joe needed to take control of the situation. He regained his composure and in a commanding voice said. "We're all going to get out of here, the cop included! Let's work together and lift this wall off him." Without thinking, just blindly following orders, some of the trapped victims started to shuffle over.

Then Gary spoke in a soft voice, "No, Joe it's over. I can't feel or move my legs. It's taking everything I have just to stay awake. I'm done. Please get these people out of here so, I don't die for nothing."

"No, Gary, we can do this. We can get you out." With tears welling up in his eyes Joe called over again to the scared people trapped with him. "Please, help me. He's my friend. We have to help him." Joe broke down and sobbed. The victims stood motionless. They didn't know what to do.

"Joe, it's do or die," Gary said, his voice even weaker than before.

Joe looked down at his dying friend, tears falling from his eyes onto Gary's bloody face. "Okay, just let me stay a few more seconds?" Joe asked. Then he looked down at Gary and continued to speak. "Hey, I found out the answer to the penny riddle"

"I thought you liked nickels." Gary said.

"That's what I meant nickels" Joe said back. Joe noticed Gary's breathing was becoming more erratic. It would not be long now. Gary was now so weak he could not open his eyes. With his last breath, he spoke.

"I wish I could remember the answer to that…" His breathing stopped. Gary died in Joe's arms.

With an ache in his heart Joe spoke his last words to his friend. "Don't worry, they have all the answers up there." Joe released Gary's head and placed it softly on the ground. With his bloody right hand, he reached on to the officer's chest. He carefully removed Gary's police badge and placed it in his pocket. Then he took the bloody cravat and carefully placed it over his friend's face.

Joe stood up and looked at the scared survivors. Suddenly the ground started to shake. Dust and dirt started to enter the enclosure where they stood. A loud thunderous boom was heard and Joe yelled out." HIT THE DECK!"

They all fell to the ground and covered their heads. It seemed like forever before the noise and rumbling stopped. When it was over the miracle enclosure that saved them originally was still standing. Slowly, the men and women started to rise from the ground. They were covered in a fresh layer of dirt and dust. Breathing was more difficult as well. Joe took his flashlight and shone it on the opening that he crawled through to get to these people. It was sealed shut.

"What happened?" asked a nervous woman.

"I think the other Tower fell." Joe replied.

"Oh my God, the opening's gone!" shouted one of the men. Panic quickly filled the small room. Joe needed to take control again.

"It's alright the policeman saved our lives again. If we left and went through that hole we all would have died. Now we need to find another way out." While the survivors thought about that Joe surveyed the room for a way out. He noticed that part of the wall next to where his friend lay was missing. Carefully he walked over and saw a hole had swallowed that part of the wall. There was no telling what floor of the building they were on due to the collapse. Joe used his flashlight to look down the hole.

As Joe continued to work on an escape plan panic started to fill the small space again. People started crying and yelling, "WERE ALL GOING TO DIE!"

"NO!" Joe yelled back at them. "We have a way out." He motioned the survivors over to the hole and pointed down. "Look, I think that might be the parking garage. We can climb down this hole and get to the bottom. We should be able to get out through there."

"We'll never make it!" cried out a hysterical woman.

"We have to. The air is not breathable in here anymore. There's too much dirt," Joe replied. I'll go first. Send the women behind me. Just follow my steps and we'll be fine."

Joe lowered himself down the hole. The small ledges seemed strong enough to hold his weight. Slowly, he inched his way along. Above him one of the men helped a woman into the hole. She started to follow Joe's path. "Don't look down," Joe yelled up to her. As the first two climbed farther down the next woman was sent. As Joe got closer to the bottom he was able to move faster. The footing became more stable and easier to move along.

Finally, Joe could see the bottom of the garage. He made the short three-foot leap onto the roof of a Jeep Cherokee. Closely behind him was the woman who followed him. They jumped down to the floor and looked up to see if they could help the next person. The woman with Joe was still obviously shaken. Joe stood on the hood of the Jeep waiting to help. He looked down at the panicked woman. She was crying, and coughing, and pacing around in a circle. She was real close to losing it. He thought if he gave her something to do it would keep her mind off their situation.

"Miss," Joe yelled to her. "Can you check some of the cars and see if there is any bottled water or tools we can use? If you can find a car jack it might help to move some of the heavy debris. Be careful you don't cut yourself or get lost."

"I am thirsty; water would be good. But I don't know how to break into a car?"

"No, miss. look in the cars that have broken windows or doors. There should be plenty." The woman shook her head and slowly walked off.

One by one the survivors made it down to the garage. The last person was the Good Samaritan, who stayed by Gary while he was trapped. Just as he was jumping to the roof of the Jeep the woman came back with an armful of bottled water. The small group sat around the Cherokee as she passed out the water bottles. The light was much better in the garage and everyone got a good look at their faces and clothes. Joe suggested that they take the water and wash out their mouth and nose first. Black puddles started to accumulate on the garage floor as the survivors tried to clean their airways. After the short break the overall spirt of the group seemed to be uplifted. It was looking like they would get out. Joe took this opportunity to ask them a question he had been wondering about since he first encountered Gary pinned by the wall. "What happened back there? I mean how did the cop find you and how did the wall fall on him?"

An older woman, maybe one of the survivors' bosses started to tell the story. "Well we were evacuating our building after the plane hit. We felt the building shake. It was like an explosion went off upstairs. We tried to make a calm exit but panic broke out. The staircase started to get clogged up. People were trying to run past the people on the steps." She stopped and took a sip of her water. Joe looked on intently and she continued. "By now the power was out and the stairwell was pitch black. The noise was intolerable; everyone was screaming for their life. People had cell phones out trying to call home to say goodbye." Tears were running down the woman's face as she continued. "My legs were burning and my heart was thumping out of my chest but something kept me going. Like I said, I don't know how far down we were but we met the policeman. He had a flashlight and told us to follow him. It wasn't long before we felt the heat bearing down on us. The cop looked up and saw a fire ball heading down on us. We ran down to the next landing and popped open the door and ran onto that floor. As the fire ball passed, the door we had just gone through blew off its hinges."

She stopped to take another sip of water. It was apparent she started to realize how close to death they had come. She composed herself and continued. "Your friend was very brave. He tried to lead us to the other side of the building.

He was hoping the stairs on that side were still intact. Then it happened. A series of loud thumps. The floors were collapsing on top of each other. Next thing we know we're covered in dust with debris everywhere. Your friend gets on his radio and tells them we're still alive. They didn't care. They didn't want to help us. We all heard it; secure the other Tower. 'It's okay, he says, we don't need them,' he says. So we start to walk to find a way out. Then Nancy falls and calls for help. He tells us to keep going, he'll catch up."

Nancy looked up and continued the story. "My foot got caught in a crack; must have happened when the Tower fell. He comes in all brave and reassuring. He put his radio on the desk next to me and starts to get my foot loose. Then that awful cracking happens and the dust starts to fall again. He gets me free and pushes me up to the rest of them. He reached up to get his radio and it fell. He went back to reach for it and the floor above starts to buckle. He forgets the radio and lunges for me. He pushed me as hard as he could into that room. Then he tries to dive in, but just then the ceiling fell and pinned him. He saved my life and I was too scared to even help him or say thank you." She broke down into tears. The Good Samaritan put his arm around her.

After a few seconds of silence, the Good Samaritan looked up and asked. "How are we getting out of here?"

Joe stood up and pointed to the ground. "We can follow these."

The group looked down and saw the large yellow arrows pointing to the exit. The group formed a line behind Joe and started walking. It was uphill and they had to climb over some cars that blocked the way. Soon they started to see some light shining through and started to walk faster. They made it to the exit of the garage which was blocked with rubble but not impassable.

Joe started to help the women climb over the rock and rebar that once supported the massive building. One by one the survivors reached the safety of the street. The rescue workers in the street saw the victims emerging from the fallen structure and were overcome with emotion. Many of them started to spontaneously applaud. The television cameras caught the entire escape. Joe helped the last man climb over the rubble to freedom. Then he threw his bag over his shoulder and climbed out. He was greeted by an E.M.S. paramedic carrying an oxygen cylinder. He quickly waved him away and walked straight to the police command post.

As he was getting closer many of the police officers stopped to pat him on the back or shake his hand. A few feet before the command post a police Captain stopped him and asked him what he needed. "I want to see your chief," he responded.

The captain took him. When they arrived, the captain brought him into the makeshift office the police were using to oversee the tragedy. Joe stood in front of the well decorated officer. His face and hands were still covered in dirt and soot. He felt weak and was still coughing up thick black sputum. "Chief, this is the medic who helped rescue the trapped people in the South Tower."

"Well done," the chief responded.

Joe reached into his pocket and pulled out a dirty, bloody, police badge. He grabbed the chief's hand and placed the dirty badge into it. "This badge belonged to Gary Murphy.

He died saving those people. He was a great man and a great cop. More importantly, he was my friend. Please honor him and your brave department by never letting anyone wear badge one, nine, seven, eight, one."

The Chief closed his hand over the badge. Joe silently walked out of the office.

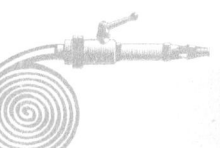

CHAPTER FIFTEEN

SEPTEMBER TWELVTH TWO THOUSAND AND ONE

By now the information on the attack was slowly coming together. Millions of people watched the gruesome events unfold on live television. It was shocking to learn about the four planes that were hijacked in a uniform attack on the United States. Many scared parents rushed to the schools to get their children, children who had left early that beautiful Tuesday morning, not knowing how the world would be forever changed. For over twenty-four hours commercial and private airplanes were grounded. Heavily armed fighter jets roamed across the skies of the country. A swell of patriotism arose throughout the country. Neighborhoods were proudly flying Old Glory in front of their homes.

The cowardly terrorist's, who only targeted innocent civilians, took the four planes on suicide missions. Two had gone to New York and crashed into the World Trade

Center buildings. One crashed into the Pentagon building in Washington D.C. The last plane crashed into a field in western Pennsylvania. It is believed that plane was heading for the White House. Manny of the passengers on board were alerted about the previous attacks on New York via their cell phones. The brave crew and passengers would not allow this jet to be an instrument of destruction on innocent people. They stood up to the cowards who hijacked the plane.

Some of the passengers had time to call the person they loved most and say goodbye. Then, in an act so selfless and brave, they rose united and fought the terrorist to win back control of the plane. With their bare hands and the bravery of a Congressional Medal of Honor recipient they fought. The jet fell out of the sky and crashed into an empty field in Pennsylvania. No one survived. The passengers and crew did win though. They kept the airliner from reaching its suicide destination. They knowingly gave their lives so others could live. They made their family, friends, and America proud. Their sacrifice along with all the innocent people who were murdered that day will NEVER be forgotten.

The day was filled with heroes such as The Police, Fire Department, and E.M.S. who responded. Many of them also died trying to save others. The victims caught in the dark, smoky buildings who stayed behind to help other people find safety in the chaos. The media who reported the events and tried to reassure America that we can rise above the fear and loss. Even the average American citizen in states not attacked heard the call for patriotism, going to blood banks to donate blood for the survivors. It seemed that every American found a way to be brave and be a hero. It was the worst attack ever on U.S. soil, but it was also our finest hour.

The next few days at Ground Zero would be spent in clean-up and looking for the dead. It would be an around the clock job. Joe was finally relieved after about fifteen hours. Like all the other rescue personnel he wanted to stay. After a quick discussion, he realized a well-rested fresh rescuer would do much more good than he would. It was about four a.m. when his motorcycle pulled into the driveway. The first thing he did when he entered his house was remove his clothes. He stripped down to his underwear and tossed his clothes away, afraid of what toxic chemicals might have latched onto his clothes' and body. Next he wanted to take a long shower. He walked into the living room and saw Michelle sitting on the couch. He was surprised that no computer sat on her lap. She stared transfixed at the television. She had a box of tissues next to her. It was just about empty. On the floor was a clump of used tissues. Her beautiful hair was a mess. She was visibly shaken and exhausted. Her eyes were red from crying.

Michelle was so focused on the television reporting the events of the day she did not hear Joe's motorcycle or the back-door open. It wasn't until he entered the room that she reacted. "Oh my God, oh my God, oh my God. I thought I would never see you again," she said as she sprang off the couch to embrace her husband.

Joe quickly pushed her away. He certainly did need and wanted a hug but now was not the time. He was dirty and contaminated with who knows what. As he pushed her away he said, "No, I need to shower; I don't know what kind of toxins are covering me."

"I don't care I need to hold you now!" she fought through his arms and hugged him. As she hugged him, she squeezed him harder.

"All right, Michelle, it's okay. Let me take my shower," Joe said in a reassuring caring voice.

They broke the embrace and Joe headed up stairs. As he walked up he gazed at the hangman's noose which he purposely never took down. Michelle followed him, wanting to get out of her clothes in case she picked up any chemicals from hugging her husband. Joe went into the hot shower. He washed quickly, the hot water taking any energy he had left. He dried himself in the steamy bathroom, put on his robe and went into the bedroom. He fell on his bed and went fast asleep.

When Joe awoke it was close to lunch time. Something wasn't right. He was pushed off to one side of the bed. He rolled over to see why and found his answer. Michelle was sleeping next to him. Not only next to him but practically on top of him. Joe quickly jumped out of the bed, his right side sending stabbing pain at him. When he got to his feet he tried to stretch it out. The sudden movement woke Michelle up. She lifted her head off the pillow and supported it with her hand. Her hair looking beautiful once again, falling to the side. "Good morning baby." She said in a sleepy voice.

Joe turned his back immediately and quickly looked for a shirt to throw on. As he looked, he said in a surprised voice, "Good morning."

She reached for the television remote and clicked the T.V. on. Every channel was reporting the terrible events of the previous day. Without taking her eyes off the screen she said, "I was hoping this was just a nightmare. Somehow when I woke up I thought I could put the T.V. on and watch I Love Lucy. But it did happen and the world will never be the same, will it?"

"I don't think so," was his short poignant response.

After a few seconds of silence between them Joe started to speak. "Michelle," he started as he turned to face her. "I have some more terrible news to tell you." Michelle sat up on the side of the bed. She shook her head to get the hair out of her face. Joe walked over a little closer to her and looked down at her. "I went into the South Tower yesterday after it collapsed. There were people trapped."

"I know. I saw on the news you got them all out."

"No, not all of them. There was also a police officer trapped with them. When I got there, he was caught under a wall or the ceiling from the floor above, I'm still not sure. He was hurt bad."

Michelle saw how upset Joe was getting telling the story. She decided to interrupt him. "It's okay I'm sure you did everything you could. You saved all those people."

"No! You don't understand. It was Gary. He was the cop trapped. He died in my arms and I had to leave him." Joe broke down, all the emotion of the previous day caught up to him. He sat on the edge of the bed next to his wife and cried like a baby. She put her arms around him and pulled him closer.

It took a few moments but he finally composed himself. As he sat on the edge of the bed, he thought about how nice it felt to have Michelle's arms around him again. Suddenly reality kicked in and Joe remembered she was going to leave him. He quickly sprang up off the bed. He did not need his wife's pity. He looked down at her. She had a puzzled look on her face. "Well, I have to get ready for work." Joe said. "They need some units on the streets while the cleanup continues."

"I'm working also," Michelle replied. "They called me last night and asked if I could go over some of our inventory and maybe help out some of the area hospitals taking care of the burn victims."

Joe just shook his head and started to turn away. Michelle quickly reached out for his hand and grabbed it. He felt her soft skin on his hand and turned back toward her. She said, "Don't forget we have to talk tonight, I have something very important to tell you."

Joe nodded back at her and walked away. "Well, I guess tonight's the night I find out about her boyfriend," he thought to himself.

Joe finished dressing and went downstairs. Michelle was sitting at the kitchen table. He was very surprised that she did not have her computer open. Instead she was watching the television coverage of the previous day's attack on America. Joe breezed into the kitchen and poured himself a cup of hot coffee. He leaned against the counter watching the news over Michelle's shoulder. He took a few sips and peeked up at the clock. All of a sudden, he was running late. He stilled needed to pour gas into his car then stop at the gas station. He put his half empty cup down mumbled a quick goodbye to his wife, and walked to the garage.

As he left he heard Michelle yell out, "Don't forget, we have a date tonight. Lots to talk about!"

"She's waiting to break my heart and she calls it a date," he muttered to no one in particular. Joe made it just in time for work. The mood as expected was very somber. Many of the medics were running on very little sleep. Joe was assigned to Brooklyn; it was an area he was familiar with. He walked to his rig and started his checklist. The mood was very much the same at the hospital that Michelle worked at. Many of the nurses and other staff looked to her for support. She did her best to remain optimistic and buoy the spirt of her staff. She stressed to them how important it was for them to remain confident and professional, especially with their patients.

Joe's shift started off very quietly. He drove through some of the East Flatbush neighborhoods. Many of the residents did not go to work on this Wednesday. The schools were closed. The streets seemed deserted. Every street he drove down had one thing in common. It seemed every house, every apartment building, had an American flag hanging. It was a sight to see both sides of the street with Old Glory waving proudly in the autumn breeze. It was a great swell of patriotism. The more he drove the more flags he saw. Today it was truly "one nation under God."

With Michelle's help the hospital was able to send out supplies to the area hospitals treating the burn victims of September eleventh. It was much needed and much appreciated. Another form of patriotism, when competing hospitals band together for the good of everyone. It was a long day for her. It was also a very rewarding day. She watched first hand as her husband suffered with severe painful burns. There was not much she could do then, but today she could help. The time seemed to fly by. She felt as though it was the best day of work she had ever done. She hoped her small contribution would help ease the suffering of the brave men and women who were seriously burned at Ground Zero.

Joe pulled into his driveway. His shift in Brooklyn had been very slow. He knew Michelle was home. He saw her car parked on the street in front of the house. He walked in through the back door. His head bowed he threw his keys onto the kitchen table. When Michelle heard the keys hit the table she yelled to him, "I'm in here, on the couch." Joe took a breath and started to walk in. He promised he would not break down. He promised he would be noble and step aside. He always felt nothing was more important than his wife's happiness.

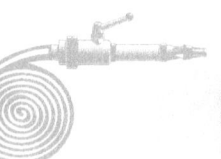

CHAPTER SIXTEEN

THE FUNERAL

As Joe walked into the living room the first thing he saw was a computer sitting on his wife's lap. He was not surprised. That's the girl he knew. "I hope she's smart enough to puts that devil's tool away and spends time with her new lover," he thought to himself.

"Oh, I'm glad you got home at a decent time. I have a lot of news for you," Michelle started.

"Let me make this easy on all of us," Joe started. "It's no secret you found a boyfriend on that stupid, shit-box computer. I know you two have been e-mailing back and forth and your little oh, I'll let you down easy, letter pretty well spelled it all out as well."

Michelle stared at him dumbfounded. Her expression was totally blank. Her eyes wide open and staring into nothing.

"Don't just stare like that. I'm not stupid. I read the note. I met some guy on the internet. I haven't felt this happy since I first met you. I see what's been going on." Joe stopped his tirade waiting for Michelle to crack, but she just kept staring. He continued, "Well I'm not going to stand in your way. All I ever wanted was for you to be happy. I have gone to great lengths, to try to make you happy. Believe me, I have gone to really, really, great lengths. I literally stuck my neck out for you." Joe paused again. Michelle still looked dumbfounded. The silence was killing Joe. He had to speak again. "So how do you want to do this? Should I pack up and leave? Or do you want to move in with him? What's the plan?"

Michelle finally made some sounds. She started to break out into laughter. It was the biggest, loudest, belly laugh you have ever heard. Every time she tried to stop she would just laugh louder. Joe looked on in disbelief. What made this tragic break up of a marriage so funny to her? "That fucking devil's tool ruined her mind," he thought to himself. He couldn't take it anymore.

He was about to walk out on her. Before he left he wanted to tell her something. "You may think this is a big joke. Oh screw Joe, he's just an asshole anyway, and you're probably right. But this asshole has feelings. He tried to make you happy. I even tried to kill myself for you. Yeah, that's right. I left everything to you the house, the insurance, the bank account. But you sit there on your high horse and laugh at the poor schmuck."

As he was taking a breath to finish his rant, he noticed the laughter had stopped. The blank stare was replaced by big wet tears rolling down Michelle's face. His mood changed immediately. Tears, a man's Kryptonite. His anger was replaced by compassion for his wife crying. He was trying to think of the right thing to say when Michelle spoke softly. "You tried to kill yourself?"

Joe was taken back by the question. He was trying to form words in his mouth. All that came out was a bunch of stammering mumbo jumbo.

Michelle was deep in thought and then an epiphany came to her. She pointed to the top of the staircase, and said, "The noose, the note, oh how stupid could I have been? All those papers laid out on the bed. Oh, Joe, I'm so sorry." She reached out and put her arms around Joe's waist. Then she buried her head into his chest sobbing.

Joe stood as his wife, sitting on the couch, had a bear hug around him. His arms were at his sides. He was more confused than ever. As she continued to sob Joe looked straight ahead. His face could not hide how perplexed he was. He was carrying on a conversation in his head. "She has a boyfriend… I find out about it …she starts laughing when I tell her… then she cries when I step aside for her." With Michelle still holding on tight he reached up to scratch his head.

Michelle finally stood up and the computer fell to the floor. Her eyes were swollen from crying. She reached up and cupped Joe's face with her hands. In a soft voice she said, "I'm not leaving you."

"You're not?"

"No, I would never leave you."

"But the note, all the e-mails?"

"Sit down, baby," Michelle's hands slid off his face. With her right hand, she grabbed Joe's and led him back to the couch. She sat real close to him and said. "A few weeks ago

Gary stopped by the house looking for you. You weren't home so he told me about some guys he knew that were relocating to Virginia. There's a town call Fairfax that has a paid fire department. He thought you might be interested. I was using the computer to do some research. I wanted to see if there were any area hospitals that were hiring. I also filled out an application for you and sent an e-mail to the chief about you. They are very interested and want you to come down and take the physical." The room was silent again; this time Michelle broke it. "You're going to be a fireman again!"

"I don't know what to say. Thank you! I mean to be honest with you, I felt like there were times you were trying to get rid of me."

Michelle turned her head away and tilted it towards the floor and said, "What would ever give you an idea like that?"

The couple hugged. After a few seconds Joe broke away and in an excited voice asked, "When do I go down?"

"This week if you want."

"I can't go this week. It's Gary's funeral"

"That's right, I almost forgot. Well let me set you up with an e-mail account and you can set something up with them yourself."

Joe pondered for a moment. He knew she was right. It was time to join the computer age, but he sure hated to give in to it. He looked at her and in a less than enthusiastic voice said, "Sure, that sounds like a great idea."

Joe and Michelle sat at the kitchen table with the computer. Michelle started to teach him some of the many functions a computer has that make the world smaller. They sat up for hours. Michelle was a very patient teacher. Joe was a very sluggish learner. It was difficult for him to put aside his prejudice against the so-called Devil's tool. He did the best he could and by the end of the first lesson he had an e-mail account and a rudimentary knowledge of how to surf the web. He also sent out his first e-mail. It was to the Fairfax Virginia Fire Department. He was setting up an interview.

That night Joe and his wife slept in the same bed again. They fell asleep hot and sweaty, and in each other's arms. By the morning they were cool and dry, and still holding each other. They awoke smiling. Maybe it was the physical activity of the previous night. Maybe it was the lessons on the computer. Probably it was both. To Michelle's surprise Joe kissed her and ran to the computer. He opened it up and logged on. There it was; a response from Fairfax. He would visit them next Monday. He told Michelle the good news. She was thrilled for both of them. They were both so excited they could not fall back asleep, but that didn't stop them from going to bed.

The day of Gary's funeral arrived. It was Friday, September thirteenth. It was held in a beautiful old-fashioned church in Rockville Center, Long Island. The church was packed. Policemen, fireman, paramedics all in dress uniform. Joe was selected to give the eulogy. Like most churches this one was dimly lit. Sunshine tried to enter through the large, thick, stained glass windows on either side of the church. The funeral mass started with a procession down the center aisle. Many of the mourners who were not familiar with Catholic ceremony were surprised to see the priest dressed in white robes. It's the last sacrament in the church and is considered to be a time to rejoice. Gary would now be with God in Heaven.

The Cathedral was overcome with the smell of incense, and smoke wafted over the pews in the dark church. The funeral mass proceeded in the usual manner. The priest performed his duties flawlessly. The church remained quiet except for the occasional sob or sniffle. Looking up at the altar from the pews you could make out Joe's outline. He was off to the right side sitting in a high-backed chair made of solid oak. It was covered in a deep red velvet. He found it very comfortable as he nervously waited for his chance to deliver the eulogy.

Joe continued to go over in his head the points he wanted to make during his remarks. He and Michelle had stayed up most of the night trying to find the right words and correct phrases to sum up the life of his friend and hero. His mind had drifted to another place during the service and then suddenly was brought back when he heard the priest say his name. "Joe," the priest repeated. Joe looked over to the podium where the priest was standing. His long arm was outstretched beckoning to Joe with the snow-white robe hanging majestically down.

Slowly he stood. His legs were not firm under him. For countless years he could run into burning buildings and his legs would not shake. Today it was different. He started to slowly walk over to the podium. As he walked, he checked his pockets for the notes he and his wife had made the night before. He reached into his right jacket pocket and pulled out several index cards. He tapped them down on the podium and cleared his throat. Then right there on the altar he had an epiphany. He put the index cards back into his jacket pocket. He looked out upon the packed church and he knew that Gary would not want anyone to be sad about his passing. It was time to celebrate his life not mourn his death. A smile crossed Joe's face and he started to speak.

"My uncle Reefer once said to me, 'You show me your friends, and I'll show you, the rest of your life' "Now uncle Refer was a hard drinking, bike riding, pot smoking, hell raiser who couldn't hold a job, and so were his friends. I never thought much about that until recently. Our lives are very much molded by the friends we make. My friend Gary was a brave, kind soul who tried to do the right things and had no tolerance for people who didn't care about other people. As we grew up I was smart enough to watch and learn. He taught me to be brave. He taught me to protect those who could not protect themselves. Soon I discovered that being around him made me a better person. I don't want to stand here and tell everyone he was a perfect person. He had his flaws too. Anyone that knew him, knew how much he loved to sleep. If you were counting on him for a ride early in the morning you'd be better off calling a taxi. I learned that in high school. He used to drive me to school when we were seniors. Our entire day at school hinged on whether or not he would have a green light on Sunrise Highway. Green light and we would get to school just as the bell rang. Red light meant late for school and possible detention. It would frustrate the hell… oops sorry Father… the heck out of me. Just get out of bed three minutes earlier!

Gary could also be a bit of a hot head. But there was no one more righteous. A man who always looked out for those who could not defend themselves. No one who took a deeper stand for what he believed in. He was also the bravest, toughest, and most compassionate person I have ever met.

It all comes back to friends. Show me your friends. It is because of him I have a bright future. When we were kids we used to sit on the rail fence outside his house. We would talk for hours and never run out of things to say to each other. People would see us sitting, talking, trying to solve the world's and each other's problems. They used to say that there's nothing I wouldn't do for him, and there's nothing he wouldn't do for me, so together we never got anything done. We used to laugh at that. All these years later I respectfully disagree. It wasn't flashy, but we got a lot done. We did plenty of good. Rest in peace, my friend." Joe took one long last look at the casket draped in the American flag, then he turned and walked back to his seat at the side of the alter.

The atmosphere in the church seemed a bit lighter after Joe's eulogy. The people who knew Gary remembered his good nature and his drive to help his community. Those who did not know him as well knew their lives would have been richer if they did. Joe's eulogy was perfect. He spoke from his heart, which was slowly breaking. Still he found the correct words to honor his friend. It wasn't long before the mass was over. It was the first time a service went too quickly for Joe. Now the casket would leave the cathedral and be brought to the cemetery. It would be the last time Joe would see it.

It was a sunny, crisp day at the cemetery. Joe and Michelle held hands as the last prayers were said over the casket. In his left hand he held a red rose. When the priest gave his last blessing, and made the sign of the cross over the casket Joe released Michelle's hand. With tears running down his face, he walked over to the casket. Gently, he placed his flower on it. His hand rested a moment, and he hung his head. In a barely audible voice he said, "How's your father?"

Joe walked back to his wife. They held hands again as they watched the rest of the mourners pay their last respects. He squeezed her hand tighter as he realized he would never see his friend again. She leaned closer to him and rested her head upon his shoulder. Joe turned his head and whispered into her ear. "I'm all alone now."

She turned and looked into his teary eyes and replied, "No, baby I'm here."

They released the hold of their hands and put their arms around each other's waists. Then they pulled each other tight as if they were one.

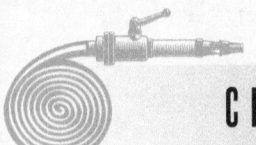

CHAPTER SEVENTEEN

STARTING OVER

Over the next few days the world was recovering from the cowardly sneak attacks on the United States of America. Citizens ran to donate blood. People volunteered their time to participate in the cleanup efforts. Musicians and entertainment moguls held concerts to raise money for victims' families. Many of the country's older generation compared this attack to the sneak attack of December 7th, 1941, that sunny Sunday morning when the Japanese bombed Pearl Harbor. It brought the United States into World War II.

Joe had taken a few days off from work. He and Michelle were getting ready to take a trip to Fairfax, Virginia. He had set up his appointment with the Fire Department. Michelle was going to scope out the hospitals in the area. She hoped there would be time to look at houses also. They were both ready to leave New York and start over.

It was a long drive to Fairfax and Michelle, who usually does not get car sick, felt nauseous most of the ride. They checked into their hotel and ordered room service. Then they hit the sack early; they both had busy days coming up. Joe needed to be at the Fairfax Fire Academy at eight a.m. sharp.

Joe got up early the next morning to stretch and have a light breakfast. Michelle slept a little longer; she had no specific appointments to keep. At seven- thirty Michelle walked down to the hotel bar which was converted into a buffet breakfast for the guests. She spotted Joe sitting alone at a small round table. He was sipping a cup of coffee. She walked over to the coffee urn and got herself a cup. She sipped on her coffee as she walked over to her husband. When she arrived, he stood up and gave her a kiss on the cheek.

"Did you sleep okay, baby?" Joe asked.

"Fine, I just feel more tired than usual. Maybe it was the long drive."

"Well, if you drop me off at the fire academy you can come back and lie down."

"I know. I'll be fine. Let me just finish my coffee and we can go." The couple sat and finished their java. Then they left the table and walked out to the car.

It was a short drive to the academy. Michelle pulled up to the front door and Joe started to leave the car.

"Good luck, baby," Michelle said affectionately.

"Thanks, I'm not worried about the written part, it's the physical I'm dreading. It's an obstacle course and I think I'll have a hard time keeping up with some of these kids." Joe replied.

"You'll be fine honey. Don't hurt anyone."

Joe laughed as he closed the car door and walked up the steps of the building. Michelle watched as he disappeared behind the door, then she drove off.

Joe took the elevator up to the third floor and went into room 303. He saw a lot of young faces already sitting, ready to take the written part of the exam. He scanned the room and found an empty seat. He walked over and slid into it. It was obvious to him he was the oldest person there. He reached behind his ear and grabbed his number two pencil and sat waiting for instructions. It was only a few short minutes before a tall well-built man entered the room.

With his entrance alone he made the room go silent. His uniform was perfect. His shoes were shined like black mirrors. His dark blue pants had a crease so sharp it could slice ham. The applicants sitting in the first row could see their reflection in his belt buckle. His torso was covered by a light blue shirt that fit snugly over his muscular physic. Over his right breast pocket was a gold nameplate with the name Collins. Over his left was a shiny silver badge with the number 721. He had a dark blue tie running down the middle of his shirt, held tightly by a silver tie clip. His hair was perfect not one out of place. His face looked worn with dark wrinkles. All eyes focused on the firefighter. He cleared his throat and spoke in a deep, deliberate, commanding voice.

"Good morning, I am Firefighter Collins. I will be the proctor of this part of your exam. You will have two hours to finish the test. It is two hundred questions. When you are done you bring me your test and answer sheet. I will give you a number. That number is your slot to take the physical part of the test. You will need to report to the downstairs gym at one o'clock. I believe those instructions are very specific. Are there any questions?"

Joe glanced around and saw about six hands shoot up with questions. Fireman Collins scanned the room, looking at all the fresh faces and hands in the air. He took his stack of test papers and started to hand them out. As he walked up and down the aisles he said spoke again with his deep, commanding voice.

"Great so if there are no questions you may start your test as soon as you receive it. Good luck." All of a sudden, all the hands went down and the sound of test booklets opening filled the room.

Joe sat and worked on his test. The room remained quiet with only the sound of pages turning and pencils scratching paper. He found the test very easy. A few simple math problems, some common-sense questions. He actually let out an audible laugh at one question. It read;

You pull into a gas station to fill your car. You smell a strong aroma of gas. You turn around and notice one of the gas pumps is leaking. What should you do?

A. Leave the station as soon as possible without paying.
B. Notify the attendant and call the fire department.
C. Don't worry about your car and just leave
D. Light a match and drop it on the leak to make sure it's gasoline

After about thirty minutes Joe heard a noise behind him. Someone getting up from his desk. He looked up to see a young man two rows over shaking his head in frustration. He angrily closed his test book, pushed his chair back, stood up and marched out of the room. As he left he was heard saying, "Man, my dad's gonna be pissed at me!"

After about an hour people started to finish the test. The room started to empty out. Joe had been done for some time also but he was in no rush. He went back to double check his math. Then he got up and turned in his test. The proctor gave him a number. It was eleven. He looked at it and stuffed it in his pocket. He left the classroom and walked out of the building. It was almost eleven o'clock. He did not need to be back until one o'clock so he took a walk.

Michelle visited several hospitals. She met with a few human resource people and left copies of her resume. She seemed impressed at the level of care many of the hospitals provided. She also stopped by the local real estate office and spoke to one of the agents. She asked about the neighborhoods and the school districts. It was a busy day for her with a lot of driving around.

At one o'clock Joe was sitting in the downstairs gym with about twenty other people waiting to take the physical part of the test. Many were talking amongst themselves about the written part of the test. Suddenly a voice cut through the air. It sounded like a voice that was used to giving orders.

"May I have your attention please?" The gym quickly became silent. "Thank you. I am Firefighter Styles. I am here to give you your instructions on this part of the test. It is designed to test your endurance and strength. It is also set up to use skills firefighter's need to perform their job. As you can see it is an obstacle course. We will put you in a firefighter's turnout gear, that is to say the coat, boots, gloves, and helmet. You will also have an oxygen bottle strapped on your back and you will carry the main hand tools all firefighters need, an axe and halligan tool. In all you will have over thirty pounds of gear."

Joe looked about the room and saw a lot of blank faces. He felt confident though. He had worn that kind of gear for many years in New York, while he was a firefighter.

Fireman Styles continued. "After you are dressed we will place you on the starting line. When you are ready you will hit the green button on the wall and the clock will start. First, you will run up the two flights of stairs directly in front of you. You will go to the window and pull up fifty feet of hose. Then you will run down the stairs and go to the red table and put the oxygen bottle on. Then you go to the seven-foot wall and climb over it. The next station is on the other side of the wall where you will drag the one-hundred-pound mannequin across the line seventy-five feet away. The last part is at the yellow table. First, you must crawl under the table. When you come out on the other side pick up the sledgehammer and hit the tire on the table across to the other end. Then you can run over and hit the red button to stop the timer. There will be firefighters at all the stations to observe you. You must finish the test with all your gear on. If you forget your tools you must go back for them. I do not think I could explain it any clearer than that. And I do not like to repeat myself. Any questions?"

Just like during the written test hands flew up to ask questions. Styles ignored the hands and said, "Good. Number one get dressed." A young man not much more than twenty-two nervously stood up and walked over to the firemen who had the turnout gear.

Joe sat and watched and studied the course as each candidate took his turn. He knew his experience would help but his age would work against him. He watched as many of the candidates fumbled through the course. He also saw some terrific athletes breeze through it with little difficulty. Finally, his number was called. He walked over and put his gear on. It felt good to wear it again; it was like being hugged by an old friend. The gear even had the smoky smell that all firemen knew.

He walked over to the starting line. He held the tools in his left hand, the axe fitting nicely into the fork of the halligan. He kept his right hand free to hit the green button.

Styles looked at him and said, "Whenever you're ready hit the button."

Joe took one last deep breath and hit the button. He ran straight up the steps taking them two at a time. When he reached the window he put the tools down on the floor and put his left foot on top of them. Then he reached down and started to pull up the hose. Many of the candidates though this would be easy, but Joe knew how heavy it was to hoist fifty feet of hose up two stories when it was still coupled to another length of hose. Still he got the hose through the window in a reasonable amount of time. He bent down, grabbed his tools, and ran down to put on the oxygen bottle.

He quickly put the oxygen pack on and picked up his tools. The wall was next. He was starting feeling tired now. He was making good time but the wall would be tough. Many of the guys who went before him had a very difficult time getting over it. Joe ran up to it and threw his ax over the top. Then he reached up with his halligan tool. The end opposite the fork was shaped like a bird beak. Its main use was to pry open doors. He placed that end on top of the wall and started to climb up. When he was high enough he swung his leg over and made it to the top of the wall. He jumped down, picked up his axe, and took off to the next obstacle.

When he reached the one-hundred-pound dummy he slid his tools across the floor. Then he grabbed the dummy and slid him to the other side. He picked up his tools and went to the last station. By now he was spent. He pushed on and crawled under the long wooden table. He popped up on the other side and grabbed the sledge hammer. He was so tired if felt like it weighed a hundred pounds. He grabbed it, surprised at how heavy it felt. He reared back with it and as hard as he could, he swung at the tire lying on the table. He made solid contact but the tire did not move. He hit the side of the table. The sledge hammer vibrated in his hands and down his body. He felt like one of those cartoon characters shaking all over. He regained his focus and with shorter, more controlled swings moved the tire across the table to the finish line. He picked up his tools and ran to hit the red button.

The physical part of the exam was over. He peeked over at the time clock. He needed to finish the course in under four minutes to qualify. He looked at the red dots that formed the numbers. They were blurry. He was still huffing and puffing hard from finishing the course. He concentrated harder to bring the numbers into focus. Three minutes and thirty-seven seconds. He passed. With a sigh of relief, he walked off the course. In the background, he could hear many of the firefighters clapping for his accomplishment. Still breathing heavy, trying to catch his breath, he dragged himself over to the rest area. A tall, black man wearing a Fairfax firefighter's uniform stood waiting for him.

Joe unbuckled the harness holding the S.C.O.T. unit he was wearing. It felt good to get that off his back. The firefighter helping him took the unit and said to him, "Congratulations, you made it." Joe smiled; he was going to be a fireman again.

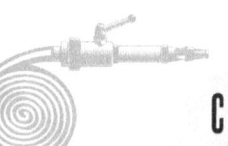

CHAPTER EIGHTEEN

GOOD NEWS

Back in New York, Joe and Michelle were getting along better than ever. Joe was very pleased with his test results. He was hoping he would hear soon from Fairfax. Possibly within the next few months he would be sworn in as a firefighter again. Michelle could not have been happier either. She cut down considerably her time on the computer. She and Joe were talking more. They were going out more. They were sleeping in the same bed together. Unfortunately, nobody has a perfect life. Over the past few weeks Michelle had not been feeling well. She did not mention it to Joe. He had been so happy she did not want to upset him.

It was late in October. It was a sunny, crisp, fall day. Joe and Michelle were both up early. Joe was getting ready for work. His mood was still cheerful. Michelle had the day off. She seemed a bit more distant. She hadn't told her husband, but today she was going to the doctor. She did her best not to appear distracted. Michelle grabbed the pot of hot coffee from the coffee maker. Joe went to the cupboard and took down two mugs. As he passed the refrigerator, he reached in and took out the milk. They met at the table and placed their items down. Then they sat at opposite ends of the small table.

The early morning sun was shining through the large bay window above the kitchen table. It separated the couple as it shone down like a laser beam.

"What are you up to today?" Joe asked his wife.

"Um, I'm not sure. Clean up a little bit. Maybe lie down again. You know just have a lazy day."

Joe took a sip of his coffee without taking his eyes off Michelle said, "So I heard you get up earlier this morning and go to the bathroom. Do you feel okay?"

Michelle felt her hands start to shake. She carefully placed her coffee mug down. "I'm fine, just a little heartburn is all."

"Oh, all right then, but if it gets worse let me know. You may have to go to the doctor." Joe replied.

"Don't worry I will," Michelle said in a cool confident voice.

"Well I'm off to work. I will see you later probably around four. Don't forget to call me if any mail comes from Fairfax."

"You know I will, baby," Michelle said cheerfully. Joe gave his wife a kiss and left. Michelle sat and finished sipping her coffee. She became lost in her thoughts. She had been sick for about two weeks and she feared the worst. Her life was just becoming what she always hoped for as a young girl.

In a few hours, she would be sitting at the doctor's office. I can hear him now, she thought to herself.

"I'm sorry, Michelle. It's worse than we thought. You may have three, but not more than six months left. I'm so sorry." Tears were rolling down her face as she snapped back to reality. She stood up and reached for Joe's empty mug. She cleared the table and took the mugs to the sink. She kept herself busy puttering around the house to keep her thoughts from wandering. Soon it was time to take a shower and get ready to leave.

It was ten o'clock on the dot when she signed in to the doctor's office. He was a nice man and a good doctor. Michelle knew him very well from the hospital. She especially liked his bedside manner. Schedules meant nothing to him. He would not leave a patient until he was convinced that they understood what was going on and what the plan was. So many doctors nowadays see so many patients they just don't take the time to see a person. It becomes volume over value.

Michelle sat thumbing through a People magazine waiting to be called in. Then a nurse in a colorful scrub outfit called her name. Michelle's heart skipped a beat and she took a gulp. She sprung up and threw the magazine to the side. Her legs were shaky, but she followed the nurse to the exam room.

"Okay, Michelle, if you take your clothes off and put the gown on Doctor Coco will be in shortly," the nurse said.

Michelle walked into the room and picked up the hospital gown from the foot of the exam table. Behind her the door closed. The nurse placed Michelle's chart into the plastic holder attached to the wall and walked away.

It took about twenty minutes before Doctor Coco made his way around to Michelle's room. He took the chart out of the plastic rack and started to read through it. When he felt he had enough information he tucked it under his arm and opened the door. Michelle was sitting on the exam table. She was dressed in the blue and white hospital gown. Her legs were crossed and her arms folded on her lap. Her eyes were puffy as if she had been crying.

"Hi Michelle," he said in a cheerful voice. "What's going on?" As he spoke, he reached behind himself, and closed the exam room door.

After about thirty-five minutes the door opened. Doctor Coco left the room and carried the chart with him to the nurse's station. Michelle was standing and looking for her clothes. She found them neatly folded on a chair. She picked them up and then walked over and closed the exam room door. When she finished dressing she opened the door and made her way to the nurse's station.

"Okay, Michelle, here is the lab work the doctor ordered. You can have that done today and we can call you later with the results."

Michelle took the paperwork and replied, "Yes, I will go right now. Thank you."

"You're welcome dear, I hope its good news."

"Me too," Michelle replied.

Joe's shift was coming to an end. He was still in a good mood, but disappointed he didn't hear from Michelle about Fairfax. Still, he could not wait to get home and see her. Maybe tonight he would take her out. It would be nice to have a date night. Perhaps a quick dinner then ice skating, he thought. Those were the kinds of things they did when they first dated. Joe turned in his rig and signed out. He just about ran to his car. It was colder than the morning and the darkness came quicker each day. It was perfect ice skating weather.

It was almost four-thirty when Joe arrived home. Michelle's car was parked in the driveway. Joe parked on the street in front of the house. The first thing he noticed was that the house was dark except for the light in the kitchen at the back of the house. He closed his car door and walked around the front of his car. As he passed the mail box he opened it to peek if Michelle missed any of the mail. To his surprise there was a stack of letters sitting in there. He reached in and grabbed them. With a spring in his step, he bounced up the driveway and into the house.

The first thing he did was flip on the light and start going through the mail. There it was, the third letter. From Fairfax, Virginia. Joe ripped it open. He reached in and pulled out the letter. He read the first word and his hear leapt, Congratulations. He continued reading. It was short and to the point. Another class of firefighters was being call to the academy. It was a small class compared to New York; only fifteen people were accepted. The important thing was that one of them was Joe. His class would pair up with other classes in the Fairfax area to make one big class of about seventy-five.

Joe finished the letter and held it tight to his chest. He closed his eyes and bowed his head. In a soft and reverent voice, he said, "Thank you, God." Then he jumped for joy and yelled for his wife. "MICHELLE!"

He ran to the kitchen. He found her sitting at the table holding a worn piece of paper. He was so excited he never noticed the expression on her face.

He blurted out, "I made it! I'm going to the academy; I'm going to be a fireman again." Michelle did not react the way Joe expected. She sat still, staring at the paper in front her. Now Joe knew something was wrong. His heart beat started to slow.

He moved closer to her. "What's going on baby? What's wrong?" he asked her.

She looked up at him expressionless. "Well, over the last few weeks I haven't been feeling too good."

"You mean the heartburn you had this morning?" Joe asked.

"It's more than heartburn. I've been sick for a few weeks now. Today I went to the doctor. He examined me and sent me for blood work." Joe stood silent. Michelle continued. "These are the results." Michelle stood up and looked her husband right in the eyes. "Joe, I'm pregnant!"

Michelle smiled her beautiful smile. Joe looked dazed, and then passed out.

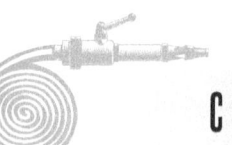

CHAPTER NINETEEN

FOR SALE

Several days had passed. Joe was wandering around the house like a zombie. His heart was filled with mixed emotions. There were so many life changing scenarios running through his brain. He was thrilled about the new chapter starting in his life. They would move to Virginia and have a fresh start. They would put the past year behind them. It would be like it was when they were first married. He would be a fireman again. On the other hand, he was still feeling woozy about becoming a father. As usual Michelle had enough strength to carry them both through this transition.

Michelle had seen several houses when they visited Fairfax the previous month. She e-mailed her resume to several hospitals that were in the area. The next step was to get their current house in shape to be sold. That would be Joe's job. He planned on having it sold before the New Year started. He needed it sold by then since the Fairfax Fire Academy started on January seventh. The first order of business was to clean up. He started with the basement. It was cluttered with several years of accumulated memories. Joe worked tirelessly humping the junk from the basement to the curb.

Pickup was Tuesday mornings. Monday night Joe took the trash down the drive way to the curb. Along with the usual trash they put out he had quite an extra pile of garbage. Michelle peeked out the front window, watching as her husband arranged things just right at the curb. Several minutes passed before he came back into the warmth of the house. He was greeted by Michelle who said, "Baby, they are never gonna take all that shit you put out."

"What do ya mean? It's their job. They pick up shit"

"Sweetheart," Michelle continued in a soft understanding tone, "they have limits. You need to call for a special pickup for all that."

"No way they charge extra for that. Garbage is garbage, that's the job. They'll take it. Tomorrow when you wake up the curb will be clear." Then he ran his hand along her beautiful face and said, "You'll see."

The next morning Joe awoke in the bed alone. Michelle was up early. He pulled the covers down and noticed the house was chilly. He sat on the side of the bed and shook the cobwebs out of his head. Slowly he started to rise and stretch his side out. Then he remembered it was garbage day. He threw his robe on and ran down the steps. He went right to the front room and peeked out the window. The sun was shining bright. He squinted his eyes and focused on the curb. It was full of all the trash he put out the night before. As he looked closer he noticed that his trash cans were missing. He went to the front door and opened it. He was immediately hit by the cold autumn air. He stepped out to his stoop and looked right and left. Then he saw two aluminum cans rolling down the street. He pulled his robe tight and ran down to get them.

When he came back into the house his face was red and his hands were cold. He walked into the kitchen where Michelle had a hot cup of coffee waiting for him. He picked up the hot mug and took a warm sip. He held the mug with his right hand and looked at his wife. He used a quote from one of his childhood heroes. "Of course, you know this means war!" Michelle just rolled her eyes.

Joe stewed all week about the sanitation department. He did not want his wife to think she was smarter than him. They both knew she was. He was too stubborn or cheap to call and pay for a special pickup. Then it hit him; a way to save face and save a buck. Just cut out the middle man. Monday night the following week he set his scheme into motion. He set his alarm clock for four a.m. He kept the volume low so as not to disturb Michelle. He slept on pins and needles waiting for the alarm to go off. Three fifty-nine. Four a.m. the clock alarmed. Joe quickly shot his arm from under the covers and silenced the clock at the first sound.

Ignoring the pain in his side and the cold of the room he sprang out of bed. He grabbed his robe and flew down the steps to the front room. He stood in front of the window, opened the blinds, and waited. At about four forty-five the bright headlights turned the corner. He waited as the big noisy truck made stops at all the houses before his. He timed it so he could run out as they pulled up to his. The time had come and Joe ran out into the cold air. He stood in front of his pile of trash in his bathrobe and slippers ready to greet the boys. The truck stopped in front of his house and two guys jumped off the back of it. They ran past Joe to the huge pile of trash he put out. He could swear he heard one of the guys say "asshole" as they passed. Joe walked around to the driver side of the truck.

"Good morning," he started. "I know I put a lot of stuff out but we're trying to sell the house and I need to get rid of this shit."

"Call for a special pickup, Mack, they'll take all of your stuff," was the reply from the driver.

Joe, shivering in the cold, continued, "I was hoping you guys could help me out." Joe reached into the pocket of his robe and pulled out some cash. He handed the driver sixty dollars.

The driver took the cash and stepped out of the cab of the truck. He passed by Joe and gave him a tap on his shoulder. "No problem, buddy, we'll take care of this for you." The burly driver walked around to the area where the pile of garbage is and told his crew, "Take it all boys!" In a matter of seconds, the curb was clear and the truck drove off. Joe stood at the empty curb and smiled. He turned and swaggered back into his house.

A few hours later Michelle walked downstairs and saw Joe asleep on the couch. She walked to the front window and saw all the trash was gone. She was surprised and proud of her man. He said he would get it done and he did. She walked over to him and nudged him slightly. "Hey, baby. Hey get up, baby. You did it! They took all the garbage."

Slowly Joe came out of dreamland and back to his senses. "I told you I would take care of it." Joe said proudly.

"Yeah, that's great!" Michelle replied. "I called to find out about the special pickup and it cost thirty bucks. I agree that's a rip off to pick up some extra garbage."

"How much does it cost?" Joe said in anguish. "Thirty bucks!"

"Yeah that's a rip off. I'm glad I didn't pay that." Michelle bent down and gave her man a kiss on the cheek. Joe slumped back into the couch.

The autumn days passed. Joe forgot about his garbage fiasco and continued working to clean and fix the house. Michelle had that special glow that women get when they're expecting. It did not stop her from working around the house as well. She cleaned and began the process of packing up. The house had been on the market for less than a month but already several people were interested. Things could not have been going smoother.

It was the first Tuesday in December. A young couple were coming back to look at the house again. They seemed eager to buy. It was close to where the man taught grammar school. It was also nearby to the young lady's mother's house. That's always a selling point. They were going to stop by with the real estate agent around four o'clock. Joe and Michelle were up early. They planned to clean and pack to make the house look less cluttered.

Michelle was working in the pantry when Joe heard a blood curdling scream. He knew immediately it was his wife. He ran to the kitchen as fast as he could. His mind raced did she fall? Did something happen to the baby? He was expecting the worst. As he arrived in the kitchen he felt relief. Michelle was standing. Her right hand was up by her mouth. Her left was holding a box of cereal. The cereal was leaking from a corner of the box onto the floor.

"What happened here? Are you, all right? Why did you scream?" Joe asked exasperated Michelle looked truly terrified and said. "Mmmmouse!"

"What? I don't understand?" Joe replied.

"There's a mouse in the closet!" Michelle said franticly.

"Oh my God, you scared the shit out of me. Big deal! A mouse. No problem, I'll catch him."

Michelle appeared to become more relaxed. She placed the cereal box in the trash and said. "That's fine. You stay here and catch him. I'm going inside to clean. And don't let the people buying the house see we have mice!" I'm going inside while you take care of him.

Joe went right to work. He cleaned all the food out of the pantry, checking for infestation as he went. He did see some mouse droppings on the floor of the pantry. Then upon further inspection he found a small hole in the wall where his little friend could be coming from. He went to the cabinet under the sink to grab some steel wool to plug the hole. He opened the door and reached in. Out of the corner of his eye he saw the rodent. It was a small, gray mouse with a tiny patch of white on the left side of his pointy face.

Joe smiled, "Well, my little friend, the game's afoot." he said. He took the steel wool and plugged the hole. Then he called to Michelle. "Baby, I need to go to the store and get some mouse traps." He grabbed his car keys off the table and walked into the living room. Michelle was vacuuming the carpet. He tapped her on the shoulder. She turned and shut down the vacuum. "I'm going to the store to get some traps for the mouse," He repeated.

"Don't go anyplace local. We don't want the neighbors seeing we have mice. There's a nice little mom and pop place about thirty minutes from here. I think it's called Paul's. Try that place." Michelle said.

"NO!" was Joe's knee jerk response. "Um, I mean I think I know a closer place." He certainly wasn't going back there. "Okay, I'm leaving, be back soon." Joe said, and he grabbed his keys and left.

It took less than an hour but Joe returned with enough gadgets to catch a six-foot mouse, let alone a four inch one. As was his custom, he did not want anyone including but not limited to rodent's thinking they were smarter than him. He did not want to place his traps so the prospective buyers could see them. He took three conventional mouse traps baited them with peanut butter, and placed them under the sink. One on each side and one across the back. He closed the doors and finished straightening up the house.

It was close to four o'clock and Joe and Michelle were sitting in the living room. Michelle was on her computer looking up her new neighborhood in Virginia. Joe was sitting browsing through a Cosmopolitan magazine. They were both startled by a loud SNAP that came from the kitchen. "I got the little bastard!" Joe yelled. Then another SNAP! Joe and Michelle looked confused. Were there two mice? He rose from the couch to see. He rushed to the kitchen. He stood in front of the sink and bent down to open the doors. Just before he touched the knob, SNAP!

With Michelle standing behind him he opened the door. Systematically, he scanned the bottom of the cabinet.

He looked to the right. The trap against the wall was tripped and flipped on its side, empty. He looked to the back wall and found the same result; no mouse but the trap sprung. He looked to the left wall; and no mouse and a sprung trap. He turned and looked over his shoulder to his wife. He was extremally puzzled. As his eyes locked on Michelle, he saw her pointing to the cabinet. He quickly turned back and saw a small gray mouse, with a touch of white on the left side of his pointy face. He was standing on top of the steel wool box. Their eyes locked. Who would blink first? Then the little gray mouse lifted his little gray hand and flipped Joe the finger. In the blink of an eye he was gone.

Joe dropped to his knees. He started to rip the cabinet apart. Suddenly, the doorbell rang. Quickly, he came back to his senses. He threw the stuff he ripped out of the cabinet back into it. Michelle composed herself and went to answer the door. Joe closed the cabinet doors and collected himself. As he stood up he shook his finger at the doors and said, "This isn't over yet!" Then he turned around and brushed himself off and collected his thoughts. He put a smile on his face and walked out to meet the prospective buyers.

The young couple toured the house with anticipation. They asked many questions and took notes as they walked through. Michelle was sure they would make an offer on it. Joe lagged behind the group, constantly moving his head back and forth, like an ice hockey goalie protecting his net as he watches the puck fly back and forth. When the visit ended, Michelle walked the couple to the door. The young woman turned to Michelle and said. "Thank you very much. You have a lovely home. I do have a question though. Why do you have a hangman's noose over your staircase?"

Michelle stammered for a second, then an answer came to her, "My husband is a bit eccentric. You see he loves old western movies and the rope is like a memento to him. Don't worry we're taking it with us."

The prospective buyer looked perplexed but replied, "Jim and I have a lot to talk about but we will be in touch. Thank you."

Michelle answered, "You're welcome, we look forward to hearing from you." With a big smile on her face she closed the front door.

By the next day the couple had made a generous offer on the home. It was only five thousand dollars less than Joe and Michelle were asking. They quickly accepted. The next step was the home inspection. It was set up for the next Wednesday. That gave Joe less than a week to catch the rodent who had taken up residence in the house. He accepted the challenge. Like most firemen he worked best under pressure. He immediately went to the store and bought more traps. He came home with every trap imaginable. He had sticky boards, spring traps, poison bait, and live traps. It took some time but the traps were set. Most were in the basement with some in the kitchen. He set up so many he had to make a map to remember where he placed them so he could check them all. Feeling sure he would find a dead mouse in the morning he went upstairs to take a shower and go to bed.

Joe was in a very sound sleep, dreaming of his and Michelle's new life in Virginia. They put a down payment on a beautiful four bedroom house. It was on three acres of land and had a built-in swimming pool. Nothing could stop him now. Slowly he found his sleep being disturbed. His dream started to change. The house started to make funny noises. As he was becoming more conscious he was feeling something lightly moving across his chest. The noise was getting louder and Joe awoke. He opened his eyes and his vision slowly focused on something sitting on his chest. It was a pointy little face with a small blotch of white on the left side of his face. Quickly his blurry vision started to clear and he could make out his nemesis smugly sitting on his chest. As his eyes grew more focused the mouse had his eyes closed, and his nose was all wrinkled up. It looked like he was straining. Like he was pushing something out. Like he was taking a shit. Joe picked his head up off his pillow and the mouse ran off. Then he looked on his shirt where the mouse was sitting and he saw a small black lump.

"Oh shit!" he yelled, and kicked the blankets off and jumped out of bed. With his right hand, he was sweeping the mouse dropping off. Michelle was startled and looked over to him. By this time, he already had the bedroom light on.

"What happened? Did you have a nightmare?" Michelle asked.

"No, that mouse was here, in this room sitting on my chest. I think he pooped on me." Was Joe's reply.

"Don't be silly, you were just having a bad dream. You'll see tomorrow. You'll find him in one of your traps in the basement. Now go back to sleep." As she finished her sentence she rolled back over to sleep.

"Yeah, you're right. It was just a dream. Sorry I woke you," Joe replied. He turned off the light and tried to get back to sleep.

The morning arrived. Joe barely slept after his nightmare. It was very early and Michelle was still asleep. He sat up on the side of the bed and started to stretch. He looked down at his feet as he started to rise off the bed. "I knew it," he said in a low barely audible voice. Down on the carpeted floor he spotted the clear evidence of mouse droppings. That little bastard was here last night. Joe refocused. He became obsessed with the mouse. He was like Captain Ahab looking for the white whale. He even gave the critter a nickname. He started calling him The Phantom, because of the patch of white covering his gray pointy face.

Time was running short on Joe. He needed to catch The Phantom before the inspection. He did not want to blow this deal. He had set traps in all the rooms of the house. The Phantom found a way to avoid them. In desperation, he decided to set all his traps in one room. It would be like setting up a mine field. Tuesday night he took all the spring traps, the live traps, and the sticky boards and laid them across the kitchen floor.

Joe slept uneasily that night hoping to hear a trap spring. By four a.m. he finally fell asleep. Hours later he was awakened by the screams of Michelle. He jumped out of bed and ran downstairs to her. As he hit the last step of the staircase he rounded toward the kitchen. He saw Michelle standing with her back to him. She was in her bathrobe and her hands were up by her head. He ran to her side and gasped. Every trap in the kitchen was sprung. They were also all empty.

"How does he do that?" Joe said.

"Look baby!" Michelle said, pointing to the kitchen floor.

Joe looked but was confused. "What? I don't see anything."

"The floor, look how the traps are laid out."

Joe looked closer and then he saw it. "Oh my God!" he gasped. On the kitchen floor the traps were tripped or move in to position to spell, PUTZ.

Slowly, Joe entered the kitchen. He suddenly had the feeling he was in over his head. Then in the far corner of the room he spotted one of his live traps moving. He walked over and peered inside it. He got him! The Phantom was caught inside with no way to get out.

Joe smiled. "Michelle quick get me a shoe box." She ran to the closet and brought him one. He took the live trap and placed it inside the shoe box. Then he went upstairs to get dressed.

When he got back downstairs, he noticed that Michelle had cleaned up all the mouse traps. Joe took the shoebox with The Phantom. "How are you going to kill him?" Michelle asked.

"I thought about that, but he put up too good a fight to be killed. I am going to take him to the woods and set him free. Maybe he'll find some other guy not as smart as me and terrorize him," Joe said as he tucked the shoebox under his arm and walked out.

Joe walked deep into the woods. It was an open area with a small stream running nearby. "This will be a good spot for you." He knelt and took the trap out of the shoe box. He laid it on the grass and opened the small door to let the mouse out. The Phantom quickly ran out. He got about fifteen feet away and stopped. He looked back to Joe. Joe could just about make out the small patch of white on his pointy face. Joe raised his right hand up toward his forehead like a military salute. "Well done, my friend. I salute you," he said. The mouse turned and started to run away.

Suddenly, Joe spotted a huge bird diving toward the ground. It had the wing span of a seven-foot basketball player. The mouse had no chance. In the blink of an eye the hawk grabbed the mouse and was flying away. Joe watched as the bird got smaller in the distance, the little mouse dangling from its talons. He stared up at the sky until he no longer could see them. Then he turned and headed back to his car. As he walked he said, "I feel sorry for that hawk."

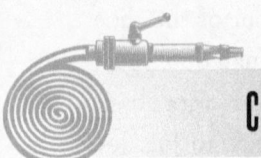

CHAPTER TEWENTY

SEPTEMBER ELEVENTH TWO THOUSAND AND TWO

It was a mild day in Joe and Michelle's new home state of Virginia. They had lived here a little less than a year. They both adjusted to their new lives very well. Joe was done with his fire academy training and was stationed with a rescue crew. The monster that once drove him to throw away his life was now tamed. He was a stubborn Irishman who learned that with patience, time, and love all things are possible. Be careful when you look into a mirror and judge yourself, you will never live up to your own expectations. We are not always fortunate enough to see what's beneath the surface. We are fortunate that other people can and help us bring it out.

Michelle was home, waiting for Joe to come home. It was getting close to dinner. She had the television on all day, watching the ceremonies of the one year anniversary of 9/11. She had been very busy these days taking care of their new baby, working part time at her new hospital, and trying to keep up with a new, larger house. She was more tired than usual and had little time to sit with her computer. Today the house had a very hearty aroma. Michelle had been cooking stew in her crock pot all day and it was just about ready.

At five-thirty the front door opened and Joe entered. He was in a very good mood and started to call out right away. "Where's my girl?" he started in a very playful voice. "Where are you? Where's my little girl. Daddy's home." He stood in the doorway looking back and forth waiting to be greeted. Suddenly, he heard some rustling coming from the next room. With a gleeful, surprised tone he yelled out. "There's my little princess. Come on, Pipemma come to daddy."

Michelle stood dumbfounded in the kitchen doorway, as the cutest little brown and white puppy dog ran to Joe. Her little tail was wagging and she tried in vain to jump up to him and give him kisses. Joe immediately stooped down to her level and picked her right up. "There's my girl! There's my girl! Daddy loves you, yes he does."

"Oh my God!" Michelle interjected. You know you have a son now, don't you?"

Joe gave Pipemma one last kiss and gently put her back on the floor. "Of course, I do," he replied. "Where is little Gary?" he asked.

He's taking his nap. Michelle replied.

"Oh, great when he gets up I'll feed him, and you can take a break." Joe said as he crossed over to kiss his wife. "Something smells delicious," he said after the smooch.

"I have a nice Irish stew in the crock pot. It will be ready soon. Go wash up."

Joe walked over to his favorite chair and sat. He picked up the paper and started to browse through it. As he flipped the pages something caught his eye. "Hey, baby, come here and check this out," he yelled to her.

Michelle came in and sat on the arm of the chair. She slid close to him and put her arm around his shoulders. "What's up, honey?" she asked.

Joe looked back down at the paper and said, "I was just breezing through the paper and I saw this article. Your Uncle Jerry escaped from prison. Apparently, he sweet-talked one of the cafeteria ladies and she helped him escape."

Michelle suddenly felt all the blood rush out of her head. In a heap, she passed out into Joe's lap.

Joe stroked her soft beautiful hair and said. "It's okay I don't think he knows we moved."

THE END

www.ingramcontent.com/pod-product-compliance
Lightning Source LLC
LaVergne TN
LVHW041906070526
838199LV00051BA/2513